Linda Orken

A Novel

by

Edward Michael Turrian

DORRANCE
PUBLISHING CO
EST. 1920
PITTSBURGH, PENNSYLVANIA 15238

The contents of this work, including, but not limited to, the accuracy of events, people, and places depicted; opinions expressed; permission to use previously published materials included; and any advice given or actions advocated are solely the responsibility of the author, who assumes all liability for said work and indemnifies the publisher against any claims stemming from publication of the work.

All Rights Reserved
Copyright © 2022 by Edward Michael Turrian

No part of this book may be reproduced or transmitted, downloaded, distributed, reverse engineered, or stored in or introduced into any information storage and retrieval system, in any form or by any means, including photocopying and recording, whether electronic or mechanical, now known or hereinafter invented without permission in writing from the publisher.

Dorrance Publishing Co
585 Alpha Drive
Suite 103
Pittsburgh, PA 15238
Visit our website at *www. dorrancebookstore.com*

ISBN: 978-1-6495-7187-8
eISBN: 978-1-6495-7696-5

For Janice, who never minded the time it took in writing this.
And Peg, gone now, but always with me.

Easter

Chapter One

It's the first warm night of an all-ready month old spring. My windbreaker flaps in the breeze as I pedal my ten-speed up Hoover Street. My friend Tommy Hulse trails behind me on his beat up banana bike. It's Thursday night after supper before Good Friday and the start of the Easter week recess. Thoughts of freedom from school for an entire week lifts my spirit as much as the warm breeze passing over me does. As my bike climbs the crest of Hoover Street I look up and see there's still some pink daylight left in the sky.

Nearing the crest of the road I stand up on my bike and pump the pedals as fast as I can. I take a quick peek behind me and see Tommy struggling to keep up. He disappears from view when I cross over the crest. I sit back down on my bike and stop pedaling and lean over the handlebars and coast down the street, windbreaker now flapping furiously. When the street levels out and the bike slows down, I begin pedaling again, effortlessly. A few houses down on my right I see the Henderson brothers, Dale and Brett, in their driveway under their lit up carport working on their race car. The Henderson brothers yellow Barracuda race car with the black number **8** on the hood and doors being worked on under the carport is as sure of a sign of summer coming as unfurling green leaves and sprouting green grass. I stop in front of their house and watch as they tinker with the car. Tommy catches up to me a few seconds later. They acknowledge us watching them and Tommy yells over, "When's the first race?"

"Hopefully the Memorial," Dale yells back. "You guys gonna make one this year?"

We both shrug. "Hopefully," I say.

Near the end of last summer Tommy and me went with our friend Broccoli and his dad to White Rock Raceway to see the races. Broccoli's dad got us all down onto the field and we watched the races from the pits. Dale and Brett's Barracuda was in the fourth heat and they did pretty good too. They finished in third place and won a trophy and the next week a picture of them smiling and holding the trophy was in the paper.

Tommy and me start pedaling away. I churn the pedals as fast as I can and gain some speed and once again lean over the handlebars and coast the rest of the way down the street towards Krauszer's convenience store, Tommy trailing. At the end of the street Highway 55 approaches. Old timers call it the new highway, but it's been there as long as I can remember. Before the highway I hang a left and lift one leg over the frame of the bike and ride sidesaddle into the parking lot of a small strip of stores that includes besides the Krauszer's, a nurses' clothing store called Scrubs, Steiner's small used appliances, and a Chinese restaurant. When I see Krauszer's red sign I jump off my bike and run it to a complete stop. I stand the bike up on the sidewalk in front of the store and peer through the front window, waiting for Tommy. A few seconds later he appears in a screeching halt as he skids his bike across the black pavement. He stops right in front of a divider where he drops the bike and jumps off, back tire still spinning. He walks up to the front door.

"Why do you treat your bike like a piece of junk?" I ask.

Pulling open the front door, Tommy says, "Maybe 'cause it is a piece of junk, ever think of that Birdyboy? Should've been thrown in the trash long 'go." He walks into the store.

"Well it doesn't help none with you throwin' it around like that," I say, following Tommy into the store. "Maybe try greasin' the sprocket once in a while. Get'r a kickstand. They're only like a dollar."

"Sure Birdbeak," Tommy says, walking down the aisle to the magazine rack in the back of the store, adding, "maybe we can trade bikes this week and see how much time and money you'd want to invest in it."

Maybe Tommy has a point there.

Steve who works here is behind the front counter. He nods at us and keeps his eye on Tommy striding towards the magazines. Tommy hardly ever buys anything because most times he doesn't have any money. I have a dime in my pocket and I scan the choices in the candy aisle and choose a Baby Ruth bar and bring it to the counter. Once there I add two Bazooka Joes and slide the dime across the counter and get two cents back. With the candy and gum in hand I start for the door.

Outside the store I'm sitting on a divider when Tommy plops down next to me. I split the Baby Ruth seventy/thirty and give Tommy one of the Bazooka Joes. We eat the candy and chew the gum and read the comic strip that's inside the wrapper. They're always a dumb riddle or joke with stupid characters and stupid advice at the bottom, like from a fortune cookie. And they advertise things for free but they're really not 'cause last year I sent away for a small telescope and it arrived with a three dollars due price tag. I crumble up the waxed paper and flick it to the ground. "Hey," I say to Tommy, "did you happen to get a good look at Diane Lindsay today?"

"No," Tommy says. "Why?"

"Well she had on one of her summer dresses and when the light hit her just right you could almost see right through."

"Whaddya mean almost?"

"Well," I say. "You couldn't actually *see* anything, but you could certainly see the whole shape of her legs and everything."

Staring out toward the highway and chewing his gum like a horse Tommy says, "Well when you can actually see somethin', you let me know. I'll bring my camera."

"You don't own a camera."

"I'll steal one," Tommy says, "just for the occasion."

And Tommy would probably do just that. He does some daring things at times. Brazen things, as mom would say. Last summer he dislodged a huge wasp's nest from under the awning of his house and walked it down the street to Mr. Nunzio's house who everybody hates and with a big stick he rang the doorbell and whacked the nest and ran like hell. Summer time he likes to bury balloons down by the river in the soft sand and watch as they blow up under unsuspecting feet. At the Two Guys or Shop Rite parking lots he'll disable people's car by loosening a spark plug wire or a starter wire and then ride up on his bike offering to help the stranded motorist, usually getting rewarded in the process. So stealing a camera to get a picture of a near naked Diane Lindsay hardly seems out of his line. Heck, for that, I might even help him.

Traffic out on the highway starts to back up at the recently installed traffic light at the intersection of the highway and Hoover Street. One of the newer Road Runner's is waiting for the light to turn green. It's parallel from where me and Tommy are sitting. I figure it's either a '70 or a '71 because it's shorter and wider than previous Road Runner's. The new models are okay but I like the older ones better. They're sleeker. The new ones look the same to me as Mach Mustangs. I see that the windows are open in the car and I yell over to the driver to give the horn a honk. The driver turns and spots me and Tommy and obliges us with a *Meep Meep!* We give the driver a thumbs up and the light turns green and the cars pull away.

"My cuz has got one of those," I say.

"Oh yeah," Tommy says. "Which one?"

"Which cuz or which car?"

"Either," Tommy says.

"My cousin Gene," I say. "Well, technically he's my uncle, but I call 'em cuz. I mean, he's about Tam's age, a year older, I think. But anyway, I'm not sure which Road Runner he got. I just heard my mom tell dad that Gene got his Road Runner. I asked if she knew which one he got, but she said she didn't know." Tommy nods. "Won't matter much to me which one he got. As long as I get a ride in it."

The flavor of the gum is already gone. That's just how Bazooka Joes are. Short on flavor, long on bad advice and bad advertising. Good thing they're only a penny. The sky's growing darker with a rolling tide of clouds in patches of grey and black. Tommy and me stand up, throw the gum on the ground, and reach for our bikes. As soon as our hands touch the handlebars we hear the low murmuring of an approaching motorcycle. We listen closer. Its two motorcycles, actually. Coming from…Hoover Street. Tommy and me know who it is: Dean Magnumson and Bruce Rutter. Two of the Harding Street Manor Kings. Probably the two toughest Harding Street Manor Kings. Two people who we definitely don't want to meet up with in a darkening and empty parking lot.

Tommy and me are quickly on our bikes and head for the dirt path on the other side of the strip mall. It's a fairly large path, more like an unpaved road with woods on both sides that lead back to Constitution Street and the neighborhood. Once on the path we pedal as far and as fast as we can until the dirt becomes too soft to ride through. When that happens we jump off the bikes and begin to push them through the sand, huffing and puffing all the way. We push a little further and then begin to slow down. Tommy and me turn around and look behind us, still pushing the bikes, catching our breath. We stop for a second and only hear our breathing. There's no sound of any motorcycles. We take a deep breath, turn back around, and start leisurely pushing our bikes again.

The surrounding woods start to thin out as we near the end of the path. We can see the approaching street lights on Constitution Street. Through the still mostly bare trees early evening shadows carpet the ground in different shapes of silver and grey. "Hey Tommy," I say. "Have I tol' ya about my great idea? How I can make some money this summer?"

"No," Tommy says without any enthusiasm. "What's the great idea?"

"I'm gonna start my own lawn cuttin' business."

"Lawn cuttin' business," Tommy says, frowning questionably. "Doin' what?"

"Duh," I say. "Whadda ya think doin' what. Cuttin' lawns Horsehead. Maybe other kinds of yard work too. I could even make it a year round thing. Ya know. Leaves, snow, stuff like that."

"Isn't havin' to do your own yard enough?" Tommy says.

That's a true statement, but, "Yeah, well, at least with this, I'll be makin' money. A lot more money. More than a dollar and half, that's for sure."

"Think so?" Tommy says in a rebutting tone.

I can't say for sure since it's just an idea, but I say, "Yeah, I think so."

"Well, good luck with that," Tommy says without spirit. "It still could suck though. Gets hot in the summer Birdyboy. And ya could get a real pain in the ass person who says you ruined their yard *after* you did all the work. An' then won't pay ya."

I know Tommy has a way of seeing the dark side of things, but I have to think about for a few seconds before I say, "Well, maybe, but, maybe not. It's worth a try. Still beats standin' out in the sun all day tryin' to outdo everybody else at the carwash."

"Yeah," Tommy says in a relinquishing tone. "*That* really does suck!"

"How would you know?" I scoff. "You only did it once!"

"And that's how I know it sucks, Birdleg!" Tommy says. "Two hours out there in the broilin' sun and for what? Five quarters? And not one girl in a bikini. And I'm pretty sure that cuttin' lawns is gonna suck too," he adds.

I always kind of expect a little negativity from Tommy. It's just the way he is, or can be. He doesn't mean anything by it. We're nearing the very end of the path where a thin trail snakes behind the fences and backyards off Constitution Street. The trail leads all the way out to the Big Woods. Down the trail some of the yards are lit and some are dark. Tommy stops and stares. "Know what I recently heard?" he says. "Very recently."

"No," I say, also staring down the trail. "What's that?"

"That Reimer's got a whole bunch of *Playboys* stashed out in the woods behind his house." Tommy nods down the trail. "Somewhere out there."

"Oh yeah," I say, interested, but doubtful that it's true. "And jus' how do you know that?"

"Broccoli' tol' me."

"Broccoli?" I say. "How does Broccoli know that?"

"He said his brother put a whole stack of 'em in the back garbage the day he quit the 7-Eleven. Was gonna take 'em after he left. When he went back to check on 'em he said he saw, was pretty sure he saw Reimer ridin' away with 'em."

That almost sounds believable. "Huh," I say. I watch as Tommy continues to stare down the trail. I know what's on his mind. "So what then? You're gonna go back there and try and find 'em?" As Tommy continues to stare, I already know the answer to that. "Well, what makes you think he has 'em in stashed the woods Horsehead? Wouldn't the garage or the attic or somethin' like that be… safer?"

"With three sisters in the house?" Tommy says. "Doubtful. Good spot in the woods would be the safer bet."

Figuring Tommy's already committed to this, I say, "Reimer kill ya if he catches ya."

"Piff," Tommy snorts. "Reimer. Piff." He turns to me. "Do you think I'm really scared of that fat a…."

Tommy's defiant tone is shattered by the returning sound of the motorcycles, and two headlights at the other end of the path heading our way. Without a word, we jump back on our bikes. We start pedaling. We're back on pavement and Constitution Street. I look back. The motorcycles are halfway down the path. We're pedaling as fast as we can and we make a left onto Truman Street. We're pedaling furiously with Tommy falling a little behind. I look back again. The motorcycles have turned the corner onto Truman. Finally

Tommy and mine's street comes up and we bear right. Tommy's house is two houses down and we ride across the grass and stop near the driveway, panting. Waiting. Seconds later the motorcycles pass by our street, continuing down Truman Street. "Close one," I say, catching my breath as the sound of the motorcycles fades.

Tommy nods, turns and says, "Got time for a ping-pong game?"

"Ah, I better not. I'm sure mom's already waitin' for me near the front door."

Tommy nods. "Okay See ya."

"Yeah, see ya," I say.

I start to pedal down the block towards home.

. . .

Daylight's faded but I'm pretty sure I'm home before curfew. Or close enough anyway 'cause Mom's not standing near the front door when I ride up the driveway. I put my bike in the garage and walk up the walkway and climb the steps and walk through the front door. Yellow light is spilling out of the kitchen entry and onto the dining room floor, but otherwise with evening shadows creeping up the walls and no television on, the house has a desolate feel to it. Mom's probably downstairs in the laundry room or pantry room and Tammy's room is dark and quiet. I stride over to where the yellow light leads into the kitchen.

When I walk into the kitchen Dad's sitting at the table and still in his work clothes. He's always extremely busy this time of the year. He's in his usual posture with a yellow pencil stuck between his teeth and another one behind his ear and one hand writing something down and the other working his calculator. His briefcase is open on the table with papers of assorted sizes and shapes strewn about with other papers and booklets that have **1040** in bold type on them. He's got his yellow legal pad out with his black ledger book and pencils of various colors. Paper from the calculator runs off the table and almost touches the floor. I walk past all this to the refrigerator and choose a Shop Rite Lemon Lime over a Fresca or a 7-Up. Mom's been on this no cola thing for a few weeks now. Probably Tammy's idea. I grab a couple of Hydrox cookies from the jar and join dad at the table.

Sitting there, I pick up some yellow papers that are in front of me. Brice's Auto Service, they say. I know where that is. There's a whole stack of them.

They must be some kind of worksheet or something because they have people's names and addresses and phone numbers on them with a list of things that were done to their cars. Oil change and tire rotation one says. Rear brakes linings with drum cut says another. I look through a few more. "This is stuff that people had done at Brice's?" I ask. Dad doesn't answer me. He's staring at a sheet of paper and writing blindly on his yellow pad. I put the yellow papers down and pick up a stack of white ones right next to them. I thumb through them and they all have different names on them and things that apparently were sold to Brice's Auto Service. I look at the white papers in my hand and down at the yellow ones on the table. "Do these two things go together?" I ask.

Dad lets out a huff and stops what he's doing and reaches over at snatches the papers out of my hand, putting them back down on the table. "Robby, leave all this alone, will you. And stop getting cookie crumbs all over the place." He goes back to what he was doing.

Sitting there, watching dad work, finishing the second cookie and the can of soda, an idea comes to my head. Maybe I could make my own forms just like these in front of me for the lawn cutting business I want to start. I peer down at the slips of paper in front of me. Sure, I could do that. I could have a list of things that I could do for a yard, cutting, raking, gathering, trimming, whatever, with a price right next to it. Maybe put some pictures of nice yards on the top and a cool slogan like Brice's has. Theirs says Brice's Auto Service. Where your car is our car. I'll have to think of a good slogan. As I get up to throw the empty can of soda in the garbage there's a group of papers behind dad's briefcase that catches my eye. There's a few of them, pale blue in color, and neatly folded into threes like an accordion. There's a dark red covering over them like on a school book and as I look closer I notice there's a stamped gold star on the blue papers. I also notice the very fancy cursive writing on them. Without dad noticing I lift one of the papers from the table. I try to read what it says but I can't even understand the first sentence. So without thinking I ask, "What's this Dad?"

Dad looks at me and sees the papers in my hands and stops what he's doing and throws his pencil down on the table and once again snatches the papers from my hands. "Robby, will you get the hell out of here and leave these things be," he growls, putting the paper back from where it came from. "Why do I always have to say things more than once to you?" he says in a huff, sitting back down.

I get when I'm not welcome so I continue out of the kitchen when Mom comes up from the basement with a basket of laundry in her hands and says, "Robby, leave your father be. He's busy. You got laundry on the couch. Get it and put it away. *In* the drawers." She flicks the hallway switch on. "And start getting settled," she adds.

"Why do I have to start getting settled?" I ask. "It's not a school night."

"Just start getting settled," she says, heading down the hallway towards Tammy's room.

I walk into the living room, gather my bundle of laundry from the couch, and walk to my room. I put the laundry down at the end of my bed and go to my desk and turn on my record player. I stack the records I want to hear and sit down. I open the top desk drawer and look for some pieces of construction paper that I know are in there. I pull out a white sheet and a light blue one. I take out my markers and my sketchers. I look at the clock on my night table. I have a good twenty minutes before my TV show comes on. I start to think of ways on how to make my lawn cutting business forms.

Chapter Two

Easter Sunday morning. I wake up as the sun clears the houses across the street and pierces through the small opening between my window curtains, settling on my eyelids. I lay there for a few minutes and in the quiet room I can hear the low din of preparations going on in the kitchen. I get out of bed and scratch and yawn my way over to the window, opening the curtains fully and looking out onto the quiet street. I yawn again and head for my bedroom door. Once opened, the kitchen sounds become louder and the scents of coffee and toast waft in the hallway air.

When I walk into the kitchen, Dad is at his seat of the table with his face buried in the Sunday paper, mom is at the sink washing something, and Tammy's sitting in her spot cleaning vegetables from her prized garden. When she looks up at me she instantly starts to laugh. A mocking laugh. That prompts Mom to turn from the sink and she also begins to smirk. "Robby," Mom says. "Your hair."

I plop down at my seat. "I just got up," I say. "K," I add, reaching for a piece of toast.

"Would it make any difference if you've been up for hours?" Tammy snidely says.

I pour myself a glass of orange juice and take a sip and stare at Tammy who's glibly staring back. I want to spit the orange juice across the table and into her bowl of peas, or smack the turnips she's cutting onto the floor, or sneeze all over those green things she calls kale. But I just sip the orange juice and chew on the toast.

"You know," Tammy says, looking at her vegetables and then at me, "it amazes me how one person can be such a twerp from the second they roll out of bed."

I swallow the toast and I'm about to lace into Tammy when Mom, finished at the sink, turns around and says, "Knock it off, you two. No arguing today. Tammy, finish with the vegetables and leave your brother be. Robby, finish what you're having and go and start getting dressed."

With a mouth full of toast I say, "Why do I have to start getting dressed already? It ain't time yet."

"Robby," Mom says with a hint of exasperation, opening up the refrigerator door, "just finish and go and get dressed."

"And do something about that hair," Tammy adds.

"Quiet, Tammy," Mom says.

"Yeah," I say. "Quiet. Do what Mom tells ya. Stick to your stupid vegetables and leave your nice brother alone."

Tammy smirks at me again and says, "You said that backwards."

I finish my piece of toast and the glass of orange juice. As I get up to leave, I figure out what Tammy just said. But its way too late to say anything back.

. . .

I love Easter recess from school but I'm not real fond of Easter day. There's lots of things I don't understand about Easter like why every year it comes on different dates or why the celebration is always at our house or why I have to wear a suit and tie and listen to an hour plus long boring sermon or why we used to get Easter baskets and now we don't. But there's one thing when it comes to Easter, or anything else church related that I don't understand and irks me to no end: and that's the fact that I still have to go, and Tammy does not. That irks me as much as her constant annoyingness, her constant mocking comments, or her constant monopolizing of the bathroom.

Now granted, we Birdsalls don't go to church as much as we used to, mainly just the big ones, today, Christmas, Thanksgiving, Mom and Dad's anniversary, maybe another time or two. And I'm not sure if they'd still let me play on the basketball team if I just quit going altogether, but I find it incredibly unfair that I still get dragged to *all* these things and Tammy doesn't get dragged to any of them. And it happened basically overnight. Like a flick of a switch. Tammy just walked into the parlor sometime last fall and told mom and dad that she wasn't going to go to our Methodist Church anymore. Poof!

Just like that. I think what amazed me even more than that was Mom and Dad's response. They calmly asked why and she said she didn't have to anymore because that was her right and they just kind of nodded and went back to whatever they were doing and she went on her merry way. So right after she left the room I asked for the same thing and was met with an emphatic, double-throated NO.

Actually what happened with Tammy, I think, is that this kid who calls himself Brother Davis started coming around last fall and picking her up after school in a beat-up, old ratty looking Beetle, pumpkin orange in color. And hanging around the house with some kid name Don, who comes around because he likes Tammy's friend Debbie Hutton. When all that happened next thing was Tammy's not going to church anymore. And then also she's wearing very different clothing, much that look as if they came out of the old clothes bin behind the Shop Rite. And she, with them, talk about the maharishi and some guy named Watts. Everything's according to this guy Watts now. And the music she listened to has changed from at least normal songs to sounds that I'm not even sure are instruments. All that happened, and vegetables. She also started growing vegetables. Her and Brother Davis. Lots of vegetables. All of which I have to eat.

So I think about this while I'm buttoning up my stiff white shirt, clipping on my clip on neck tie, lacing my uncomfortable dress shoes, and putting on my dress jacket. And the best I can figure out is one has to be at least Tammy's age to garner such religious freedom. So I guess I got a few more years plus to go.

. . .

Forty five minutes later I'm sitting right next to mom in church in our usual pew. The place is packed like at a game seven and since Easter came late this year, the thing I don't get, it's an unusually warm late-April day. Inside the church the air feels stuffy and stagnant. I ask Mom if I can go and open up one of the windows and I start to get up but I'm met with a firm mom grip, silently telling me to sit down. As I sit back down dad glares at me. I'd really like to move somewhere else, if just for a few minutes, because the old lady next to me smells like grandma twice over and the kid in front of me has turned around and told about three thousand times already that he's three years old.

I try the bathroom excuse but again I'm turned down, this time with mom's silent and firmly clenched lower jaw. There's nowhere to go. I'm boxed in. So I sit and wait, and wait. And wait. And finally, miraculously, Pastor Mark strides down the center aisle. He walks to the pulpit with the Lay Leader and in his all white robes he stands majestically out against all the colorful Easter flowers and purple-laden crosses and palm leaves.

Of course the sermon is long and boring so I keep busy by scanning the pews for familiar faces. I know Tup's here somewhere but I don't see him and Fig's probably here too but I don't see him either. I spot two pretty girls that I've never seen before an aisle down on the other side of the church and as I keep turning around to look at them I'm told to stop looking that way. I huff and turn away as Pastor's rambling on and on, something about a missing body. I start flipping the pages in the bible, trying to guess what page I'll land on until mom's hand closes the book for me. I grab one of the pencils in the holder in front of me and one of the cards and start doodling. Mom stops that after a while. Giving up, I'm fading fast. I think Pastor Mark says something about fear and just as my eyelids can't stay open one more second his voice booms out, "Blessed be to God." I spring back to life. That's the usher's cue. Thank God, it's almost over. Moments later, eight people have fanned out along the pews from all sides with their baskets and as they pass our pew Dad throws two dollars into the basket. I'm incredulous. That's more than my allowance! I watch as the ushers finish collecting and are standing at the back of the church, waiting on Pastor Mark to summon them forward. I turn back around. Pastor Mark scans the congregation. He raises his hands summoning the ushers. He stands in the middle of the altar. "Friends," he says, "we're so grateful for all those who have entered today's covenant with the Lord, and the bounty in which we're about to receive. And as I look out amongst you today," he says, scanning the congregation, "I see some new faces, and some faces I see throughout the year." He stops scanning when he looks my way and says, "And some faces just unseen for a while." He smiles. I recoil. What the hell was that? Did he just say that to *me*? I look over at Mom who seems unfazed. I look at dad. No response. My eyes dart left and right, seeing if anyone else is looking at me. I can't tell. Then in his booming Pastor voice Pastor Mark says, "Christ has died. Christ has risen. Christ will come again. Alleluia. Blessed be the Lord."

Alleluia is right. It's finally over.

Linda Orken

. . .

With the place as packed as it is, as we're waiting in line to greet Pastor Mark, I start to slowly distance myself behind Mom and Dad. And when they get into a conversation with the people in front of them, I'm quickly down one of the aisles and out the side door. Once in the walk way between the chapel and the rec room, I stand near the back door entrance and look around. I don't see where the two pretty girls went off to and I don't see Tup or Fig or anyone else I know. I head toward the middle of the walk way to peek into the rec room. There's a lot of bustling going on in there. It looks like walking into a wedding reception, just without a band. I scan the room but again don't see anyone I know. So I turn and walk back to the middle of the walk way as mom and dad walk out of the chapel. Glaring at me the whole way she sternly asks, "We're have you been?"

"I've been right here," I say as taken back and nonchalantly as I can. "I really did have to use the bathroom," I add.

Mom shakes her head and I get another glare from Dad, but otherwise we walk silently down the hallway to the rec room, me in the lead this time. When we walk in the near-filled room there's a steady stream of conversations going on from the thirty or forty round tables and the long tables set against the far wall. As I pass some of the tables I can tell that some run the full gamut of a family history. Great grandparents and grandparents and parents and kids of all ages. Probably cousins and second cousins too. We walk up to the front of the room where cafeteria tables are set up with all kinds of food. Waiting in line I scan the walls behind the cafeteria tables that are filled with drawings and paintings of colorful eggs and Easter baskets and bunnies and Jesus and crosses and angels and last suppers. The line moves and I'm at the first cafeteria table where I grab a plate and utensils. I walk along the table pondering the choices and I decide on one of those breakfast sandwiches where all the stuff is cooked all together. I take a waffle and a pancake and two pieces of bacon and two maple syrup packets. At the next table I grab two of those Danish things, one blueberry and one raspberry, and a cup of rice pudding. Before I leave I'm able to stuff a brownie in my coat pocket. At the last table, to make Mom happy, I take two quarter pieces of an orange and choose apple juice over orange and before Mom and Dad are finished selecting, I'm turned and scanning the room. There's got to be someone here I know and….

From the back of the room, near the kitchen, I hear, "Hey Birdyboy! B I R D Y B O Y! Back here!"

I look and there's Tup, big grin on his freckled face, mop of coarse red hair, waving his arms and calling me over. I smile and nod. I turn to mom.

Sternly she says, "Just mind your P's and Q's."

I nod and head Tup's way.

"Birdman Birdman," Tup says with his big toothed grin as I set my plate down on the table. "Happy Easter."

"Hey Tup," I say. "Happy Easter. Where is everyone?"

He nods toward the kitchen. "Mom and Dad are workin' in the kitchen."

"And your sis?"

Tup shakes his head and smiles and says, "She's in there helpin' too. Doin' what she can."

"How'd you get out of it?"

"I'm on cleanup detail."

I guess I should feel guilty that I'm having this big breakfast doing nothing and Tup's gonna be slaving over a hot tub of sudsy water for an hour after everyone's gone, but I don't. After all, dad did put more than a week's worth of my allowance into the basket. And Tup doesn't seem to mind either. And besides that, Tup must have a half dozen slices of French toast drenched in maple syrup and white powder and the same amount of slices of bacon on his plate, as well as a brownie and two Danish and a cup of rice pudding and a cup of chocolate pudding and a cup of mixed fruit and two apple juices. We're eating and talking about who looked nice in the church and what we're going to do on our week recess. I tell Tup about my lawn cutting venture and unlike Tommy, he says it should be a great success. Halfway through breakfast Tup's mom and dad come out of the kitchen with two cups of coffee and Tup's little sister Dana. They sit down at the table. After the hello's Mrs. Tupper asks me how I liked Pastor Mark's sermon.

With a mouth full of rice pudding I nod and get out, "I liked it."

"Did any part of it stand out for you?" she asks.

Since I have no idea what the sermon was about I pretend to be thinking about it and come up with, "Well, it's hard to say."

"Well I really like," Mrs. Tupper says, "when Pastor tells the part of the story when the women go to Jesus' tomb. And what happens when they find out that the body is gone." She's looking at me and slowly nodding her head. "And what the angels said to them. Do not be afraid," she says to me, "that this is the right thing." She stops and looks at her coffee and takes a sip. Then she looks at me again and adds, "And that's for us too."

I guess so, so I shake my head in an approving manner.

"Well," Mr. Tupper chimes in. "I also like when Pastor reminds us that if we were to go to the tombs of Buddha, or Muhammed, or even to Lenin's tomb in Russia, that you'd find those tombs to be occupied. And as Mrs. Tupper just said, go to Jesus' tomb, and you'll find that tomb is empty." He's looking at me nodding in a paralyzed state. "Empty indeed," he adds.

I smile. Mr. and Mrs. Tupper are nice people. Just a little church crazy.

Mr. Tupper gets up from the table, grabbing his and Mrs. Tupper's coffee cups. Mrs. Tupper gets up. She asks Dana if she wants to stay with her brother or go back to the kitchen. She chooses the latter. "Finish up here, Brian," Mrs. Tupper says. "Ten minutes. There's plenty to do."

"Almost finished," Tup says.

"It was wonderful to see you today, Robert," Mrs. Tupper tells me. Mr. Tupper tells me the same. I smile back and reciprocate their words.

Tup and me finish eating and push the plates aside. We're playing tabletop football and when Tup tries a field goal he misses badly and the paper football lands a few feet away from the table. I get up and retrieve it and as I pick it up I spot Figgy Pudding sitting across the room near a window. I sit down and let Tup know and moments later we've positioned ourselves to where we can see Fig, and he can see us, but not the rest of his family sitting at the table. And we're having a pretty good cut-up time of it. Tup's got a straw sticking out of every hole in his head and two more like antennas coming out of his mop of red hair. I'm wiggling a straw underneath my nose with pieces of napkin drooping off the ends like a walrus mustache. I have a quarter piece of the orange stuffed in the front of my mouth and I'm smiling a big orange smile and Tup's moving his head like a robot and from behind me I hear, "I saw Pastor Mark say those things to you at the end of the sermon, Robert."

My straw walrus mustache falls to the floor as I'm startled with what I had already forgotten about from the chapel. I quickly turn around and there's Joni

Iachello, standing there looking menacing. I try to say something but I can't because I have the quarter orange stuck in the front of my mouth and it won't come out. I finally put my head down and spit the damn thing out where it lands next to what looks like Joni's brand new patent-leather shoes. I pick up the gnarled orange piece and what's left of the walrus mustache and place them on the table and say, "I don't think he was talking right at me."

"Oh yes he was," Joni says with determination. "Pastor was just saying to us how he'd like to see more familiar faces throughout the year at his sermons." She turns to Tup. "Wasn't he just saying that, Brian?"

Tup looks at me straw-less now and shakes his head and says, "He actually was just sayin' somethin' like that Birdman."

I guess I'm cornered here so with nothing to say I look at the table. "You know Robert," Joni says, "that not paying proper penance to your church is a form of blasphemy, don't you?"

I'm not really sure what that means and I look at Joni who is staring down at me expecting an answer and with as much casualness as I can muster I shrug my shoulders and say, "What isn't?"

She wrinkles her nose like she's smelling something foul and snits out, "Maybe if you were here more, you'd know that answer." Abruptly dismissing me, she turns to Tup. "You remembered that bible study is Thursday this week, Brian?"

Tup, scraping the bottom of all his pudding cups, making one last spoonful and pondering his concoction says, "Sure."

"Pastor's going to be teaching about the Apostles during Pentecost, in case you're interested Robert. There's more going on here than just basketball, you know," she adds with darting eyes before she turns and struts away. I watch as she joins her parents on the way out of the rec room.

"What the hell," I say once Joni's out of the room.

Tup shrugs his shoulders, examining his now clean spoon. "What did Pastor say to you during the sermon, Birdman?"

"Just that...," I stop for a second, say, "and it wasn't directed at me personally anyway, but somethin' about seeing familiar faces more often."

Tup just shrugs his shoulders again as he gets up from the table. "Well, I guess Joni's right 'bout Pastor sayin' that Birdman. But maybe like you say, it wasn't meant just for you. Probably just was, what do you call that thing?"

"Call what thing?"

"You know. That thing," Tup says. "When you just happen to be somewhere at the right time."

"I don't know. I guess the same thing they call it when you just happen to be somewhere at the wrong time," I say. "What's it to her anyway?"

"Well," Tup says, "maybe it's Joni who'd like to see more of you, Birdman, and not so much Pastor Mark. Y'ever think of that? Maybe she likes ya and that's her way of showin' it."

That's a shuddering thought. Joni's pretty and everything, but for some reason she either resents me being in her church or resents me being in her school or just resents me being period. "I sincerely doubt that, Tup." I say.

"Hey, I can find out for ya," Tup says, big grin on his face as he starts for the kitchen. "Ya know I know 'er pretty good,"

"Thanks, Tup," I say, "but I don't think that'll be necessary."

Chapter Three

I follow Dad into the house once were back from church and fling my jacket onto the arm of the parlor chair. Mom, following right behind me, picks up the jacket and hands it to me before I get to the hallway and tells me to hang it up and everything else including the tie stays on.

I walk in my room and hang up my jacket and grab my basketball. I walk out of my room and see dad at the end of the hallway examining two bottles of wine. All I have to do is clear the kitchen and I take a breath and I'm a blur past the entrance and I'm in the parlor heading for the front door when mom yelps out, "Robby!" I freeze and slowly turn around. She's standing at the dining room entrance, looking exasperated. "Just where do you think you're going?"

"I'm gonna shoot some hoops before everyone gets here," I say dead-panned.

"With your good clothes on?"

"Mom,' I say in exasperation. "I'm just shootin' hoops. I'm not playin' in a game."

Mom stares at me then looks at Dad who is walking toward the dining room table with the bottles of wine and he nods that it's okay. So then Mom says, "Well, at least do *something* to help out today." There's a brief pause. I hope she's not waiting on me to come up with something. "Why don't you set the silverware," she finally says, walking back to the kitchen and getting the big brown box with the good silverware and handing it to me. "Here. Go see what a nice table your sister set."

I put my basketball down and take the big brown box of silverware and walk toward the dining room and for the first time since I got home realize that Tammy is home and in the porch room. As I pass the door I see she's sitting with Debbie and they're in there listening to that Watt's guy. I really can't stand hearing him talk. He's got a really annoying voice and talks about absurdity. Right now, he's saying something to the effect that we don't exist. That's what he's saying. That we don't exist. If we don't exist then what the heck are we? I open the box of silverware and grab a handful of knives and forks, mumbling about the stupidity I hear coming from the porch. From the kitchen mom says, "Forks go to the left."

I stand there for a few seconds, utensils in hand, staring at the table. Logically, I ask, "To the left of what?"

"The plates, Robby," mom says.

"Okay," I say, still staring at the table. Then, again logically, I say, "but what if someone's right handed?"

Dad walks into the dining room and looks at me and smirks and shakes his head. Mom tells me just to put the forks to the left side of the plates and the knives and spoons go to the right. From the porch Tammy chirps, "What a twerp. Still doesn't know anything."

Unconsciously I say, "Well I know who's gonna be named Three Brooks High School's worst dressed junior this year."

"Oh really?" she responds. "And who would care about such a thing? And anyway, twerp, for your information, these clothes are recycled. If everyone recycled more things the earth wouldn't be so polluted."

"What does recycled mean?" I say. "Hideous?"

"No, twerp, it means earth conscious. Oh, and by the way, I love the white tube socks and suit look. Real classy," she says with another snidely laugh.

I'd love to barge right now onto the porch and grab Tammy's stupid Watt's cassette and throw it right in the pot with Mom's Easter soup. I don't even get the chance to respond. From the parlor, Dad tells me to keep quiet. From the kitchen mom tells Tammy to stop antagonizing me. So I ignore Tammy's existence. I finish setting the table. I put the brown box on the kitchen table. I go and grab my basketball and head for the front door. Passing through the parlor, dad's watching the *Bowery Boys*. Not one of my favorites. Sunday morning television always ends for me with *Abbott and Costello*.

• • •

I'm out in the driveway shooting hoops and I'm Meadowlark Lemon. The Middle Man. All dressed up in a suit and tie and playing tricks against the hapless Washington Generals to a raucous Garden crowd. I turn my tie into a blindfold and I'm shooting free throws, talking to the crowd as I do. I put my tie back on and pretend to continually tighten and untighten it, like I'm finished getting dressed, letting the ball bounce in front of me until the last bounce and then scooping it up and tossing it into the basket, again telling the crowd what I'm doing. Then I'm turned away from the basket and talking to a waiter who is taking my order and flinging the ball over my shoulder, making Meadowlark remarks. As I take apart the Generals, a few cars with neighbors pass by, coming or going, all in their Easter best. I wave to the Martins across the street when they get home. Even though it's warm out they still have their winter coats on. Our neighbors the Varleys are out in their yard hunting Easter eggs. From time to time Mom's face appears at the front door just to make sure I'm still out front. Then my court is cut in half as Uncle Steve and Aunt Mary arrive with their two six year old twins, Richard and Jeffrey.

The combination of the car pulling into the driveway and the subsequent slamming of its doors and my uncle's boisterous greeting brings Mom and Dad to the front door and then out onto the steps. Uncle Steve takes the ball from my hands and takes a shot and even though he's close to the basket he misses everything. Richard and Jeffrey go chasing after the ball. They retrieve it and try make some baskets but they can't barely reach the rim with the ball. Aunt Mary greets me and tells me I've grown another few inches and hands Uncle Steve a brown paper bag. Richard and Jeffrey are tussling over the ball and only promises of Easter goodies that are inside the house deters them. Uncle Steve smiles a big smile and opens the brown bag and tells me to reach in and grab. I do and pull out a plastic orange whistle that's on a plastic orange chain. Then he tells me to be careful on who I blow the whistle on, whatever that means, and then follows everyone into the house. I look at the plastic orange whistle. I like my uncle Steve. I know he's Dad's younger brother and everything, but this is junk that's on the pegboard at the back of the 7-eleven. I can't even give this away in a school grab bag.

I get a few more minutes of the shortened driveway before Aunt Lorraine and Mario arrive with their two year old daughter Maria. Aunt Lorraine is mom's younger sister. I'm not sure by how many years. I remember asking dad at her wedding a few years back if I had to start calling Mario Uncle Mario, since I've been calling him Mario ever since I've known him. Dad just shrugged his shoulders and said it didn't matter. So I still call him Mario.

There's a small patch of driveway by the hoop but I know better than to take another shot. Too many cars, too many little ones. Mario passes me on the driveway with a firm handshake and Aunt Lorraine, holding Maria's hand, gives me a hug with her free arm. I say hello to everyone. This time it's just dad at the step holding the front door open. I'm lagging behind and after everyone's in the house, Dad gives me the discernible thumb to get inside. Slowly I follow everyone into the house.

When I walk in the front door Richard and Jeffrey are looking behind the couch and the chairs and under the dining room table or in the parlor closet or anywhere else they might find hidden eggs. Mom is helping little Maria do the same. Mario and Uncle Steve are standing and talking by the back picture window. Dad comes out of the kitchen with three bottles of beer and they step out onto the back yard. Aunt Lorraine and Aunt Mary are on the couch sitting opposite of Tammy and Debbie, who are sitting Indian-style on the parlor floor, having a conversation. I bring my basketball ball to my room and dilly-dally in there as long as I can until Mom appears at my doorway and tells me she's setting out the hors d'oeuvres.

I'm the last one to the parlor and I find a spot at the end of the couch. I'm sipping on a Shop Rite lemon soda, cola still outlawed, and I stare at the table. These are hors d'oeuvres? I watch and frown as everyone helps themselves to either that droopy asparagus thing mom makes every Easter, or a plate of celery sticks with various colored centers, or a plate of Tammy's radishes with some kind of sauce on the side, or plates of those tasteless Easter crackers surrounded with slivers of olives and peppers and dried fruit and jars of some kind of topping. The twins and little Maria have it made because they're eating candy from the small baskets mom got for them. Along with the hors d'oeuvres, Mom and my aunts are sipping glasses of wine and Dad and my uncles are on a fresh bottle of beer. I have no idea what Tammy and Debbie have concocted in their glass. I'm avoiding everything on the table and sipping my soda and listening to talk about not being overly concerned if one of the two twins develops sooner than the other, and talk of the hidden trap of the terrible twos. I'm listening to talk of teenagers that bring all new difficulties. I'm listening to talk about senior year and college on the near horizon. I'm listening to talk regarding middle school. There's talk of work problems and the cost of groceries and how to make this or that out of this or that and whatever sales at whatever stores are occurring. With little Maria now on Aunt Lorraine's lap, she asks Aunt Mary when she got the twins involved in Sunday school. Aunt Mary says three years old and I look at Tammy and see some agitation. See, more than just quitting going to church, Tammy has had a resentful opposition to it ever since. I don't know why, well, I actually do know why, it's boring, but I'd be happy with what she has already: Not having to go anymore. Mom has asked her if she wanted to go on the few occasions we've gone since she stopped and the answer is always been a firm no. But sitting there and seeing the small storm brew in Tammy, and for no other reason other than to agitate, I say, "So, Mom. What did you think about what Pastor Mark said to us at the end of the sermon?"

That gets a stare from dad that stops him from sipping his beer, and a bewildered look from mom. "What Pastor said to us?" she asks in a confused tone, wine glass in hand.

"Remember? At the end?" I say, then turn to Tammy and add, "When he said he's like to see more familiar faces at the sermons," I can see Tammy can't wait to have a rebuttal.

"I don't think, Robby," Mom says, sipping from her glass, "that he was talking directly to us."

Pressing, I say, "I don't know Mom. I mean," again turning to Tammy, "he was looking directly at us when he said it. I think he meant us."

Mom scoffs, but doesn't say anything.

Finished with my soda, getting up from the couch, heading for the dining room and the kitchen, I look at Tammy and say, "Well, it is a form of blasphemy, I guess. Not ever going to church." Tammy's says something to me about being brainwashed and I smirk on my way to the kitchen as my little spark starts a debate between Tammy and Debbie and my aunts about church values and Tammy's newfound…whatever they are values. Once in the kitchen I throw the empty soda can in the garbage can and head for the hallway entrance and my room. Mom meets me there. Calmly, but firmly, she asks me if I'm happy with what I just caused. I am. I just can't say it.

· · ·

Turns out that that little escapade was the highlight of the rest of the day. Other than Easter dinner and the desserts. After everyone's done eating and the dishes are dried and stacked and percolated coffee dominates the air, Dad turns on the television and everyone gathers to watch *The Ten Commandments*. Even Tammy sits and watches for a while. But nobody makes it to the end. Nobody ever makes it to the end. The movie is like four days long and immensely boring. That snake scene is pretty creepy and scary and I really don't know why we watch it every year, but we do. So as Easter day fades and Charlton Heston drones on and on, the later day sun cuts through the picture window blinds, creating golden angled slices of light on the parlor wall. And one by one, everyone leaves.

Chapter Four

Next morning there's a solid rap on my bedroom door and in a half-conscious state I hear Mom in the hallway telling me to get up. I take a few more minutes before I flip off the covers and sit at the edge of my bed. I stay there for a few minutes more before I saunter over to my window and look out the curtains. I see that the sun has also decided to sleep in a little later this morning, as it hides behind giant puffs of white. Moments later there's another rap on my door, this one a little more forceful with a louder command from mom to get up. "I'm already up," I say in an exasperated tone.

I walk out of my room and head for the kitchen. It's empty except for what's left of Mom's and Dad's breakfast on the kitchen table. I take a piece of half-eaten toast from Mom's plate and eat it on my way to the cabinet that holds the cereal bowls. I open the cabinet door, grab a bowl and the Cocoa Puffs next to them, fill up my bowl with milk, bringing the puffs precariously close to the brim, grab a spoon and head for the parlor.

I turn on the television. *Green Acres* comes on the screen and it's the one when Oliver's car blows a head gasket and he makes a new gasket out of Lisa's hotcakes batter. I head for the couch. I watch the show and chew on the Cocoa Puffs. During the commercials I notice some of the paper's in Dad's briefcase sitting on the other side of the couch. Those yellow and white one's from Brice's Auto. I slide over to get another look at them before dad leaves for work but in doing so some of the milk with a few Cocoa Puffs splash over the top of my bowl and splatter into the briefcase. I quickly dry the papers but dad's shuffling down the hallway prevents me from getting any of the Cocoa Puffs. I quickly slide back to where I was. Tying his tie he looks at me and as he heads for his briefcase, he asks in an unconcerned tone, "Are you supposed to be in here with that?" He grabs his briefcase and locks it shut.

"It's just the bottom of the bowl," I say, showing dad the bowl.

He doesn't look. He finishes tying his tie and straightens his jacket.

Seconds later Mom emerges from the basement. She's got a box in her hands that says curtains. She looks at me and in an instant rage says, "Robby! How many times! Huh? How many times do I have to say it?" I stare at her. "Off the couch with the cereal bowl!"

I huff and get up, wanting to say that just yesterday everyone was eating on the couch, but I keep quiet.

"And I better not find one of those Cocoa Puffs on the couch either," she adds.

On the couch? No, they won't be any found on the couch. Not today, anyway, I think to myself on my way to the kitchen. I hear Mom and Dad say their good-byes at the front door. I walk into the kitchen and before I cross the back door entrance, Tammy comes hurriedly in carrying a basket full of some still wet and muddy green spear-like things and I guess what looks like spinach. We both head for the kitchen sink. "I see you started your day off with the usual garbage," she says, looking at the bowl with a bit of brown milk left.

"What's wrong with Cocoa Puffs?"

Like the bird in the commercial, Tammy mocks out, "*I'm coo-coo for Cocoa Puffs, coo-coo for Cocoa Puffs.*"

"Funny," I say and give a half-beaten smile. Then I quickly put my bowl in the sink and walk away. "How funny's that?" I say.

Holding her basket full of muddy vegetables, Tammy snorts out, "Hey twerp. How about washing your own damn bowl!"

I turn and look at her and smirk and turn back around and head for my room.

. . .

Once in my room I forget all about Tammy as I actually have some work to do today. I sit at my desk and turn on my transistor radio, 66 WNBC joining me, and make some of the slips for my lawn cutting empire that I plan to hand out throughout the neighborhood. I've already come up with a name, **FOUR SEASONS LAWN SERVICE**, and using my large stencil I stencil it in black on the very top of the construction paper. Right underneath that I put the slogan

I came up with, **YARDS SO NICE THE BIRDS'ALL WANT TO STAY**, stenciled in red with a smaller stencil. From some of Mom's old magazines I've pasted pictures of well-kept yards with bird baths and bird feeders on them. Next to the pictures I made a list of things I can do. And in my smallest stencil in green color I stenciled my name and my phone number. A little more than hour passes and I've made three. I think they're pretty good. I roll the best one up like a baton and head for Tommy's. When I get to the parlor Mom and Tammy are at the front door getting ready to leave. Tammy heads for the car as Mom looks at me and says, "Robby, I'm taking your sister to work. I'm stopping at the store on the way home. Lunch is then. Be here. And wash your cereal bowl," she says as she walks out of the house, Tammy smirking at me following right behind her.

. . .

I keep the peaceful house to myself for a bit, then with my rolled up lawn cutting slip in my hand, I hop on my bike and head down to Tommy's house.I ride my bike under the carport and rest it against the back of the rusted Chevy Impala with the hood that won't close and an engine that never starts. I walk up the steps and knock on the door. Mrs. Hulse answers. "Oh, hello Robby," she says with her nice smile.

    Mrs. Hulse has a pretty face. But she always seems sad. I presume because of Tommy's dad. He's not around much and when he is it's always an uptight feeling. Sometimes when I'm walking up the walkway I hear him yelling. At her. At Tommy. At everybody. At nobody. When that happens, I turn around and leave. "Hi, Mrs. Hulse," I say as she opens the door and steps aside.

    "How was your Easter?" she asks.

    I shrug my shoulders and say, "Pretty good. How 'bout yours?"

    "Quiet, but nice," she says.

    "Oh. Well we just had family over," I say.

    "Well," she says, still smiling, "Family's nice." She stares at me for a few seconds and says, "Well you know where Tommy is."

    I shake my head that I do. Through the closed basement door I've heard Tommy slamming a ping pong ball around down there.

    "Hey Horsehead,' I yell out as I descend the wooden steps, the familiar musty concrete basement smell taking over. The overhead light mixes with daylight coming though the basement windows, giving off a dingy yellowish hue. And just as I figured, Tommy's got the ping pong table pushed against the far wall and he's playing a game against himself. He does this because he says the wall never gives, or hardly gives, a true bounce. Its great practice he says. For some reason he thinks he's gonna be the next person who goes to China to play ping pong against the Chinese. He says his name will be all in the papers. I constantly have to remind him that there's no ping pong tournaments around here.

Without interrupting his game, he says, "Birdyboy. How's it goin'? Pick up a paddle. We'll go a few games."

"Sure," I say, "but let me show you somethin' first."

Tommy hits the ball against the wall and catches it and turns and says, "Okay. What's that?"

I unfurl the slip I made and show it to Tommy. "Whadda ya think?"

He puts the paddle and ball down and takes the slip and looks at it. He scans it. "So I guess you were serious about this," he says. I nod that I am. "Slogan's kinda stupid," he says, handing me the slip back.

I disregard Tommy's remark. "I'm gonna make a lot of 'em and put 'em around the neighborhood and stuff," I say.

Tommy makes a face like it doesn't really matter. "Good luck with it," he says, again without any heart. "Tell ya what, Birdhouse, pick up a paddle, let's see if you got any game in ya today, then I've got somethin' to show you."

We play best two out of three which means just two games, of which I lose both by more than ten points each. Tommy is very good at ping pong. I just don't think he's ever going to go to China. When the second game ends Tommy tells me to follow him to the other side of the basement. Once there he dips underneath his dad's long workbench that's set against the back wall. I hear him moving what sounds like a cinder block and he emerges with a brown shopping bag. He hands it to me.

"What's this?" I ask.

"Open it up and find out," he says. "And try not to get too big a boner."

I open the bag. I can't believe my eyes. I pull out a small stack of *Playboy* magazines. Six in all. The one on top has five gorgeous girls on the cover with their knockers staring right at me. "I can't believe this," I gasp. "These Reimer's?"

"*Were* Reimer's," Tommy says. "And Broccoli's brother before that."

I'm thumbing through the magazine covers. There's one with a girl all curled up on a beach. You can't really see anything other than she has no clothes on. One has a beautiful dark haired girl with a red sweater and white gloves on. One has a pretty blond girl with an Indian-like head band on and she's making the peace sign. Another is wearing a very short and very tight black dress. "I can't believe this," I say again, in a trance.

"Well believe in one of 'em Birdbrain and pick it out and take a look." I pick the first one I saw out of the paper bag. I hand the rest back to Tommy. I thumb through the pages and get to the centerfold. I unfurl the page and oh my God. There it is. Right in front of me. Everything. A completely naked and beautiful girl. Staring and smiling right at me. "So where'd Reimer have 'em stashed?" I ask, not removing my eyes from the page in front of me

"Where I figured," Tommy says. "Along that path out in the woods behind his house. The one that leads out to Emerald's."

"That's a lot of woods," I say, still staring at the centerfold.

"Not really," Tommy says. "Brock took one side of the path, I took the other."

"Huh," I say, folding the page back up and thumbing through the rest of the magazine. The centerfold girl has a few more pictures of her and there's another naked girl a little further on in the magazine, but not another centerfold. "Think Reimer knows yet?"

"Who cares?" Tommy says, shrugging his shoulders. "Me'n Brock found 'em. An' we split 'em up. Six each."

"Whadda ya think Reeimer's gonna do when he finds out they're gone?"

"I don't know," Tommy says, not caring. "Cry probably."

Turning the pages, a picture of Raquel Welch comes up. I know her. She's the girl that was on that poster for the caveman movie a few years ago. I read the headline. *"Raquel Welch. A candid interview with Hollywood's hottest sex symbol and the improbable star of 'Myra Breckenridge.'"* She's just as pretty, prettier even I think, than any of the girls in this magazine. I start to read about Raquel when we hear the basement door open. Footsteps begin to descend the stairs. Quickly Tommy grabs the magazine out of my hands and has all of them back in the brown bag. In one swoop he's under the workbench with the bag and seconds later reemerged without it. We're sitting at the work bench when Tommy's mom walks in. She's carrying a basket of laundry. Tommy's slides his Brig of War model he's been working on toward him and starts to work on it.

I have to say, he's convincing. And that's really because the model's really coming out pretty good. He's got all the masts set up, four levels of them, with all the rigging. It's very intricate. He's got little men on the decks working on different equipment. Mrs. Husle puts the laundry into the machine and on the way out stops and asks me if I'd like to stay for lunch. I tell her thank you but mom's expecting me back. Once she's gone, Tommy gets the magazines out again. I look through them all. Every one of these girls is gorgeous. I get the one with Raquel again and as I begin to read the article, Tommy's mom calls him upstairs for lunch.

. . .

I ride my bike back home and after lunch I make two more slips. It's the last two pieces of construction paper I have. Now with five in all made, I decide on where best to leave them. I'll show one to ol' man Martin across the street, though he actually still cuts his own grass. He pushes this little electric mower around the yard with this orange snake of a cord following him everywhere. Takes him all morning to do it, but he does it. I'll leave one at the Lampman's around the block. I pass their house everyday on the way home from school and they've always been friendly. And they're kinda old. I'll leave one with the crazy lady down Brock's street. Mrs. Agrusa's her name, or something like that. She lives by herself but every once in a while we see people stopping at the house. I've shoveled her driveway a few times with Broccoli after it snowed and she gives us each a dollar each time. And her yard always looks like it could use some work. And she's not like, crazy crazy, just a lil' crazy.

So I walk across the street and show the Martin's the slip and wouldn't you know it, they want to keep it. Leaves me with only four. I ride down the block and onto Truman Street and the Lampman's aren't home so I leave one tucked into the big **L** on the front door. I turn and head the other way down Truman toward Brock's street and turn on to it and ride to the near end and fold a slip up and leave it the crazy lady's paper box. I decide to keep the two I have left and make some more during the week. I figure the best thing to do would make at least ten or more slips, keep a book like dad does, and write down the addresses where I dropped the slips off. On my way home I stop at Brock's house. I'm hoping to get a look at his stack of *Playboys*. I knock on the door. His mom answers. She tells me he went over to Tommy's. So I ride back over to Tommy's. I don't see Tommy's bike in the carport so I figure they're riding their bikes somewhere so I ride around the neighborhood trying to find them. I try Krauzer's, Necci's, Branch Park. No sign of them. I ride out to Roosevelt Street and cross the highway and try the 7-Eleven. They're not there either, so I head back home.

Chapter Five

Next day, mid-morning, I leave the house for the Two Guys department store out in the Plaza. I need a pack of construction paper to make the slips for my lawn cutting enterprise and though it's a bit of a ride out to the Plaza, it'll be worth it. For fifty-cents I'll get a pack of twenty-five sheets of paper of various colors instead of the measly ten I'd get at the 7-Eleven. So I start out for Two Guys.

I hop on my bike and head down my block. I figure I'll stop at Necci's on the way and see if they got in any of those cinnamon flavored toothpicks that come wrapped in waxy paper. They've been the hottest thing since Necci's started selling 'em last month and when they do get them, they sell out almost immediately. And besides that, sometimes, even a few days after Easter, Necci's still has some Danish or something left over that I can get either for free or for real cheap. Mere pennies. I ride past Tommy's house to see if he wants to tag along but don't see his bike under the carport so I turn onto Truman Street and then out to Constitution Street and then over to Van Buren Street. Necci's is at the end of the Van Buren Street, sort of caddy-cornered to the highway, and when I ride up the little ramp and onto the wood framed porch, who's sitting there but Tommy and Broccoli on one of the two benches by the telephone booth.

"Hey guys," I say, riding up to the bench. "What's happ'nin'?"

"Free cannoli," Broccoli says, showing me a half-eaten cannoli. Tommy shows me his free cannoli.

"Any left?" I ask.

Taking a bite of his cannoli, Broccoli says, "There was. But a few people have come and gone since we got here."

"Huh," I say, kicking down my bike stand and standing it near the unoccupied wooden bench. "I'd better get in there then," I say. "Any cinnamon sticks yet?" I ask as I head for the door.

Brock and Tommy both shrug their shoulders. "Dunno. We just came for the free stuff," Broccoli says.

I walk in the store. The cowbell over the front door clangs as I open and shut the door. Then the overwhelming smell of cheese hits me. There are a lot of smells inside Necci's, but cheese is by far the strongest. And it's everywhere. There's different colored cheese in the glass encased counter. There's blocks of cheese in colorful wrappers in baskets hanging from the ceiling. There's different sized jars with different grated cheese on the front counter. There's melted cheese in crock pots behind the counter on the stove. Necci's has other stuff too, like different shaped and sized and colored bottles with all kinds of oils in them. Loaves of different kinds and different colored breads. They have a small deli section with fresh salads and stuff and an aisle full of delicacies. They have a real cool freezer in the back full of sodas that I can't get anywhere else. They have fair candy section. And another thing they have here and nowhere else is newspapers and magazines in both English and Italian.

Mrs. Necci is behind the counter wiping down the near empty glass encased counter. There's one Danish left. She sees me through the cleaned glass. "Roberto, Buongiorno."

"Hi Mrs. Necci," I say. I walk to the front counter. I start looking for the box with the cinnamon toothpicks. I push this and that out of the way and I look over this and that. I don't see them.

Watching what I'm doing, Mrs. Necci says, "Roberto, what are you looking for?"

"Cinnamon toothpicks."

Straightening up, wiping her hands on her smock, Mrs. Necci mumbles something under her breath in Italian and walks to the small stock area at the side of the front counter. She emerges with a brand new box of the red-striped, waxy packages of fire hot cinnamon flavored toothpicks. I'd buy two but the Neccis will only sell each kid one. She opens the box, hands me a package, and puts the box down on the front counter. I take a dime out of my pocket for the toothpicks and place it on the counter. I have a nickel and a few pennies left so I ask Mrs. Necci how much the Danish is. Mrs. Necci goes and gets the

Danish. I reach in my pocket for the pennies and the nickel. Mrs. Necci puts the Danish on the counter, slides the dime her way and says. "Roberto. Abbastanza," motioning that a dime is enough.

I stop digging for money. I grab the Danish and with my cinnamon sticks in hand say thank you. I go and join Tommy and Brock on the small porch in the front of the store. I sit down on the empty wooden bench and in short time, mere seconds, devour the Danish. I take the package of cinnamon sticks and unfold the top. Now you only get twelve toothpicks in these packages, but thinking sharing will get me another look at the magazines, I take three out. One each for me, Brock and Tommy.

"Thanks there Birdman," Broccoli says, taking the toothpick. "So Horeshead here tells me you're startin' your own kind of lawn cuttin' thing," he says.

"Yeah," I say. "I'm actually on my way to get some construction paper to make some flyers to pass around the neighborhood."

"Birdbrain's gonna be the next *Lawn King* of Branch Manor," Tommy says, taking his toothpick. "Or he thinks so."

"Huh," Broccoli says. "How much you gonna charge?" Brock asks.

"Guess it depends," I say.

"On?" Broccoli asks.

"On how bad the yard is. Or the size of it." Sounds smart.

"Huh," Broccoli says again. He turns to Tommy. "Think we should tell 'em what our plan is there, Horsyhead?"

Tommy shrugs his shoulders with indifference. "Birdclaw there already knows a lot anyway," he says.

I'm waiting in anticipation as to what their plan is though I figure it has to have something to do with the magazines they found and sure enough, Broccoli says that they're gonna sell the magazines for two dollars each. Now I know I remember seeing the cover of the magazines and them saying they're only one dollar. So I mention that.

Broccoli just smiles and says, "Sure, they're only a dollar in the store, Birdyboy. But if you walk into the 7-Eleven with a dollar, or even two, are you walkin' out with one?"

I don't answer because I know that of course the answer's no.

"What does the ol' Kazoo call that in math class, Horsehead?" Broccoli asks Tommy. "In business? Caveat somethin'."

"I don't know what he calls it," Tommy says. "I call it if you want a magazine its two bucks."

Broccoli looks at me and smiles and asks, "Wanna be the first to get one Birdy? You'd have the pick of the litter."

"Maybe," I say, knowing that I don't even have two dollars, but figuring I can get a glimpse at Broccoli's stash, adding, "But I've only seen Tommy's."

"So then let's take a ride to my house so you can take a peek. It don't matter who you buy from 'cause Tommy an' me are splittin' the profits. Fifty-fifty." Tommy and Brock slap hands in agreement.

Sounds fine to me. So we get up from the wooden benches. I grab my bike and walk it down the ramp to the side of the store where Tommy's and Brock's bikes are resting against the wall. Just as we're about to get on them we hear screeching car tires out on the highway. The piercing sound lasts for a few seconds. We look down the highway in both directions. Even Mr. Necci has scrambled out onto the front porch. We don't see anything, we don't hear anything. No sound of crumpling metal, or shattering glass. No yelling. Must have been a near miss.

As I turn away from the highway, out of the corner of my eye, I think I see Brother Davis and his ratty orange Beetle heading our way. It's a few blocks down the highway, and there's lots of those Beetles on the road nowadays, but I'm pretty sure it's Brother Davis. "Hold up a sec guys," I say.

Tommy and Brock hold up and seconds later I see that indeed it is Brother Davis. And it looks like that kid Don that hangs around with Debbie at the house is with him. I'm expecting them to drive by so I back up against the wall so not to be seen but Brother Davis pulls his car right into Necci's, windows down, music blaring. And right behind Brother Davis there's that gray four door Nova I've seen a few times around my house, also pulling into Necci's, also with the windows down, also with the music blaring.

The parking lot's instantly quiet when they shut off the car engines. Brother Davis and Don emerge from the Beetle and I recognize the driver of the Nova, I'm sure from one of Tammy's weirdo Watt's gatherings. I've seen that stupid yellow tee-shirt he has on that says **SAVE THE HUMANS.** I've never seen the other kid. He has on those moccasin-style shoes that all the hippies wear with a plain white tee-shirt and one of those Indian-style vests where the bottom is all frayed. I try to make out what they're saying as they make their way into the store, but I can't.

As soon as they all walk into Necci's, Tommy dashes over to Davis' Beetle and looks inside. I guess he sees nothing of interest, so he dashes over to the Nova and peers in. Then he half jumps into the car, his feet teetering off the ground, reaching for something. He stretches, stretches, stretches and teeters back to his feet and dashes back to the side of the store. He's holding a pack of cigarettes. A few seconds later we hear the cowbell ring and watch as the four of them leave the store and get back into their cars. We hear them say something about meeting each other somewhere and then the music is blaring again. Seconds later they back up out of the parking spots and pull back onto the highway.

The cigarettes Tommy has in his hands are a soft pack of Winston's and when he opens the package his eyes grow wide. "Now would you look at this," he says, pulling out a cigarette that does not look like a regular Winston cigarette.

"Is that what I think it is?" I ask.

Tommy holds it up to his nose and takes a deep breath. "Certainly is Birdman. Oh and look at this," Tommy says, big smile on his face, "another one right next to it. And another one right next to that," he says, almost giddy with excitement. "Oh and two more behind the silver." He takes them out of the package. "Smell this, Brockworst." He hands one to Brock

Taking a deep breath of the funny looking cigarette, Broccoli says, "Yep. No doubt about it. That's the real McCoy." He hands me the funny cigarette.

I smell it but I'm not sure what the smell should be like. "I can't say I've ever smelled this before," I say, handing it back to Tommy. "Are you guys, like sure?"

"Sure we're sure. I've smelt this 'round Mark more than once," Brock says, looking at Tommy who is nodding in agreement. "You never smelt it 'round Tammy cakes or her Beetle drivin' boyfriend?"

"No," I say. "Not that I can remember."

"Well, take a sniff when she's around, Birdyboy," Brock says. "Or when she's with her groupies. I bet they're burnin' a lot of incense when they're all together."

Come to think of it, they actually are.

"Probably chewin' a lot of gum, too," Brock adds getting on his bike. "Like Mark does."

"Well, that I never noticed," I say, hopping on my bike. "So what are you gonna do with 'em anyway?" I ask Tommy.

Getting on his banana bike, Tommy looks at Brock and says, "I don't know. Whadda ya think, Brock?" he says as we start to pedal down the street. "Maybe give one to Mark for being cool about the magazines?" Brock nods that that would be a cool thing. "Maybe sell some. Maybe keep some."

I'm not sure why Tommy would want to keep one unless he's planning on starting to smoke that stuff, but as we're pedaling down the street, going to get a peek at Brock's stash of magazines, I'm thinking that between the *Playboy* magazines and the funny Winston cigarettes, Tommy and Brock have quite the illicit business going on.

Chapter Six

Now I know that yesterday I should've gone, at some time, up to the Two Guys and bought the construction paper that I need to make my slips and hand them out throughout the neighborhood. If I really think I'm going to have any kind of lawn operation going on. But once I got to Brock's house yesterday I ended up hanging around there with Tommy all afternoon. I got to see all Brock's *Playboys* and they were all just as good as Tommy's. I'd like to buy one, I just don't have two dollars. I barely have the fifty-five cents for the construction paper that I still have to buy, and I don't get my allowance till later in the week, and that's only a measly dollar and a half anyway. I'd have to scrimp and save at least for two weeks to get one. And even if I did save the money, they'd probably be gone by then. Then Mark came home later and smelled the funny cigarettes that Tommy said he "found" and happily took the one Tommy said he'd give 'em for letting him keep the magazines. Mark said that that was really cool of Tommy and then bought another one for a dollar. He said it smelled like good bud, whatever that means. Tommy said he was gonna keep the other three and decide later what he wanted to do with them. Mark told Tommy to seal them up real good and keep them in a cool dry place, and if he ever wanted to sell them, he'd give him five bucks for all three.

So that's what happened yesterday afternoon, so I guess it was my fault for not getting to the store. But today, with the day being over now, and as my favorite TV show *The Mod Squad* is set to come on, it's only partially my fault for not going, and even the partial bit is understandable. And that's because two things happened.

First, when I woke up in the morning, I heard the pattering of rain on my window. Not a drenching rain, but rain nonetheless. The kind of rain that I didn't feel like riding my bike all the way out to the Plaza and getting drenched in the process. Then carting the construction paper in the shopping bag under my windbreaker all the way home. I figured I'd see what the afternoon brought. Sometimes the day turns out nicer than one thinks it will. So I lay there for a few minutes, slowly got out of bed, and shuffled over to the window. I yawned and stretched and looked out the window. Gray skies. Light rain. Wet roads. Damp weather. Certainly wasn't a morning for taking a ride up to the Two Guys.

So I had breakfast, which was very pleasant because Tammy was nowhere to be found and I didn't have to listen to any of her Cocoa Puff remarks or look at any of her muddy vegetables. Dad must have left early for work and the only blemish during breakfast was when Mom appeared out of nowhere and in one pass through the kitchen said for me to make sure I wash my cereal bowl and to drink my orange juice and wash the glass and put my damn clothes away and don't think for one second I'll be traipsing in and out of the house all day with any wet sneakers. I eat a spoonful of cocoa puffs. It always amazes me how much mom can be thinking about at one time.

I kept the peace by doing the things I was asked to do, which really didn't take all that long anyway, and then headed out the front door, telling Mom I was on my way to Tommy's. I was hoping he'd be home and that he'd let me take another look at his magazines. I'd like to see the one with Raquel Welch again before it gets sold.

I walked briskly down to Tommy's and Mrs. Hulse answered the door and I instantly heard Tommy downstairs in the basement playing ping pong. She smiled her usual smile and I said my usual 'I know where Tommy is' and moments later I was helping Tommy pull the ping pong table away from the wall to play a best two out of three, which after, I'd get to look at the magazines.

Of course I lost both games, rather handedly. And of course I didn't care. I never really care and I especially didn't care then. All I cared about was getting another look at Tommy's stash of magazines. And Tommy was true to his word for right after the second game I was sitting at his dad's workbench looking through with the *Playboy* magazine with Raquel Welch in it. And even at this third time of seeing her, and even with all her clothes on, she's still the most pretty girl in the whole magazine. I started to read the article that was about her.

Apparently, this movie that she was just in, this *Myra Breckenridge* movie, is a very strange one. Her character had some kind of sex change thing which I don't even understand how that can happen, but apparently it can. Anyway the character Raquel played went to Europe to have the operation, to stop being Myron Breckenridge, and then came back to America, after the operation, and was then Myra Breckinridge. Tommy, working on his Brig of War model, looked at me while I was reading and said, "Birdbath, you're supposed to look at the pictures, not read the stuff."

I guess Tommy's right but I ignored him and read on a little bit more, but I couldn't really understand much of the article. The person who was talking to Raquel in the magazine was asking her how she felt about the movie's negative reviews and something about exploitations and something about redesigned gender roles. I had no clue as to what any of that meant so I stopped reading and took one more look at beautiful Raquel and started to flip through the magazine when Tommy and me both heard the sound of a car pulling into the driveway. Tommy dashed over to the basement window, looked out, and with the devil in his eye, dashed back. "Dad's home," he said. Instantly, I handed the magazine to Tommy who in mere seconds had it back in the brown bag and back in its hiding place. Then Tommy went back to working on the model. Minutes later we heard his father descend the basement stairs. I smiled the best smile I could and said "Hello, Mr. Hulse," when he walked over to where we were sitting.

"Hello, lad," he said, with not a trace of friendliness in his voice. "Son," he said to Tommy.

"Dad," Tommy said back, not turning around and still working on the model.

Mr. Hulse stared at Tommy for a moment, who kept working on his model, and then at me. I had even a weaker smile then when he walked in, and then thankfully, Mr. Hulse plainly turned around and went back up the stairs. I didn't stay much longer after Tommy's dad came home. He wasn't yelling at any one or anything, but it was close enough to lunch time anyway and for one reason or another, somehow or another, Tommy's dad always brings some kind of uneasiness into the house with him.

As I walked back home and I could see the skies were beginning to clear up. And when I neared my house, I could see Brother Davis' ugly orange Beetle parked out front in the street. I walked past the car, peeked inside, seeing nothing but strewn papers and strewn books and empty plastic cups and straws and wrappers. I walked up the driveway. Mom wasn't home yet and when I walked in the house, I could hear whoever was here in the porch room. The slatted door was closed but I could still hear them. Even over the blasting record player.

    I wanted to see if I could smell anything coming from the room so I quietly slunk over and put my nose up to the wood-slatted door and sniffed. I couldn't smell anything. I tried peeking through the slat to see who was in there, but I really couldn't make anybody out. I'm sure it's Debbie and Don and it sounds maybe like Katie and I knew Tammy's and Brother Davis' voices when they sang out really loud in unison, *Tell me what is my life, without your love? And tell me, who am I, without you, by my side?* That George Harrison song that they love so much. I was still near the porch trying to listen when I was startled by the front door opening and mom walking in. She stared at me for a second and then with complete exasperation, said, "Robby! What did I tell you! Huh?" I just stared back and then felt relieved that she yelled at me for not taking off my sneakers and getting her clean floor all marked up, rather than for eavesdropping. Mom hates eavesdropping. She shook her head and said, "Well, since they're still on I have the new ironing board in the back seat of the car. Go and get it, please."

    Now if I knew mom was going up to the Plaza, I would've hitched a ride. Would've saved me the trip. I wanted to ask Mom why she didn't tell me she was going, but I don't 'cause I know what I'll hear in return. So I bit my tongue, being happy enough I didn't get caught eavesdropping. And about this ironing board? I head for the front door and Mom's car still in a state of disbelief that Mom and Dad saved green stamps all winter long just to get a new ironing board. With all the cool things in the catalog to get, like dart boards or radios or wall posters, they chose an ironing board. So I put the thing in the garage and before I got in the house, the mailman came and along with whatever stuff that was for Dad and Mom, my new edition of *Street and Smith's Basketball* magazine came. So I walked back in the house, this time removing my sneakers at the front door, and glided over the floor and down the hallway and into my room with the magazine. Lew Alcindor is on the cover. Game four of the finals is tomorrow night and the Bucks lead the series 3-0 against the Bullets. One more win and they sweep the series. And I'm really rooting for the Bucks to beat the Bullets. I've hated the Bullets since they knocked my Knicks out of the playoffs week before Easter. The Knicks lost game seven by two lousy points. One bleepin' basket.

I'm engrossed in the magazine when mom rapped on my door and told me it was lunch time. She set a plate for me in the kitchen while in the dining room sat Tammy, Debbie, Brother Davis, Don, Katie and the kid from the Nova. Not the one driving, the other one, with the Indian vest on. I didn't catch the name. Anyway, I ate my peanut butter and jelly sandwich and my bowl of chips and the small fruit cup and drank my glass of cherry Kool-Aid and listened to the six of them talk about the Beetles and who was gonna have the best solo career. Debbie's a Paul fan and Davis and Tammy like George and Katie's still too broken up to have a favorite and Don and the other kid said John will have them all beat. I guess nobody likes Ringo. Then they went on to the space thing and the rocket ship thing that they all hate. In that they're in unison, that it's a complete waste of time and money. Besides all that poison that we're blasting into the atmosphere, they say, what will we ever get out of it? I do have to say one thing on that one, and that's grandma, who is quite sane, also believes that sending these rocket ships into space is a bad thing. She says all kinds of strange events happen on earth every time we send one of those things into orbit. Hurricanes and earthquakes and floods. Then the anti-space talk leads to the military thing. For some reason, they're all convinced that the army has something to do with all this space travel. Something about weapons from outer space. I just rolled my eyes. And then it went on to Watt's and the earth and everything we need is here and the earth as a spaceship moving at colossal speed and…I'm done. I take my last bite and last gulp and put my glass and the bowls into the sink. I went back to my room, finished the article on Lew Alcindor and the Bucks, and was on my way up to the Two Guys.

And then the second thing happened.

I went back to Tommy's and thankfully his dad was gone and I asked Tommy if he wanted to take a ride up to the Two Guys. He said he was up for it and we decided to ride down the utility road instead of the highway. Well we hadn't even got to the utility road when Billy Cutro and Johnny Pawin came flying by on their bikes and yelling that Dean and Bruce were gonna race two kids from the other neighborhood out in the Zone! Right now!

So we pedaled like hell over to Brock's house and picked him up. Then we raced over to and down the utility road, which is really nothing more than a hardened dirt road that runs the entire length of the neighborhood, all the way from the power plant out to where our neighborhood ends, or begins. That's where what we kids call the Forbidden Zone is. We call it that because the piece of land looks just like the Forbidden Zone from the *Planet of the Apes* movie. Land unmoved with time. Land that is just a barren lot about three football lengths long and maybe just as wide, made up mostly of soft sand and scrub brush and weedy grass and buffered by thin woods three quarters around. When we got there, kids from both neighborhoods were milling about, waiting for the race. Small arguments broke out about who would win. Bets were placed. Crow would be eaten. Bragging rights would be won. We waited and argued. We waited and challenged. We waited and waited and waited and nobody showed up. So I guess I did sort of waste the afternoon away, but that was solely because of a false rumor.

Chapter Seven

Today I'm going to go. No matter what. I'm going to avoid stopping at Tommy's and getting distracted with ping pong games and *Playboy* magazines. I'll ride along the highway instead of taking the utility road and going anywhere near the Forbidden Zone. On the highway I won't stop at Necci's for anything. In fact, I'll avoid going past it all together. I won't watch any television after breakfast and right now, even as I'm eating it, I won't get into an argument with Tammy who is now making fun of Cap'n Crunch. First it's Cocoa Puffs, and now it's Cap'n Crunch. "Aye aye sir," she's saying to me. "I'll eat this garbage, aye aye sir," she saying with a salute my way. I just eat my cereal and ignore her.

Right after breakfast I do my Thursday chore of collecting all the garbage in the house. The small can on the porch and the small can downstairs by mom's pantry and the can in my room and the small one in the bathroom and the bigger can in the kitchen and the can out in the garage. I don't dare go near Tammy's room. I get that all bundled up and put it into the silver can on the side of the house and drag it all out to the street. That's my Thursday chore, whether I'm in school or out of school, all the time, all year round, except on holidays. Later in the day, I have to bring the silver can back to the side of the house and make **damn sure** that the lid is on tight. I caught slack one time for not making sure that the lid was on tight on a windy day and it got blown out to the street and run over by a few cars and dad had to go buy another one.

Done with my chore, I'm riding my bike down Constitution Street all the way to Roosevelt Street, thus coming out onto the highway well after Necci's. I begin the long trek down the highway to the Plaza and Two Guys.

I'm riding with the traffic to get some push from the draft of the cars zipping by me. I get to the circle and wait for an opening. I can smell coffee brewing from the Dunkin Donuts in the little strip mall on this side of the circle. There's a break in the traffic so I dash across the two lane round road and walk my bike across the grassy center of the circle. There I wait for another opening and when I do I dart across and hop back on my bike, this time going against the traffic. From there there's a big long dip in the road and I pick up as much speed as I can and as the road starts to climb, I stand up and pump the pedals. When I get to the crest of the road I can see the giant **Two Guys** sign and the approaching Plaza.

At the light at the big intersection I turn onto and then cross over Cornerbridge Road that leads into the Plaza. From there I leisurely ride into Lower Brook Plaza that besides the Two Guys has a twin movie theatre which today has *A Clockwork Orange* playing, which must be pretty good 'cause it's been there a while now. I'd like to see it but I can't 'cause it's rated R. I hear it's a really weird movie. The other movie playing, *Willie Wonka and the Chocolate Factory*, I saw already and it was really good. There's an H.L Green's department store here which is a small, but actually pretty neat store. They got lots of stuff there and cheap and that's where mom and dad usually trade their stamp books in for something. The latest something the ironing board. I still can't believe that. An ironing board! There's also a Burger Chef and a Baskin Robbin's and a Town's Drugstore.

The Two Guys is at the far end of the Plaza, set back from the rest of the stores. It has an extremely large parking lot that believe it or not, can get completely filled up. I ride my bike under the big overhang that covers the twelve doors leading into and out of the store. I leave my bike behind the phone booths, check the coin slots for any left change, which there isn't any, and head into the store.

Now Two Guys department store has everything. And I do mean everything. They have clothes for work and clothes for dressing up and just plain clothes. Work shoes, dress shoes, sneakers, slippers, sandals. Pajamas, socks, underwear. Washers, dryers, air conditioners, fans, humidifiers. Clocks, radios, records, record players, tape players. Jewelry, furniture. Lawn mowers, shovels, rakes. Automobile stuff. Bicycles, toys, and stationary, where I'm headed. Some stores have some of this stuff, but none of them have it all. There's even a small restaurant in the back of the store.

Linda Orken

I walk down the aisle where the multi-colored packs of construction paper are. There's a few different brand choices and I find one with a fifty cents tag on it and that's the one I grab. With the pack in hand, I walk over to the sneaker section and take a look around. I like the new Converse One Star sneaker. They're a sleek red color with a white star between two white stripes. Adidas has out these Americana's which are really cool. Blue and red stripes with a blue edged back and some kind of reinforced toe. The Pro Keds Royal Master are sort of like the Americana's, just without one stripe and a blue back. I like the Nike Cortez with the red swoop but they're mainly just for running. Chuck Taylor High Tops are in a real cool green color this year, but I don't really like Chuck Taylor High Tops. And here they are: The crème de la crème. Puma Clydes. Gold in color in that suede Puma fabric and a black Puma stripe going down both sides and black laces. The same colors as my school. And endorsed by my favorite basketball player, Clyde Frazier. I look at the price tag. $22.00. That's a lot of money. I put them down by my feet. I stare at them. I imagine I'm bringing the basketball up the court at Lower Brook Middle School, and then dishing and swishing, as Clyde would say. I stare at the sneakers a little longer and pick them back up. I inspect them closely. I look at the price tag again. It still says $22.00. That's a lot of money.

I put the sneakers back on the shelf and start to head over to the records. I'm not buying any but I want to see the top 40 and take a look through the ten cent bin. Last week *Joy To The World* was number one and *Never Can Say Goodbye* was number two. I head for the main aisle. The record department is on the other side of the store in the back. Walking down the aisle I stop in my tracks. Quickly I dash into an aisle. I peer out from behind hanging pots and pans. That can't be her, but just in case, I ditch going to the records and head for the registers. When I get there there's only two open and one has an old couple in line with stamp books in their hand. I think they're green stamps. I avoid that line because old people in line holding stamp books of any color usually ends up in an argument with the cashier. They either have the wrong stamps or the wrong product and it always takes forever to convince them otherwise. I move to the other lane where there's two people ahead of me, but not with any stamp books. I scan the magazines in the racks as I'm waiting in line. There's a large rack with magazines that Mom reads: *Ladies Journal*, *Red Book*, *Good Housekeeping*, *Family Circle*, *Better Homes and Garden* and stuff like that. There's another rack with today's newspapers and *Life* magazine and *People* magazine and *Harper's Magazine* and stuff like that. The person ahead of me moves up so I move up. The last magazine rack before the conveyor belt and checkout has *Sports Illustrated* and *Baseball Digest* and *Golf Digest* and *Pro Wrestling Illustrated* and stuff like that and below those there's *Tiger Beat* and *True Romance* and *Right On!* and *16 Magazine* and stuff like that. I see that David Cassidy and the Osmonds are on the cover of *Tiger Beat*. I don't care for either one of them, though Marie is kinda cute. Just in an Osmond way. There's somebody else at the bottom of the magazine that I don't recognize and it looks like maybe they're wearing a dog collar or something. I bend down to take a closer look and recoil slightly when I see that it is indeed a dog collar. I'm scanning over the cover of the magazine trying to figure out who it is that's wearing a dog collar when from behind me I hear, "What's so interesting down there, Robert?"

Hearing my name spoken like that instantly starts a cringing in my back that slowly ratchets me upward. I know who it is. I guess it was her in the main aisle. When I stand up straight and turn around Joni's standing there, different color spools of yarn in her hands. I look at Joni, then back at the magazine. "Ah, nothin', I guess."

"Must of have been something interesting," Joni says accusingly. "The way you were staring at it."

"Well, no," I say. "It's just that," I point to the magazine, "whoever that person is there, it looks like they're wearing a dog collar." I say, turning back toward Joni like I've just given the most defensible plausibility ever for staring at the magazine.

Joni doesn't look at the magazine or even blink. "You do know that those magazines promote promiscuous behavior, don't you Robert?"

That I did not know. I'm not even quite sure what that means. Joni's mom walks up behind her. She smiles and says hello to me. I say hello back. By the grace of God the person in front of me is done. I smile and turn away. I put the construction paper down and the checkout lady rings it up on the register and tells me fifty two cents of which I hand her. She puts an orange paid sticker on the paper and I pick the package up and start to head for the exit. Before I round the checkout lane Joni says, "There's a bible study tonight, Robert. Seven o'clock. In case you didn't know."

I turn toward Joni and her smiling mother and nod indiscriminately and then turn back and head for the exit.

Chapter Eight

Now yesterday when I gathered all the trash from the house, I purposely left the old magazines that Mom leaves in a box in the parlor closet when she's done with them where they were. I figured on using them for the pictures I need for nicely kept yards to put on my slips. But now, after I've sat down and stenciled out a few new slips, I go to the closet to retrieve the magazines and find that they're gone. Now I know it was Tammy who took 'em 'cause ever since this year's Earth Day she's been collecting them, among other things, bottles and clothing and returning them or doing something with them where she works. She works at this strange store called Mokunai that sells gypsy-like clothing and Indian-like jewelry and weird sculptures and strange books and wall posters and tee shirts and just overall weird stuff that apparently was something else before it became what it is now.

Now I know I can't really blame Tammy for anything, I should've just put them in my desk yesterday, but it still irks me that somehow she's always in my way. Or annoying me in some shape or form. So I decide that I'll head on over to Tommy's to see if his mom has any old magazines I can use. I walk in the parlor and turn on the television and lace up my sneakers. The game show *Concentration* comes on and I watch the first ten minutes of it. The top part of the puzzle might be a torch which gets me to think it could be the Statue of Liberty, but the puzzle hardly ever turns out to be what I think it is. And only one letter so far has been revealed. A commercial comes on and I'm contemplating watching the rest of the show before I head over to Tommy's when mom walks in the parlor, rummaging through her pocket book in a way that I know can mean only one thing. "Where ya goin'?" I ask.

Still rummaging through her purse, pulling her coupon book out, not looking at me, she says, "Food shopping."

Green light alert! Shopping! Food shopping! Probably old magazines there! In the big green dumpsters in the back of the store! "Can I come?" I ask, half jumping up from my chair.

Still looking at her coupons and her list, Mom says, "Robby, I just want to go and get what we need and get back. I don't need you pestering me up and down every aisle."

"I won't be any pester," I say. "Really. I'll just stay up front and look at some of the newspapers."

Mom puts her coupon book back in her purse and looks at me like I've just said he most obscure thing ever. "Why?" she asks.

"I want to read about the Bucks sweeping the Bullets," I say. "Our paper had hardly anything on it." Which is partially true. But I really want to see if I can get any magazines and I don't want to tell mom about why. Not yet. That'll just start a whole round of new questions of why.

Mom shakes her head and snaps her purse shut and in a somewhat annoyed tone says, "Let's go then."

The car ride helps me out a lot 'cause the Shop Rite is just as far away as the Plaza is, just in a different direction. It's out on the old highway past Heron Pond Road. I can ride my bike and save some time if I cut through the power plant at the back of my neighborhood and ride down Juniper Street in the new neighborhood, but it's still a bit of a hike, even from there. So the car ride helps.

Mom and me get to the Shop Rite and Mom grabs a cart and tells me to be here when she's done because if I'm not I'll be hoofing it back home. I acknowledge her threat and head for the newspaper rack at the end of the checkout lanes. I scan the papers and it turns out none of them really have much to say about the Bucks either. Just that they swept the Bullets and won the NBA Finals. Their first as a franchise. I don't know how long Mom's gonna be so I quickly walk out of the store and slip down the side of the building. The two big green dumpsters are behind a ten foot high green chain-linked fence that has a clasp and a lock but never is locked up. I swing the giant gate wide open and it scrapes against the pavement. I walk inside the enclosure and there's cardboard boxes all over the place and garbage bags half in and half out of the dumpsters. Like they were just thrown over the fence. There's empty soda cans and empty bottles and mashed up cigarette butts and Burger Chef bags and Dunkin Donut coffee cups all over. And between the two dumpsters is a solitary chair. Now why would anyone want to sit between two smelly dumpsters? I look inside the dumpsters and don't see anything but garbage bags and trash and I look under the dumpsters and don't see anything but more trash and just when I'm about to give up I see against the far corner of the fence a small bundle of magazines. I walk over and pick up the bundle and rip the string and in the middle of the bundle lo and behold there's two *Better Homes and Gardens* and one *Good Housekeeping* and one *Family Circle*. I take the magazines and throw the rest in to the dumpster. Before I walk back into the store I put the magazines in the car under the front seat.

I'm hoping as I walk back into Shop Rite that Mom's not at any of the checkout lines yet and luckily, she's not. A take a seat on one of the benches by the free handouts and the community bulletin board and wait. As I do I see that the crazy old man that I sometimes see is here again. What this crazy old man does is he walks around all the checkout lanes looking for cigarette butts. He looks in the ashtrays at the end of the lanes for cigarette butts. He looks under the benches and down by the newspaper racks for cigarette butts. He looks under the chairs outside the store and in the entrance area and out by the carts. All for old cigarette butts. And when he finds one he deems smoke worthy, he lights it. And I just can't understand why. Why would anyone smoke and old cigarette butt after somebody else has smoked it and put it out on the floor? Or in an ashtray? So I just assume that he's just some kind of crazy.

Mom shows up at the checkout and I help her bag the groceries. As I'm doing this I know that at some time I'm gonna have to run this great lawn cutting idea of mine over with Dad. I also know it'll be better if I can get Mom to, if at worst, say that it sounds like a good idea but it'll be up to Dad, or maybe, at best, she'll tell Dad what a great idea she thinks it is. How I'll be working a little and making some money and learning how to be responsible and all that jazz. So as we're walking out of the Shop Rite on our way to the car, I decide I'll tell her on the way home.

I begin by pulling the magazines I found from underneath the front car seat. Mom notices them and asks where I got them from. I tell her. So I get the first, "Why," from her astonished face,

"Well," I say, "I've been thinking, actually preparing, on having my own lawn cutting business."

"Lawn cutting business," Mom says. "What does that mean?"

I can't believe I have to explain this to Mom like I had to with Horsehead. It seemsed self-explanatory to me, but I tell Mom my idea. I tell her about the slips I'm making. I tell her that's why I need the magazines. For the pictures of nice yards that I'm putting on my slips. I tell her I'll show her one as soon as I'm finished with it. I tell her a few are already mostly done. I tell her I've already handed out a few throughout the neighborhood. I tell her to who I left the slips with. She listens. She shrugs her shoulders. She says it sounds okay but adds that it'll be up to Dad.

After lunch I hunker in my room and finish making some slips. I add the best pictures I can find to the few I've already stenciled out and then I make a few more. When I'm finished I have five nicely made slips. I walk out of my room with them in my hand looking for mom. She's sitting on the couch in the parlor folding laundry and watching that afternoon television show she always watches, *As The World Turns*. I show Mom the slips and she takes them and looks at shuffles them and nods approvingly. "Well, you did a good job with them, that I can say," she says. "And I love what you did with the slogan," she says with a smile, handing them back to me. "Good luck with your father," is all she adds.

I take the slips back. "Think I should ask, tell dad my idea tonight?" I say.

Mom's already back to watching her show and blindly folding laundry. "Good as night as any," she says.

So later as supper arrives, during it I'm waiting for when I think will be the best time to tell dad about my idea. It's Friday so he came home in a good mood. During supper he was telling mom some of the jokes that went around the office. Like 'What's big and brown and looks good on an IRS agent? A Doberman.' Jokes like that. Mom made Dad's favorite supper of meat loaf and mashed potatoes and creamed corn and even Tammy's been tolerable. So near the end of supper I'm about to talk when Dad looks at Tammy and says, "Let me know if you want to take the car out this weekend. Your test's coming up quickly."

Tammy's taking her driver's test next month. Last year when she got her permit Dad bought her an old Dodge Dart that he's been fixing it up little by little ever since. "I know," she says. "Maybe Sunday morning?" she asks. "I don't have to be at work till twelve."

Dad nods. "That'll be fine. We can go out to the Plaza and practice K turns and parallel parking while the lot's empty. Maybe get on and off the circle a few times, which can be…difficult, as you know," dad says.

"Just got to be careful," Tammy says, confidently.

"Careful yes," Dad says. "And sometimes lucky," he adds. "Just don't be in a rush. Anywhere. Give yourself plenty of time and stay focused on the road."

Tammy nods her head. "I know, Dad. I'm very careful."

I'd like to add my advice for Tammy, like if she's wearing her clown clothes while driving people might think that the circus is in town so, maybe she should put something else on, but I refrain. For one, Dad, Mom too, but more Dad, is taking Tammy's driver's test very seriously. They're happy about it and worried about it at all at the same time. Somehow, they can't believe that she's driving already. And besides all that, I've got more important things to discuss with Dad right now.

So I wait for that conversation to end and when supper's over and the table has been cleared and Tammy has gone on her way and Mom is beginning to wash the dishes, she turns and gives me a look as if now would be a good time to ask. So I look at Dad, take a small breath and say, "Ah, Dad."

Looking at his evening newspaper, "Robby," he says.

"Ah, well, I have this great idea that, well, ah, Mom said I should run past you." I slyly put mom in there positively.

"Okay," Dad says folding his paper, putting it on the table, and turning my way.

Well, here it goes. "I've been thinking, trying already actually, on maybe having my own lawn cutting business. Over the spring and summer. Maybe into the fall. Cutting grass and taking care of lawns in the neighborhood."

Dad reels all that in and takes a deep breath. "Interesting," he says with an approving gesture, giving me a brief moment of exalted triumph. Then quickly, he adds, "But what's more interesting to me, is that every summer and fall I have to constantly remind you to cut the lawn and rake the leaves that's right here." He looks at me for some response.

A moment of mental paralysis comes over me and it's like I have the quarter piece of orange stuck in my mouth again 'cause I can't talk. A few seconds pass and I stammer and stutter and finally get out, "Well…ah…this would be…different."

"Oh? How so?" Dad abruptly says.

I have to be careful here because I don't have much room to maneuver so I say, "Well, I'll… I'll be makin'…money. And like I said, I kinda already started. I mean, let me show you," I say, getting up from the table and dashing to my room, grabbing my slips and dashing back. I sit back down and hand them over to Dad.

Dad takes the slips, looks at them pretty thorough, nods his approval, hands them back to me and says, "They're very good. But it still doesn't answer the question though, about why I have to remind you all the time about cutting your own lawn, Robby. In fact, I, we," he looks Mom's way, "have to remind you on just about everything round here."

There's a simple answer to that and that is that I'm underpaid. I mean, look at the facts. I'm the only one who cuts the lawn all summer and I still get the same measly allowance that I always get all year! Seems to me I should get the same cost of living thing over the summer that the adults are always complaining about. I know I can't spew out one word of that out so I say, "I just think it'll be a lil' different. Earning some money from outside my allowance."

Dad actually seems pleased with that answer. He thinks for a moment or two and says, "Well, let me tell you a few things you probably hadn't thought about, if you're…if you're really *serious* about this."

Here it comes. The serious part. Dad's always big on being serious.

"First, if you're going to be using my lawn mower, and rakes and whatever else, I expect you to keep them in good use."

I nod 'cause, that's all I can do.

"Even now, Robby," Dad emphasizes. "That pull cord on the mower will not last the season. And if the mower's getting used more you'll have to keep an eye on the oil and check the filters. And I'll expect you to use your earnings, if you do this, for any gas you need, or repairs" he adds, looking sternly at me.

I nod 'cause that's all I can do.

"And you have to be careful, Robby, very careful. If you break something in someone's yard, they'll expect you to pay for it."

On that I actually have something to say. "Well I haven't broken anything here," I say.

Dad smirks. "No, I guess you haven't. But take heed, Robby. Be very careful, if you do this."

"I will," I say, slowly coming to the realization that dad seems okay with my idea.

"And just one more thing," Dad adds, with his "one more thing" forefinger raised.

I take a long breath, waiting for the one more thing.

"What do you do if someone's not happy with the work you've done and won't pay you?"

Now I have to admit that that thought never crossed my mind but I say the first thing I think of. "I guess find out what they didn't like and try and fix it."

Dad's looking at me as if I've just made a transformation of some kind. He gets up from the table. "Well then good luck with this, Robby. Work hard, be safe, don't take on too much, and do a good and honest job."

. . .

So later that night I made twelve really good new slips and the next morning after breakfast, just as the whole house begins to smell like Windex from Mom's springtime window cleaning, I ride around the neighborhood handing them out. I left two on my dresser, one for Mom and the next time she goes to Shop Rite. She can put one on the community bulletin board. I see things like that there all the time. And I'll give one to Tup next week and ask him to put it on the church bulletin board. Another good spot. Other than that, I'm riding around the neighborhood trying to try remember where old people live 'cause I figure that would be a good place to leave a slip. That and I'm looking for yards that look like maybe they need some work. I've ridden up and down the neighborhood save Harding Street 'cause that's where the Manor Kings live. I've handed out all of my slips save one and I'm all the way down Constitution Street on the corner of Roosevelt and I know that old people live in the corner house. I see them all the time sitting on their porch when we turn the corner in the car. I ride my bike in front of the house, walk up the walkway, am about to put a slip in the hole in the big **R** on the door when all of a sudden a giant German Sheppard dog comes out of nowhere and is snapping and snarling and slobbering from behind the door, lunging up at me on its hind legs. I stand frozen for a few seconds. I realize that no one's coming to the door and this dog looks as if he's gonna break the door down. I walk briskly backwards to my bike and hop on. The dog's still in a frenzy at the door. I pedal away.

School

Chapter Nine

Time is a funny thing. Here I am, sitting at my desk in A-wing, looking up at the clock that reads 8:12. I've been sitting here since 7:50 and it already feels like I've been here for two hours. How can one whole week off from school whisk by like on a breeze, and then in one day, in one morning back at school, Friday and the weekend feels like it's an eternity away? How can that be?

Well for one reason, and a very strong reason, is this is math class. And I hate math class. I'm not good at math, and I don't want to be good at math. And somehow this year my schedule put me in for math class the very first thing in the morning. Something like that should be outlawed. And another reason for this slow drip of time, and also a very strong reason, is this year my math teacher is Mr. Kazcynski. The Great Kazoo, as we kids call him. Now Mr. Kazcynski, besides having a perpetual menacing demeanor and taking this math stuff way to seriously, constantly squeezes a pair of annoyingly squeaking hand strengthening grippers all class long,

The one lucky thing I have in this year's math class is Pete Glenn's in it. Pete, Space Man as we all call him, and me were last year's backup backcourt on the Lower Brook Middle School Golden Eagles basketball team. Mike Driscoll and Jeff Sikora were the starters but they're graduating in June so Pete and me think we'll be next year's starters. So at least with Space Man Pete in class I have some relief from this unrelenting math wizard standing and squawking and squeaking at the blackboard under the portrait of George Washington.

Now what the Great Kazoo has been yammering about in class for the last two weeks is this thing called stagnation. Which has something to do with the economy. So I don't even know why we're studying it here. Seems like a topic for another class. But For two weeks I've, we've, been looking at a blackboard full of white and yellow and green and pink chalk lines going all helter-skelter. We've been given mimeographed papers with equations of this plus that and minus this and minus that followed by this divided by that and then divided again and that all ends up equaling this and that. And somehow this and that always leads the Great Kazoo in challenging us to go to the stores and observe all the things left on the shelves, month after month, because people don't have the money to buy them. Or even if they have the money they're spending it on other necessities. He prods us to ask our parents how much more they're paying for a week's worth of groceries, or a month's worth of utilities, or even how much more filling up the gas tank is, compared to just a few years ago. He tells us to ask our parents if they can still afford the things they need. I personally never do because that would only lead dad to suggest that I give up my measly weekly allowance. I know Pete doesn't talk about this stuff to his parents and I'm pretty sure nobody else talks to their parents about this stuff either.

So as the Great Kazoo goes on and on about stagnation and being taken off the gold standard and frozen wages, he showing us how the green line plummeted and the yellow line rose, and the white line was erratic and the pink line trailed off. Between peeks at the blackboard Pete and me have hidden behind our math books my new *Street and Smith Basketball* magazine and a copy of the newspaper clipping and the box score of game four of the finals when the Bucks completed their sweep of the Bullets, with the overall box score of the series as well. First I thumb through the pages of the magazine until I get to the section that shows the perspective stars coming out of college this year and I show Pete. He looks over it and whispers to me asking what do I think of Austin Carr coming out of Notre Dame? I give an emphatic thumbs up. Pete points to Sidney Wicks from UCLA. Another thumbs up. I whisper I hope he doesn't go to the ABA. Pete goes down the list of players and I give my silent opinion. The Great Kazoo is squeaking with one hand and writing on the blackboard with the other as Pete and me have turned our attention at the box scores of the finals. Pete is writing down the combined points and steals and assists of the Bucks backcourt of Bobby Dandridge and the Big O and I'm doing the same for the Bullets back court of Pearl Monroe and Mad Dog Carter. Pete and me add all this up and we look at the figures. It's no wonder the Bullets didn't win a game. The Bucks outrebounded them, had more assists, and had a better shooting percentage both at the foul line and from the court. The only thing the Bullets led in was taking more shots. Pete points to Kareem Jabbar's (last week his name was Lew Alcindor) stats compared to Wes Unseld's and I say, louder than I apparently should, "Ha!"

Mr. Kazcynski, who had just finished whatever he was doing on the blackboard turns and looks at me and says "Oh? Mr. Birdsall?" Silence for a few seconds. "I guess since you've been following along so intently, maybe you'd like to tell us the figures you came up with." A few more seconds of silence. He takes the chalk in his hand and points to the blackboard. "For the green line?"

I look at the blackboard. Pete cleverly lets the magazine and the clipping slip down and inside his desk, just in case. I look at the figures in front of me. I guess one choice is as good as any so I choose assists. "19.5," I say.

Mr. Kazcynski turns and looks at the board, then turns back to me, asks, "And for the yellow line?"

I again look at the paper. "23.3," I say.

Again Mr. Kazcynski turns to look at the board. He rumbles through the equation in his brain, I guess to see how I came up with those numbers, slowly shakes his head, turns back to me and says, "Close, Mr. Birdsall. Surprisingly close. Just do your math again."

Ha! I say again, this time silently.

My next class is social studies over in C wing with Mr. Kilcommins. Tommy's in my class and he's the band leader for leading the class in driving Mr. Kilcommins absolutely crazy. At least once a week it seems Tommy organizes a day and time when everyone in the room will either cough or sneeze or belch or snort or slam our books or clear our throats or say something like "Sergeant Pepper" out loud in unison. A few times we've all barged into the room at the same time at the very last second, almost running Mr. Kilcommins over in the process. And 'cause Mr. Kilcommins' first name is Joe, Tommy really gets under his skin when he says, "Say it ain't so, Joe," to something he's talking about. The first two times Tommy did it, Mr. Kilcommins sent him to the principal's office. The third time Tommy said it Mr. Kilcommins asked him why he keeps calling him by his first name and getting sent down to the principal. Tommy said he wasn't. Tommy said that it was just an expression. So, from time to time, he still does it. And though Mr. Kilcommins still doesn't like it, Tommy no longer gets sent down to the principal's office. The week before Easter break we did something that really unnerved Mr. Kilcommins: We all let our heads fall onto our desks making a last gasp of breath sound. When that happened, Mr. Kilcommins had a startled look at first, then ripped his glasses from his eyes and threw them on his desk and got up and stormed out of the room. A great cheer went up in the room and like a bolt of lightning he was instantly back in the room with a slammed door behind him. It was terrifically hard not to laugh at him as he stared at us. Today though, probably because everyone is feeling the Easter recess is over blues, there's no coordinated antics. We've been studying world geography and we all sit and listlessly listen to some information about languages and how they travelled and how they're as much of a part and reason for the world geography that we have today. Mr. Kilcommins explains to us the uniqueness of language. How language is really just vocal symbols that people use as a societal group to interact. How before that it was visual and hand symbols that constituted societal agreement. He tells us that there's various theories has to how language began, proto-language he calls it. He tells us to pay attention because there's going to be two pop quizzes and an essay on all this. From Tommy's desk, "Say it ain't so, Joe" rings out. I hold in my smirk, watching Mr. Kilcommins trying to ignore Tommy's comment. It's now an official week of classes.

    History is next, just down the hall in B-wing. On the way I pass Diane Lindsay at her locker. She always dresses nice. Today she's wearing a black and white plaid skirt with two rows of three large buttons in the front. A tight black sweater with silver bracelets on her wrists and black Adidas sneakers with three white stripes on the sides. A lot of times she's there with Robyn Luft, who happens to be in my science class just two desks away, but not today. I think, most of the boys think, that Diane Lindsay and Robyn Luft are the prettiest girls in the whole school. I smile at Diane when I pass her, but she never smiles back.

    I have Mrs. Stanton this year and somehow Mrs. Stanton is both stern and nice. It's like she has a sense of humor with us, as well as an easiness in handing out bad marks and looks of utter disbelief to our incomprehensiveness. And even though Mrs. Stanton is older, somewhere between Mom's and Gramma's age, she still has a prettiness to her. She has shoulder length blonde hair in a style that she calls a beehive. I know that because one day in class the girls asked her what kind of hairstyle she has and that's what she called it. She always wears nice dresses and nice outfits and smells of nice perfume and she has a nice smile. Many times that nicely scented smile comes accompanied with an F, but still, there's a niceness about her.

Now I know already, that before class even begins, the very second I get in my seat, Todd Sasso will be coming over to my desk and let me and Curt Clayton who sits next to me hear that his Bucks won the NBA finals. Even though me and Curt told Sasso before the series started that we were rooting for the Bucks to win. Sasso said that was just our sour grapes talking. He said the only reason we were rooting for the Bucks was because the Bullets just beat our Knicks. He reminded me and Curt how much we ribbed him last year, when our Knicks knocked his Bucks out of the playoffs, on *our* way to winning the finals. All that might be true, but still, we were rooting for the Bucks all along and Sasso knew it. I walk in the room and over to my desk. Curt's already at his desk. I sit down. I say hey to Curt. He says hey back. I look across the room and here comes Sasso. Smiling a huge smile. He stoops down in front of our desks. He reaches into his shirt pocket, he takes out a newspaper clipping. "Eh eh eh," he says smugly as he unfolds the clipping. "Did either of you happen to catch this headline?" He turns the clipping our way. Curt and me look at it, already knowing what it says.

"Yeah, we know Sasso," I say. "We tol' ya all along we were rootin' for the Bucks," I say in an exasperated tone.

"Yeah, I know," Sasso says. "You an' CC here. Both big Buck fans."

"No," Curt says, also in an exasperated tone. "We just didn't want to see the Bullets win, that's all."

"Yeah yeah yeah," Sasso says, folding the clipping up and putting it back in his shirt pocket. "Looks like things turned out a lot different this year, eh? Who's on top now?" he says, triumphantly walking back to his desk, turning around once to show us the news clipping again.

I guess Curt and me had that coming 'cause we did rib Sasso pretty good last year when the Knicks knocked the Bucks out of the playoffs. And even though Curt and me really did want the Bucks to win this year, Sasso's right about the reason. A few seconds later Mrs. Stanton walks in the room and I settle in for class.

We've been studying the Civil War and I have to say it's not the most boring of subjects. We've studied some of the battles, Gettysburg, Vicksburg.

We've learned that the North referred to some of the battle names differently than the South. We've studied some of the reasons for the war and we've learned that the North was fighting the war to stop slavery while the South was fighting the war for this thing called state's rights. We've studied some about Abraham Lincoln and some about General Grant of the North and some of General Lee of the South and some on some person named Jefferson Davis, the president of the South. Mrs. Stanton told us about this one odd general for the south named Stonewall Jackson. Apparently this Stonewall Jackson would ride around on his horse with one arm raised in the air and eating lemons with the other.

Today Mrs. Stanton is telling us what happened after the Civil War ended. She explains to us that this is what's called the Reconstruction Period. She says we'll be discussing it over the next few days and some of it will be on Wednesday's short test. She says it's a very important topic to discuss and study on, and not enough school districts are doing it. She says the Civil War did not end with the end of the war. Then she outlines for us how the states of the North helped many southern cities and towns by rebuilding roads and buildings. The reconstruction. She tells us that many northerners moved to the south to be overseers and to make money from this rebuilding process. Carpetbaggers, they were called. She tells us that even after the Civil War was over, much of the south still oppressed Negroes from having any equal rights. She tells us it took another hundred years for that to happen. Stacy Latice raises her hand and asks why. Mrs. Stanton just smiles and says, "Well, changing people's hearts is…well, some people's hearts just don't change."

Fourth period is next, English composition with the Witch Whitaker. And the way I get myself through fourth period English composition with the Witch Whitaker is during it, I start thinking about lunch period, which is right after it. It also helps to have Figgy Pudding in the class, who is also in my lunch period. Great minds think alike, so I've heard.

Now, after just coming from the still very pretty and nicely scented Mrs. Stanton's class room, I'm hauled down to E-wing, the wing where someone forgot to add windows in the rooms. Windows would be helpful down here so we would at least have something else to look at rather than the barbaric figure of Mrs. Witch Whitaker. Witch Whitaker's short and heavy with fading brown hair that has no style to it at all. She wears thick glasses that are very pointy and very plain clothes and she also has a scent, I'm just not sure what it is. Sort of smells like mothballs. Her voice cackles when she talks and she constantly walks around the class with her hands clasped behind her back, one holding her world famous pointer, always at the ready to snap it down at a word or paragraph. And she's unrelenting. Because in Witch Whitaker's class EVERY WORD NEEDS TO BE PAID ATTENTION TO!

For the past week we've been reading and discussing this story called *The Pearl* by some person named Steinbeck. In the story a person named Kino has a sick kid and Kino doesn't have the money to afford the medicine the kid needs to get well. Then, miraculously, Kino finds a pearl in the ocean that's worth a lot of money. So Kino tries to sell the pearl to anyone and everyone but instead anyone and everyone wants to fight Kino for the pearl. In one of the fights Kino's kid is killed. So Kino throws the pearl back in to the ocean. So what's the point? Why didn't Kino just give the pearl to a doctor to begin with and cure the kid? Seems logical to me. I don't really see any reason for anyone to write an entire book about it and then torture seventh graders in making them read it. All this and oncoming lunch period is what's on my mind when I notice Fig's pencil tapping on the page of my book. I quickly look down at my book to try and see where Fig was pointing but much too quickly is the shadow of Witch Whitaker hovering over my desk. "Can you answer the question, Mr. Birdsall?"

I take a deep breath and worm my way upward in my chair. "Well, I'm not really sure," I say.

"You're not really sure of what, Mr. Birdsall? That you can answer the question, or what the question is?"

Another breath, this one shorter. "Probably both," I say to the guffaws of my classmates.

The next words I'm expecting from Witch Whitaker are "Fly monkeys! Fly!" She looks at me with piercing eyes and nods disapprovingly and I can hear her snapping her pointer in her hands behind her back as she says, "No doubt, probably both, Mr. Birdsall." She then stalks away, searching for another victim.

Fifth period is glorious lunch period. Now on most days I brown bag lunch because most days the school lunch really sucks. When it's pizza it's always the frozen stuff and when it's hamburgers it's always the frozen stuff and we're never really sure where those tater tots come from. The Styrofoam platter of chicken and mashed potatoes and corn are three more things that were once frozen. The tuna fish sandwich and chips? Took me to this year before I knew what that actually was. The spaghetti and meatballs is also horrible. Of the various lunch choices only a few are tolerable. Today, mom made me a peanut butter and strawberry jelly sandwich with a bag of Wise potato chips, half a red apple, cut in half again, a fruit punch Hi-C, and a few Hydrox cookies.

I sit and eat lunch at the end of the long cafeteria table with Broccoli, Figgy, and Cairnsy. Brock bought the school lunch which is a ham and cheese sandwich with a pickle and a cup of apple sauce. I guess that is one of the better of the school lunches. Figgy still has a lunchbox and we all rib him about it but he always has a good lunch. He has a roast beef sandwich with some cut up carrots and some kind of dipping sauce. He has pieces of a pear, a small bowl of tapioca pudding, and a thermos of chocolate milk. Cairnsy has a slim sandwich of who knows what with a school milk. "Any of you guys get a good look at Robyn Luft today?" Figgy asks. Broccoli, me, and Cairnsy all shake our heads no.

"But she's in my science class," I say. "So what can I expect?" I ask excitedly.

"Well," Figgy says, "let's just say better than Marcia Brady. If that's possible," Figgy says.

"Anybody see Diane Lindsay today?" I ask.

"Yeah, I did," Cairnsy says. "Unbelievably beautiful. Stuck-up as all get out, but unbelievably beautiful."

"Robyn's not like that," I say. "She'll smile at ya or say hello to ya. And she's just as pretty as Diane. In my opinion, anyway."

"Yeah, well, then wait until ya see her today, Birdyboy," Figgy says.

"Does she have one of her summer dresses on?" I ask.

"I'm not even gonna tell ya," Fig says. "I'll leave ya in suspense."

"So," Broccoli asks me, "did ya get any lawn business yet?"

"Not yet," I say. "But I got some flyers out in the neighborhood."

"Birdyboy here says he's gonna be the lawn king of Branch Manor," Broccoli tells Cairnsy and Fig.

"Really?" Cairnsy says. "Did ya leave one at my house so I don't have to cut my lawn?"

That's funny, I'm thinking, but say, "No. I only went around my neighborhood."

"Well, you get into my neighborhood, 27 Spruce Street's your first stop," Cairnsy says.

"You guys want to hear about another business venture?" Broccoli says. He sinisterly peers about and leans into the table a little, calls Mike Powell and Steve Dunn over, again makes sure no one's watching or listening, and proceeds to tell everyone that he has *Playboy* magazines to sell. "Real ones?" Powell asks in disbelief.

"Whadda ya think Powell?" Broccoli says. "I'd have fake *Playboys?* 'Course they're real ones. Birdman here saw 'em."

All eyes dart my way. "You saw 'em?" Powell asks me in a state of disbelief. I nod nonchalantly that I did. "Horsehead's too."

"Horsehead has some too!" Cairnsy gasps and quickly turns to Broccoli. "Is he sellin' 'em too?" he asks.

"Yeah," Broccoli says. "We're splittin' everything fifty-fifty."

"How much ya sellin' 'em for?" Powell asks.

"Two bucks each."

"Where'd ya get 'em from?" Cairnsy asks.

"Let's just say that I, we, stumbled on 'em," Broccoli says.

Turning my way, Cairnsy asks in an unbelieving tone, "And you seen 'em?"

"Every one of 'em," I say.

I'm asked if I liked any one better than another. "Well, there was this one with Raquel Welch in it, you know, the caveman movie girl. But she wasn't a centerfold girl. It was an interview."

"So what good is that?" Cairnsy says. "Do you at least remember the centerfold girl's name?"

I think for a moment. "Not really," I say, "but they were all beautiful."

So for the rest of lunch period deals are made. Cairnsy says he'll buy one and both Powell and Dunn say they'll buy one. Figgy says he's like to have one but not at his house. I know the feeling. Moments later Mrs. Darnold the lunch monitor tells us to clean up our areas and to get in line by the big double doors. As we do Broccoli tells everyone just name the day and he'll bring the magazines. He says cash first, then the magazine.

Gym's next and we're in the third and last week of playing basketball. These three weeks, along with the three weeks of flag football, the three weeks of floor hockey, and the three weeks of softball are the best gym classes that we have all year. I don't mind the soccer games but I'm not too keen with the track and field and I absolutely hate the gymnastics. And I'm not good at climbing that damn rope either. Pat Riley is the only one who makes it to the top and he does it in record time. It's impressive, but I don't see the point of it. But this week, and hopefully at the end of it, my three man basketball gym class team that consists of me, Johnny Walsh, and Blair Logan, will be playing in the championship game of our class.

We're all dressed and waiting for Mr. Goddard to come out of his office and blow his whistle to line us up for class. Me and Blair are playing a quick game of OUT and I already have Blair at OU. So I try this shot I've been practicing in my driveway. I walk out to the top of the key and turn my back to the basket. I bounce the ball over my head and as it descends I catch it and turn around and in one motion take a step back jumper. I watch as the ball arches toward the net and with a swoosh, it goes right through the net.

Just as Blair's about to say something about how difficult it will be for him to make that shot from the bleacher area I hear, "Betcha five bucks you can't make that shot again, Birdsall."

I turn toward the bleachers. I see its Jeff Sikora, who just happens to think he's the best basketball player Lower Brook Middle School has ever had. He's with Mike Driscoll. I act like I didn't hear him and Blair tries the shot and he misses everything and I say that's OUT and go and retrieve the ball and when I return to the basket Sikora's standing under it. "I got five bucks that says you can't make that shot again, Birdsall. Hell, I'll even give you two tries." Blair is staring at me to see if I'll take up Sikora's challenge. Driscoll has also walked over and stops and waits. "Well, Birdsall?" Sikora snickers.

I bounce the ball a few times and think for a second. Blair's watching, Driscoll's watching. Others are now watching. I take a deep breath. "You're on," I say.

I walk the ball out to the top of the key. I take another long breath. I bounce the ball over my head. It descends, I catch it, turn around and once again in one motion step back and let the ball fly. It arches toward the net, and swoosh, right through the net. I jump in the air and pump my fist just as Goddard comes out of his office blowing his whistle telling us to line up. As we go to prospective places, I tell Sikora he can settle with me after class.

"I don't have five bucks on me right now, Birdsall," he says. "Could you have paid me today if I won?" Sikora says.

Well, I guess he has a point there.

"Tomorrow," Sikora says.

"Okay," I say. "Tomorrow's fair."

Science class is next and it's my last class of the day, and I like it for a couple of reasons. I like my teacher, Mr. Molnar. *And* Robyn Luft is in the class just those two desks away. And sometimes I even like what we're studying. It's been a little boring lately because the third semester started with us studying molecules and minerals and nitrogen and gaseous stuff and how they interact and now we're onto tadpoles and toads and frogs. Mr. Molnar's a good teacher and he's calmly explained to us without going overboard on how all this information will give us a better appreciation for the earth that we live on, but I still find this larval stage earth stuff kind of dull.

The bell rings and class starts and Mr. Molnar is standing at his desk and he's letting us know what to expect on next week's test. He tells us to take notes for the next fifteen minutes as he reviews the material. He's writing things on the board and turning and talking to us. I pay attention for a bit but quickly start to lose interest. I probably won't remember all of this anyway and I figure I can pass with what I do know. So I rest my head in my hand and pretend to be looking at my book but actually my eyes are half-closed and I'm about ready to lose consciousness when I hear the screeching of a chair across the floor. My eyes bug open and I see Jack Helmstetter walking toward the back of the room and to the closet. He opens the door and drags out the projector and wheels it into the center of our **U** shaped room. He clicks and clinks and clanks the projector together and Lori Brunson douses the light and there's a few seconds of crackling sounds and a few bursts of bright white light and then the projector hums along in a steady stream.

Expecting to see a baby tadpole swimming in a creek or some flower blooming, I'm surprised to see astronauts landing on the moon. We watch as the tape shows footage of all three moon landings and the unfurling of American flags on the moon. We watch as the astronauts bounce off the moon's service and pick up moon dust. Then one of the astronauts from the latest landing is talking to one of the crew mates of the same mission. They're talking about what they and the other astronauts have already accomplished and what they can accomplish in the future. They're describing different types of rockets that can take astronauts further and longer into outer space. As the astronauts are talking the screen behind them shows astronauts riding a dune buggy on the moon and others playing golf. Then the screen goes completely black and something white starts spinning around and a narrator's voice comes on and says, "So how far can we go? And for how long can we stay?" The screen is still spinning and the narrator repeats what he just said and then the screen freezes with those words on it: "So how far can we go? And for how long can we stay?" Seconds later the film's over with the end of the tape flapping against the projector. Lori Brunson turns the lights back on. Helmstetter disengages the projector. "So, did the film surprise anyone?" Mr. Molnar asks.

We all kind of look around at each other. "Well, we all know you're a NASA junky," Helmstetter says, putting the projector back in the closet.

Mr. Molnar smiles at that. "Well, that's true, but, well, maybe this will surprise you all a little."

Mr. Molnar goes on and explains that the seventh and eighth grade classes of Lower Brook Middle School will be a participating school in a statewide competition to create a project on what we think a future NASA mission might accomplish fifty years from now. In the year 2021. Mr. Molnar tells us all three science classes will have a class winner, with prizes being handed out, and the faculty will decide the overall winner. And that overall winner will have that project on display, in competition, with other school winners during the Apollo 15 mission this summer. The winner of that gets placed at some NASA center somewhere as part of NASA history. "Forever," Mr. Molnar says. Mild enthusiasm rumbles through the class room.

"So what we're going to do," Mr. Molnar adds, "to make competition fair, and not just pair up with friends, is I'm putting the names of the students on this side of the room in this shoe box. And this side of the room will pick out a name. Whoever you say, that's your partner." Mr. Molnar shuffles the shoe box and as he walks to my side of the room, he says, "Both students will be expected to know what the full project is about, not just their part." He holds that box out in front of Rich Varley.

I sit third on my side of the room and I'm hoping that I get to team up with Vicky Carlson. Or Stephanie Fabbri. I can't team up with Robyn only two seats away because of the rules, but both Vicky and Stephanie are very pretty too. Rick Varley chooses and he says "Lori Brunson."

Lori's nice. Not as pretty as Vicky of Stephanie, but she's nice.

Ty MacIntyre sits next to me and he reaches into the box and says, "Alex Grebel."

Alex Grebel's a geek who's good at this stuff. Last year he made a tornado in some glass casing. A real tornado!

I'm next and reach in the box and take out a slip and unfold it. "Linda Orken," I say. I'm partially paralyzed. My brain freezes. Did I just say Linda Orken? I look down at the slip. It says Linda Orken. Linda Orken! Orken the Dorken! I hear names being called out but I'm oblivious. Linda Orken? I just said Linda Orken!

When the last name is called Mr. Molnar collects the empty shoe box. He tells us to think of some ideas on our own. He tells us on Friday we'll have some class time to discuss things with our partner. I look over at Linda sitting in the first desk with one of her three stained print dresses on and thick black-framed glasses and frizzy brownish hair with her bangs cut straight across her forehead and her lips that are too puffy for her face. Her hands are clasped in front of her on her desk, and she seems oblivious to any of this.

After the bell and on my way to my bus, I see Tup's mop of red hair hanging out the bus window. "Hey Birdman," he yells to me as I near his bus, "are you guys part of the science class competition?"

"Yeah," I stop and say.

"Who's your partner?"

"Linda. Linda Orken."

"You'll never believe who I got?"

"Joni," I say, as if the answer is obvious.

"How'd ya guess?" Tup asks.

"Lucky guess," I say.

Chapter Ten

Miraculously, the school week did finally come to an end. Saturday morning is actually here. Thank God. 'Cause by Friday's final bell, I didn't want to hear another word about the nation's stagnation problem. I couldn't bear to hear another reason for why we talk the way we do, and where. And Mr. Kilcommins did give us a pop quiz on Friday. I guess I'll find out Monday how I did. One good thing was I passed Mrs. Stanton's history quiz using my time-tested proven method: Study half the material, and make an educated guess with the rest. Result: 68. Passing. Barely, but passing. And wouldn't ya know it? In English, the day after she verbally abused me the Witch Whitaker threw a five question pop quiz on that exact part of the stupid Kino story she grilled me about. I got a twenty on that one. And now we have to write an essay at least one page long on it due Monday. Monday! In gym class Johnny Walsh, Blair, and me did reach the championship game but we lost 15-11 to Sikora and his team of Mike Driscoll and Steve Foglar. And I've yet been able to collect the five bucks that I won from Sikora Monday. Every day he says it'll be tomorrow. And in science class, true to his word, Mr. Molnar gave us the last fifteen minutes or so on Friday to team up with our partners and start working on some of our ideas. Mr. Molnar handed out *NASA* magazines and *Astronomy* magazines for us to look at. Linda and I silently thumbed through the magazines with not one idea between us.

So now, I'm watching the best hour of cartoons on television of the whole week. *The Road Runner* comes on at nine and right after that comes *The Harlem Globetrotters*. Luckily Dad has what he calls a "half day" so he's not here to give me "something to do" and Tammy also left early so I had my *Quisp* cereal in peace. Mom's busy bringing boxes up from the basement that's marked curtains. It's that time of year again. I have no understanding as to why, but Mom always changes the curtains when the calendar turns to May. She's standing at the dining room table spreading out a curtain and the *Globetrotters* aren't even finished yet and she says, "Robby. It's a beautiful spring morning. Are you going to sit inside all morning and watch television? And don't you have yard work to do? I'm sure your father doesn't want to come home from work and see that it isn't done."

I have all intentions on getting all that done, as soon as the cartoon's over. "My shows over in five minutes," I say. "I'll have it done." Mom just shakes her head and transfers the curtain from the table to the new ironing board, sprays something on the curtain, places a towel over the curtain, and seconds later I hear the hissing sound of steam emanating from the iron. After a few let offs of the steam, the room fills up with that ammonia-type smell. The phone rings and it's Aunt Mary and mom has the phone held to her ear with her shoulder as she continues to iron the curtains. A few minutes later the cartoons end.

As soon as the cartoons are over I silently mouth to Mom that I'm just going to ride over to Necci's and see if they have any cinnamon sticks. She makes a motion reminding me of the yard work left to do. I nod that I know. "I'll be right back," I silently mouth.

As I hop on my bike I know Mom's right about dad and how he'll react if he comes home and nothing in the yard is done. So I pedal straight to Necci's, no stopping at Tommy's. When I walk into the store, I head right for the counter where the cinnamon sticks would be. I move things around looking for the red box but don't see it. Mrs. Necci walks in from the back and sees me and says, "No cinnamon sticks, Roberto."

"Are you getting them in?"

"Molto presto," Mrs. Necci says. "Next week."

"Thanks," I say. And true to my word, I pedal straight for home.

I'm pedaling down Truman Street nearing my block and I see Mr. Lampman sitting on his front porch. I wave to him and he waves back and he shouts something to me. I stop my bike and ask what he said because I wasn't really paying attention and didn't hear him.

"I said you must be a half-hearted business man," he says. I look at him perplexed. "Didn't your sister tell you I called yesterday to see if you could cut my lawn today?"

Instantly my blood boils. "No, she didn't," I say, withholding as much venom as I can from spitting out the things that Tammy does to me that "would make the Pope swear," as Mom says.

"Well, the job's still available, if you're interested," Mr. Lampman says.

"Sure I am," I say. "I can bring my mower and stuff over anytime you want."

"How about right now, if you're not doing anything?" Mr. Lampman says. "I can show you around the yard and what to watch out for."

"Okay. All right. I'll be right over," I say, elated at the chance, and steaming for almost losing it.

The rest of the way home I'm thinking about what if. What if Mr. Lampman didn't stop me while I was pedaling by? And what if he never called back because I didn't respond? I'm thrilled at actually having my first lawn to cut, but I'm just as angry at Tammy for not telling me. When I get home I walk in the house. I look a mom who's off the phone now and hanging a curtain on the back dining room picture window. "Do you know what Tammy did to me Mom?" I say.

"No," Mom stoically says, staring at the curtain. "What did she do?"

"Well Mr. Lampman just stopped me in the street and said he called yesterday and spoke to Tammy about me cutting his lawn today. And she never told me!"

Mom nods and smoothes out the hung curtain and picks up another one from the table and places it onto the ironing board "Does he still want you to do the work?"

"Yeah, but…."

"Then just go and do his yard, Robby." Mom says, spraying the curtain. "I'll talk to Tammy."

"Yeah, well, she'd better not ever…." is all I get out as I walk out the front door.

I take the lawn mower out of the garage and fill the tank up. I pull the cord just to make sure the mower starts. I grab a rake and a broom and a pair of shears and a green garbage bag. I walk all this down the block and over to Mr. Lampman's house. I feel like stopping at Tommy's and telling him that I actually have a lawn to cut, but I don't. When I get to Mr. Lampman's house he's waiting for me on the porch.

I leave my mower and rake and broom and garbage bag at the end of the driveway. Mr. Lampman walks me around the yard and shows me where I need to be careful. At the very edge of the driveway where the mower can fling little rocks against the car. Up in the front of the yard where the walkway to the porch is. That's where Mrs. Lampman's tulips will soon be in full bloom. Be careful, he says, near the bird bath in the center of the yard. I could easily knock it over. In the backyard where the patio cement rises, so I don't chip the cement with the blade. He tells me I don't have to rake the clippings up this early in the season. The grass needs to get stronger yet. No argument from me. Then he shakes my hand and lets me do the work.

I take my time and do a good job. First thing I do is walk around the yard and pick up any branches and twigs. When I'm finished I take my time and cut the grass. When I'm done cutting I sweep off the back patio and the front walkway and the driveway. When I'm finished I leave my mower and rake and bag of twigs on the sidewalk. I walk up to the front door and knock. Mr. Lampman answers the door. "All done?" he asks. I nod that I am. "Well, let's go have a look."

Mr. Lampman walks around the yard, inspecting the areas he warned me about. He shakes his head in an approving manner. "Well, I take back what I said." He takes his money clip out of his pocket. "You're not a half-hearted business man. Now, we never talked about your charge," he says, taking two crisp dollar bills from his clip, "but I'd imagine you'll find this fair," he adds, handing me the money.

George Washington never looked so good.

"How about again in a couple of weeks say?" he says.

"Sure," I say, radiating inside.

As I walk home with the money in my pocket, I'm thinking I've earned money outside my allowance before, at the car wash, but that was just standing around waiting for someone to give me a few quarters for drying their car. This feels completely different. This feels like an accomplishment. I can see my name being spelled out on one of those big trucks I see around town that provide lawn services. I can see my slogan spelled out under my name. I can see my business phone number under that. I can see how many years of service I've had under that. Before I get home for lunch, I stop at Tommy's. I want to show him the two crisp dollar bills I just earned. I turn the corner and see Tommy's bike under the carport. I leave my mower at the end of the driveway and knock on the door. Mrs. Hulse answers and lets me in. We exchange hellos. Tommy's in his room. I rap on the door. "Birdman?" he says from behind the closed door.

"Yeah, it's me Horsehead."

"Come on in."

I walk into Tommy's room, which never changes. His bed is always in the same place and his dresser is always in the same place. Nothing ever changes on the walls either. When the Jets won the Super Bowl a few years ago Tommy pasted all the headlines he could find all over the walls and they're still there, fading away. But even before the Jets won the super bowl he had that Joe Namath jersey he made nailed on the wall over his bed with a New York Jets cap next to it and a New York Jets pennant. He's had that Huck Finn straw hat nailed onto his closet door for forever and there's a guitar with a missing string that he never plays in the corner by the window. His record player and sparse set of records are at the end of a long desk that runs a good length of the wall by the windows. There's a clock and a plug-in radio on the desk that never switch places. And I'm pretty sure that the trail of scattered papers and magazines that lead to where Tommy is sitting and looking at something on his micro tube have been there for years too. "Whatcha lookin' at?" I ask.

"Stinkbug," Tommy says.

"A stinkbug? Where'd ya find a stinkbug?"

"Where'd I get a stinkbug," Tommy repeats condescendingly. "Where do ya think, Birdbrain?"

"Is it still alive?"

"Well if he is, he's been playin' possum," Tommy says. "Considering he's been in my box since Halloween" Tommy's got a plastic box with tiny compartments where he keeps dead insects that he looks at on his micro tube. "Ya gotta see this, Birdyboy."

I walk over and look at what Tommy's has on the micro tube. It is indeed a stinkbug. "Am I supposed to be seeing something here? Besides the stinkbug?"

"Look at the center."

I do. I'm not sure what Tommy sees.

"Dontcha see it?" he says. "It looks like a face."

"A face?" I say. "I really don't see a face."

"You don't? Looks like the face of Marley's ghost on the door knob if you ask me. You saw *Scrooge* at Christmas."

I peer harder. I don't see the face of Marley's ghost on the stinkbug. I shake my head. "It just looks like a stinkbug to me." I get up and walk away from the micro tube.

Tommy sits back down. Peers into the micro tube. "You're blind, Birdcage. That's the face of Marley's ghost."

"I'll take your word for it," I say. "I gotta get home for lunch but I wanted to show you something." I take the two dollars I just earned and show them to Tommy. "My first two dollars earned in my lawn care business," I proudly say.

Tommy stops looking at the Marley's ghost stinkbug. "How 'bout that," he says. He reaches into his pocket. He takes out one, two, three, four, five, six dollar bills. "From my magazine business," he says.

Well, I guess I can't argue with his success, so I go home for lunch.

When I get home for lunch Dad's already home from work. I show him the two dollars I just earned from Mr. Lampman. "Congratulations," he says, shaking my hand. "What are you going do with it?"

"Well, I think I'll save half of it, and spend the other half."

"That sounds like a smart plan," Dad says, then reminds me of the yard work I've yet to do in my own yard.

I tell Dad I'll do it right after lunch and right after lunch I do just that. I begin with raking out the leaves left in the shrub beds that boarder the walkway and the driveway. Then I trim the hedges and rake everything up. And it doesn't take all that long. When I'm done I go to my room and pull out an empty Sucrets tin can and add one dollar to the fifty cents already in there. I'm now thinking if I save enough money, I could actually maybe buy those Clydes.

I decide to take a ride over to Tommy's to see if he feels like taking a spin up to Two Guys. I'm going to take a look at the records. I have enough to buy a top forty 45 record, or a few from the ten cent bin, if I can find any in good condition. And of course I'm going to take another look at the sneakers. Especially the Puma Clydes.

When I get to Tommy's him and Broccoli are sitting under the carport on the trunk of the old Impala. "Birdyboy," Broccoli says.

"Hey Broccoli. Horsehead," I say. "You guys feel like takin' a ride up to Two Guys?"

"Can't right now," Tommy says. "Brock and me got a lil' business goin' on."

"Oh," I say. "What's that?"

"Couple of magazines to sell," Tommy says.

"One of my magazines, and one of Horsyhead's," Brock adds.

"Huh," I say. "How much are ya gonna get?"

"Same. Still two bucks," Tommy says. "You got two bucks, Birdseye. Why don't you buy one? When I get rid of this one I'll only have two left."

I think about buying the magazine for a second, but figure it'll be just too risky of a thing to bring home. Mom can easily find it 'cause she's forever changing things in the house. And Dad's always rearranging things in the garage, so it's not safe there either. And there's always Tammy. "I think I'd rather spend it on a record," I say.

"Oh yeah," Broccoli says. Whatcha gonna get?"

"I'm not really sure," I say. "I'll take a look at the top forty. Nose through the ten cent bin. I'll decide when I get there."

I ride out to Two Guys. I leave my bike in its familiar spot behind the phone booths. On my way in I check the coin slots for any dimes. Nothing. I walk into the store and head for the record department which is in the back and to the left. I keep a keen look out for you know who. Now the Two Guys record department is actually pretty cool. It has five aisles of records fit for just about anyone who wants to listen to a record. It even has a section for those funny shaped 78 records that the old people buy. H.L Greens has records, but not like this. In the first aisle there's racks that hold the top forty records of the week and along the back wall racks that have the top 100 albums. And all along the back wall above the albums there's posters of individual musicians and posters of musical groups and posters of musical events that have happened. On the dividers separating the aisles there's guitars and violins and saxophones and flutes and even a miniature drum set. When I get to the record department it's surprisingly quiet, considering it's a Saturday afternoon. There's only a few people scanning the records and albums.

First thing I do is check out who is in the top ten of the 45s this week. *Joy to the World* is still number one and *Put Your Hand in the Hand* is now number two. *ABC* has fallen to number three. I continue to walk down the aisle and scan. *Chick-A-Boom* is in the top ten. It's such a stupid song. I see that Ringo's in the top ten. I keep walking and scanning. It goes from number one all the way to forty. This is odd. There's a song called *The Drum* at 39 and a song called *Battle Hymn Of Lt. Calley* at 40. As I start to walk toward the aisle where the newest albums are, two girls, about Tammy's age, walk hurriedly into the department and toward those albums. One has pretty long blonde hair and is wearing a white shirt with frilly sleeves and faded denim hip huggers and has a vibrant wide red belt around her waist. The clogs on her feet scrape out against the floor like tap shoes. The other girl has medium length brown hair that is held to her head with what looks like a thin piece of braided rope. She's wearing a denim skirt with a green and red checkered shirt and has moccasin style shoes on, giving her a look between either a farm girl or an Indian girl. I walk to the ten cent bin that's near the aisle. From there I can spy on them.

The pretty blonde girl goes to the end of the aisle further away from me and the girl with brown hair comes to my side of the aisle. I watch as they both begin to flip through the albums like our librarian at school Mrs. Boese flips through index cards. They're flipping through the albums so fast it's like they're burrowing. The blonde girl stops flipping and holds up an album she found and shows it to her brown-haired friend. It's that George Harrison album with the funny cover that Tammy loves so much. George is sitting on a chair in a field with I guess a bunch of munchkins or oompa-loompa's or something like that sitting around him. "Don't you already have that?" the brown-haired girl says.

"It's kinda scratched up," the blond girl says. "And this is marked down to a dollar ninety eight." She rests the album against a guitar on the top of the aisle divider and continues to flip through albums. The girl with the brown hair is still flipping through albums. "I know she put it in this aisle, somewhere," the blonde haired girl says. "I watched her take it from the rack and walk down this aisle and leave without it." I'm watching them get closer to each other when the blond haired girl shrieks and pulls up an album and shows it to her friend. I can see it's the Paul McCartney *Ram* album. Paul's on the cover holding the horns of a ram. It's a very popular album. And with a few screams, hops, and hugs, the girls leave the record department, records in hand, as hurriedly as they came. I go back to searching through the ten cent bin.

Chapter Eleven

Back in school, already. It's first period, mid-week, not even ten minutes in, and I'm nearly collapsed at my desk from both boredom and illogic. Since Monday we've been doing this crazy new math thing and I'm listening to the Ol' Kazoo who is standing at the blackboard, chalk in one hand, squeaky hand strengthener in the other, telling us to look at the clock. Squeak, squeak, squeak. "It's now eight o'clock, correct?" he says. Long squeak. We all nod our heads. He writes an 8 onto the blackboard. We all know something strange is coming. "And if we add another eight hours to that, that will make it four o'clock, correct." Squeak, squeak. Some of us take a little longer to add that up, but within a few seconds we all nod again, still waiting for the illogic. "And if we add eight plus eight, we would have sixteen, right?" He does just that on the blackboard. I can tell this is going to end up horribly. "But," the great Kazoo says, the but we all knew was coming, squeak, squeak, squeak, squeak, "there's no sixteen on the clock, is there?" He looks at us smugly. "It only goes up to twelve." Ssssqqqquuuueeeeaaaakkkk. "So in this modular arithmetic equation," he says, "the modulo is twelve. Which is also the same as zero. Twelve is zero and zero is twelve in this equation, it's a congruent relation," he tells us, squeak squeak. I shake my head in unbelief. Next to me Pete lets out an agonized breath. I look at Pete and mouth "And we thought fractions was hard," and then look out the window.

Ol' Kazoo goes on squeaking and talking about multiple integers and writing crazy equations like b-gn+r and a-pn+r on the blackboard and God knows what else because I've stopped listening. I'm never going to understand this so why bother trying. I'll figure some way to get by. So what I'm actually thinking about is what we did to Mr. Kilcommin's Monday in social studies. After we got the first of our pop quizzes back, and I actually passed with a seventy-one, Tommy had this great idea that since we've been studying languages and what they've meant to the world's geography, he said that we should come up with our own language. Something completely inaudible. He said he'll start it off if Mr. Kilcommins calls on him to answer a question, or he'll start it when he raises his hand to ask a question. And we're to follow his lead. So when Mr. Kilcommins asked the class if he was to draw an imaginary line around the globe, what would the center point between the North and South poles be called, quite stone-faced, Tommy raised his hand and looked at Mr. Kilcommins and responded in some kind of gibberish. And then Larry Gethard picked right up on that and said something in the same gibberish to Tommy who then turned around and said something back to Larry in gibberish and seconds later the entire class was talking to each other in gibberish. It went on for a few seconds before Mr. Kilcommins opened and then violently slammed shut the top drawer of his desk to shut us all up. Thinking about it, I'm actually having a hard time right now not bursting out in laughter. So I'm not sure if it's the slight grin on my face or that the Ol' Kazoo has some kind of telepathy, but in the middle of my revelry I hear, "Oh, Mr. Birdsall, something strikes you as funny about this equation?"

I snap out of my hysterical cocoon.

"You've come up with a different result?" he asks.

Unlike the stagnation grilling, I don't have any *Street and Smith's Basketball Magazine* or box scores to look at and guess numbers from. I actually have no clue as to what anything on that blackboard is about. What do they say to do when you're in a hole? Stop digging? "No," I say, defeated.

"Pay attention, Mr. Birdsall. If you don't get this early material, you're really going to struggle with the rest."

Of that I'm sure.

And then, after being accosted in Ol' Kazoo's classroom with this new and ridiculous mathematical concept, I'm accosted at my locker after class by a ridiculous claim from Joni Iachello.

I'm grabbing my social studies and history books and as I start to close my locker, there's Joni, glaring at me. "So," she says, "I guess you think you can get Brian Tupper to find some things out about me, huh Robert?"

I cringe and twist for a second or two like Dracula in front of a cross as I look at Joni's glaring eyes, then say, "I have no clue what the heck you're talkin' about, Joni."

"Oh, you don't," she sneers. "Then why would Brian be asking me things lately that would involve you?"

When I catch up to Tup after school today on his bus I'm gonna kill 'em. I know he doesn't mean any harm, but still. "Like what?" I ask in an annoyed tone.

"Like if I'm going sign your yearbook this year or if I'd want to go to the seventh grade dance with you."

Exasperated, I say, "Joni, I have no idea. Maybe you should ask Tup." I close my locker.

"I did," she says. "He said he was just throwing out names. But for some reason yours constantly was thrown. So I'm supposing that for some reason he thinks that I might like you. Now where would he get an idea like that?"

"Joni," I say in compete exasperation, "I have no clue. Ask Tup," I say again. I shut my locker and turn the tumbler and head for my next class.

My next two classes are the quizzes we were promised. Kilcommins gives us our second quiz on the language thing and Mrs. Stanton gives us our quiz on the Civil War. The only question on the Reconstruction Period was what was a carpetbagger and why were they called that. By the time it was English class I was just glad there wasn't going to be another quiz. But I did get my essay back that we had to do over the weekend on *The Pearl* from Witch Whitaker with a big fat **C-** on it. I turn the paper over a read what she wrote on the back. According to her, I neglected to mention the most important themes of the story and made inadequate connections between the ones that I did. Figgy shows me his essay. **B** his says. Both of us shrug our shoulders and throw the essay papers in the back of our notebooks. On the blackboard Witch Whitaker has the word Thesis written on it. "Can anyone tell me what this word means?" the Witch cackles, pointing to the word with her world famous pointer. Pam Moser raisers her hand. "Yes, Pam."

"Doesn't mean, isn't it your intention?"

My intention is not to pay attention.

"Sort of," the Witch says. "But not quite. Anyone else?"

All I do next is take a breath and maybe roll my eyes a little and look out the window and the next words I hear are, "I would try and be a little more engaged on this, Mr. Birdsall. Understanding what a thesis is will help you with your under developed themes."

I swear I watched Witch Whitaker's face turn green when she said that.

She goes on to tell us that a thesis is a short, one or two sentence statement that summarizes what you're writing about. But a thesis is not just one or two sentences. Oh no. A thesis *makes* a statement. A thesis *takes* a stand. A thesis *sounds off* an alarm. I can already tell already that thesis thing is going to be a real pain in the ass over the next few weeks.

At lunch Cairnsy gives Broccoli two dollars to give to Tommy for Tommy's last *Playboy* and Steve Dunn gives Broccoli two dollars for his last. Broccoli says he'll bring them in tomorrow. Then Broccoli and Cairnsy play me and Figgy in a game of two-man table top football of which me and Figgy win on a desperation, last play touchdown, 37-34.

In gym we start the track and field stuff. Monday we just did calisthenics and yesterday we ran relay races. My relay team lost to Sikora's and speaking of Sikora, I've had enough of his excuses for not paying up on our bet last week so after class I quickly change and walk up to Sikora with a slip of paper. I thrust it his way.

"What's that?" he asks, disinterested.

"Read it," I say.

He unfolds the slip of paper. He reads what it says. *I, Jeff Sikora, will pay Robert Birdsall the five dollars I lost to him last week tomorrow at gym class.* I signed the slip and had Blair witness it and left a spot for Sikora to sign. He smirks and says, "So I guess you want me to sign this?"

"Either that or pay me now the five bucks you owe."

Sikora shakes his head in a condescending way as if I'm being unreasonable or something and says, "Have it your way Birdbrain." He searches for a pencil and I have one ready and hand it to him. He takes it, smugly laughs, and scribbles his name. "I tol' ya I'd get it to ya," he says, handing me back the slip.

I look at the paper to make sure Sikora didn't sign his name Charlie Brown or something like that. He didn't. He actually signed his own name. "Well, maybe this help remind ya," I say, folding the slip back up and putting it my pocket. Happy with myself, I head for my last class.

I instantly know something's up when I walk into science class 'cause all the desks have been set up in the room in pairs of two. Rich Varley's sitting in the back with Lori and Robyn's on the other side of the room with Glen Newhouse and Alex Grebel is sitting with Ty MacIntyre and as I pass Mr. Molnar he smiles at me and says, "I believe Linda's your partner, Robert," pointing me to where Linda is sitting. I fumble with my science book and notebook and grab a pencil out of my holder and sit down next to Linda.

When class starts Mr. Molnar tells us we're to have the rest of the week to work on our science projects. He picks up a box from his desk and as he walks around the room dropping *Sky and Telescope* and *Astronomy* magazines and *NASA* materials on our desks, he says that today we're to work at our desks and come up with our idea for the project and Thursday and Friday we can either work on it here in class or at the library. But don't think they'll be any Tom Foolery going on in the library, he says. Mrs. Boese will be keeping an Eagle eye on us.

As Linda and I look through the magazines I hear Mr. Molnar walking around the room and talking to the other pairs. I hear him say "maybe you're on to something there" or "maybe that's worth some more thought." When he gets to Linda and me he sees that we've written nothing down about any ideas for the project. He pulls up a chair and sits opposite us and says, "Let's see if we can help out a little here." He picks up the *Astronomy* magazine and slowly thumbs through it. He turns the pages and then stops and nods approvingly. "Well, this is kind of interesting," he says. He turns the magazine so Linda and I can see it. The headline says **SPACE TRAVEL, ANYONE?** He puts the magazine down in front of me and Linda. "What do you think about this, Robert?" he asks me, pointing to the article.

I pick up the magazine and read where Mr. Molnar was pointing. He asks me to read what it says out loud. So I do. The article says that very maybe, in the next twenty years or so, that space travel could be safe enough and simple enough so that ordinary citizens will be able to take a trip into orbit. That we'd be able to see further than our imaginations could take us. That maybe even one day further on, we'd might find somewhere inhabitable for human beings. To visit, maybe even to stay.

"So what do you think, Robert? Do you think, say, years from now, when you're in your thirties or forties, that you might want to take a trip into outer space? Just like if you were travelling on an airplane? If you could?"

Well I've never been on an airplane and I've never thought about travelling into outer space so I shrug my shoulders and say, "Yeah, I guess so. That might be fun. I don't think I'd want to go for very long, though."

"Oh, so maybe a day trip? Or a weekend spent in outer space?" Mr. Molnar says. "That's very interesting." He turns to Linda. "So, Miss Orken, you've been listening to this. What do you think about a day trip into outer space? Or spending a weekend on the moon?"

Linda stares at Mr. Molnar, then at me. "With Robert?"

"With whomever," Mr. Molnar says. "If you could actually do something like that."

Again Linda stares at Mr. Molnar, then again at me. She shrugs her shoulders and says, "I guess so."

Mr. Molnar gets up from his chair. "Well," he says. "I think you both might be on to something there."

• • •

I search for Tup as I head for my bus after the last bell. I see his mop of red hair. I tap on the window. He sees me and with that big toothed smile of his he opens up the window. "Birdman! How's it goin'?"

"Not so great, Tup." I say.

"Oh?" Tup says, big smile turning into a small frown. "Why? What's the matter? Ya didn't have another run-in with Mrs. Whitaker in English, did ya?"

"No, Tup," I say solemnly. "It's Joni. She was at my locker earlier and she was seething at me because she thinks I'm puttin' you up to askin'…whatever it is you've been askin' her."

"Huh?" Tup says.

I stand there for a second and hear the last bell for getting on the buses. "What the heck did you say to her?"

"Nothin', really," Tup says. "I was just askin' her whose year book she plans on signin' this year and if she's goin' to the seventh grade dance and stuff like that."

I hear the gears change into drive from buses in the front of the line. "Tup, do me a favor. Just don't mention me anywhere near Joni. K," I say as I make a dash for my bus that's two ahead of Tup's.

• • •

Thursday at gym class it was easy for Sikora to avoid me and the note he signed Wednesday because I was on the track running 100-meter and 400-meter races and hurdles and Sikora was on the field doing the shot put and Frisbee throw. So when gym class ended he was in and then out of the locker room as quick as a cat. But today, with the games reversed, I'm in the locker room first and I'm quickly changed and I'm at Sikora's locker, who is already tying his sneakers in a rush to get out and avoid me again. I have the signed letter in hand. "Hey Sikora. Forgetting something today?" I confidently say, holding the note.

Finishing tying his sneaker and putting his gym clothes into his duffel bag, mockingly he says, "Forgetting something today?" He zips closed his duffel bag and looks at me. "What might I be forgetting today, Birdclaw?"

I unfold the note that's in my hand and clear my throat and read what it says. And remind him that he signed it Wednesday. "That's two tomorrow's already," I smugly add.

Picking up his duffel bag, Sikora says, "I'm sorry to have to tell you this, Birdyboy, but there is no tomorrow, according to what I signed."

I look at the note again. Still confident, I say with an incredulous tone, "And just how do you figure that?"

Sikora lets out a frustrated huff and puts his duffle bag down and points to the paper in my hand, "See, you're problem here, Birdleg," Sikora says, "is that there's no date on that there note. Anywhere. All it says it that I'll pay you tomorrow."

"Yeah…but, you signed it."

"I'll sign it again for ya, Birdbrain. If that's what floats your boat. But there's still no date on it. So there's still no tomorrow. And any changes made to that note now makes it voided. Legally. You can ask any lawyer that," Sikora says, picking back up his duffel bag. Then he sticks out his hand and says, "And that I'll bet ya a hundred bucks on right now. Just shake that hand."

I don't shake his hand. Sikora walks out of the locker room. My brain swims around what just happened for a few seconds, trying to grasp what Sikora just said, and if any of it can possibly be true. I fold the note back up. I stand there for a few more paralyzing seconds, then head for science class, not sure at all if Sikora is right about what he just did and said. So on the way to class I break all seventh grade protocol. I stop where Mr. Napier is standing outside his classroom. I take out the note and hand it to him and explain what happened. Mr. Napier reads the note, chuckles slightly, and says, "Well, I guess he does have you there, legally, Robert."

Instantly my face seethes red. "But how can he get away with that?"

Handing me back the note, Mr. Napier says, "Let me ask you something, Robert. If you had lost, would you have had the five dollars to pay Mr. Sikora?"

I guess Mr. Napier has a point there. "Well, no, not yet," I say. "But I would've."

"I bet you would've tried harder to get out of it. So maybe both you and Mr. Sikora should stop making bets neither one of you can pay?" he says, giving me that wise old teacher look.

I thank Mr. Napier and take a defeated breath and put the note back in my pocket. I head for science class.

. . .

Even though I'm steamed at what just happened, I do have to say that the science class projects have turned out to be really fun. When I get to class, just like yesterday, I sit for attendance and then me and Linda leave for the library. In our research we found out a real cool thing about the moon. There's a part of it called the Oceanus Procellarum. On the Apollo 12 mission the astronauts studied it. It's a fancy name that means the ocean of storms. And besides the ocean of storms there's other seas and smaller bays surrounding it. A giant magma thing happened like a million years ago that caused it. It's that really large gray area of the moon that everyone sees. And with a decent telescope you can see right in the middle of this area at a crater called the Copernicus Crater. And then there's these ripples extending from there called the Carpathian Mountains. It's pretty cool. So what Linda and me have done is taken Mr. Molnar's idea about short trips to the moon and came up with five or six trips people might want to take to this area of the moon. And let me say something else about Linda Orken. She is surprisingly very cool to be around. She's very sincere when she talks and she looks right into my eyes when she does. And she's got a great sense of humor. And sitting close to her like I have the last two days, I can see she's actually pretty behind those thick, black-framed glasses and puffy lips too big for her face. And her hair is not as scraggly looking up close. And I like it when our arms touch while we're working together. And I like it when our hands touch. And I like when our legs touch. And with next Friday going to be presentation day, Mr. Molnar told us we'll have one more day to work on our projects and put any finishing touches on it. I'm looking forward to that, too.

Chapter Twelve

Saturday mid-morning and I'm busy cutting the lawn. As I'm pushing the lawn mower I wish I had the nerve to hand dad one of my slips with a two dollar charge on it. I know that I won't because I know that *that* won't end up well. Not for me, anyway. But still, I would like to see the look on his face if I did. I'm finished with the front yard and push the mower along the side of the house and open up the gate to the backyard.

When I walk into the backyard I see them. They're all behind the fence in the garden. Tammy, Brother Davis, Debbie Hutton, Davis' side kick Donnie, Katie, and Alistair, the kid with the Nova, who everyone calls Mr. Speaker, even though he never utters a word. It takes me a second or two to fathom what they're doing. They're all sitting in the dirt in the garden Indian style with their hands resting on their knees, palms turned upward to the sky. And they're withering about like a worm or something, raising and lowering their necks and rocking back and forth, quietly chanting something. It's gotta be more of the Watt's stuff. I watch for a few seconds more and then, just like the Grinch, I get an idea. I get an awful idea. I get a wonderful awful idea. Quickly, I spring into action.

I dash into the garage and grab the quart of oil from its shelf. I dash back to the mower and fill, overfill, the oil tank. I start the motor and let it run for a minute or two, then head for the garden. A few feet from the garden's fence the mower begins to sputter so I throw the choke wide open and push the throttle up to max and seconds later the motor is spewing out gray obnoxious smoke. I stop right by the garden's entrance and pretend to try and understand what's going on with the mower. The grey smoke billows out. I see and hear

Tammy screaming at me to turn the thing off but I cup my ear and act like I can't hear her. Everyone's covering the mouths from the smoke and getting up and walking away when I finally hit the kill switch. "Sorry," I meekly say, walking away with the mower. "I guess there's a lil' too much oil in the motor."

That'll teach Tammy to give me any damn messages involving my lawn care business! I bring the mower into the garage and I drain the excess oil from the motor and check the filters. Everything's good. I finish cutting the back yard, the garden now empty.

• • •

Right near lunch time I'm sitting in my room listening to my records. The records I bought last week are first. I settled on *The Love You Save* and *Never Can Say Goodbye* by the Jackson Five, one of my favorite groups. They've both been out for a while as singles so I was happy I was able to dig them out of the ten cent bin. As I listen to the music, I'm making an exact replica of the 1969-70 New York Knick championship banner. I'm gonna hang it from my ceiling just like they have at the Garden. As I'm doing this, from my bedroom window I'm watching Tammy's band of now fumigated gypsies leave the house. Davis with Donnie and Debbie, Katie with Mr. Speaker. Then between songs, I hear mom's raised voice. Before the next song starts I turn my player down and listen.

"For the ninth, tenth, hundredth, and last time," Mom says, "you are taking your driver's test with your father in the car that he has bought and fixed for you and has been teaching you in!"

"But Mom," Tammy screeches, "why can't I take my test in the car I feel most comfortable in?"

Tammy has a point there.

"Because to begin with Tammy, neither I or your father have ever been comfortable with you driving that…car."

Mom has a point there about Davis' car. It is an ugly orange rat trap. Then Mom adds more.

"Secondly, no matter how important you think Martin is to you right now, your father is more important."

Mom and Dad refuse to call Brother Davis Brother Davis. They always call him Martin.

"I never said dad wasn't important!" Tammy wails. "I just don't understand why I can't take my test in the car that I feel most comfortable in!"

I hear Mom take a measured breath. Then, in her polished mom tone she says, "It's as simple as this young lady. You will be taking your test with your father in the car he has bought and fixed and taught you to drive in or there will be no test at all!"

I'm sure mom walked away from Tammy after that because I hear Tammy say something incomprehensible and I could feel the stir of air in the hallway as she rumbles past my closed door. Seconds later Tammy's out the front door and I'm sure on her way to Debbie's.

. . .

Dad gets home a little after noon and I'm still in my room listening to my records. Mom is in the kitchen fixing lunch and I can hear them talking when he enters the room. He says hopefully this is the last Saturday he'll have to put in for the season. Then mom says she's had enough of Tammy's insistent demand that she takes her driver's test in Martin's car. Dad says in a couple of weeks it will be all over. Mom says if Tammy pesters her one more time she has a good mind to tell her that maybe they'll be no test at all. Dad says again it will soon be over. Through my closed door I'm called for lunch.

Right after lunch I decide I'm going to ride over to River End Playground and see if I can get a game up. Our playground has a court but our baskets have chain-link nets. I hate chain-linked nets. So I get ready to go. I hear the phone ring and dad answer it. I put the 45s I was listening to this morning back into their jackets. I'm about to grab my basketball when I hear a light rap at my door. Dad walks in. "Looks like you got another lawn there, kid," he says.

"Really," I say, sounding more surprised than him.

"Looks so," he says. "I just spoke to a Mrs. Medina. She wants you to come over and take care of her yard."

I take the note and read it. Mrs. Medina. 37 Azalea Court. 295-4657. That's in the new neighborhood. I didn't put any flyers in the new neighborhood I think to myself. "I didn't put any of my slips on this street," I say.

Dad shrugs his shoulders. "She got your number somehow. Ask her how when you get there. I told her you'd be right on your way."

"She wants me to go over there now?" I say, basketball in hand. Dad shakes his head in the affirmative. "Right now?"

Dad kinda smirks and says, "That's business, kid."

So a few minutes later I take the mower back out of the garage and fill it with gas, grab my rake, broom, shears, and green bag, and light broom, and I'm on my way to cut my second lawn. I did actually want to go to River End and play some basketball but for one, I knew that wouldn't go over well with dad and secondly, if I get another two dollars with where I'm going, I'll add that to my Sucrets tin. That'll give me almost four dollars saved. If this lawn care business goes good enough, I'll be able to buy those Clydes for sure.

I pass Tommy's house but don't stop 'cause his dad's car is in the driveway. I turn down Truman Street. I pass McKinley Street and then Fillmore Street where Brock lives and then Garfield Street and head for the utility road. There's a little cut through behind the power plant into the new neighborhood that saves a lot of time. When I get to the end of Truman Street I push my mower onto the dirt hardened utility road.

On one side of me I pass the backyards of the houses on Garfield Street. The houses are set back some from the utility road. Some houses have fences and some are just open from the road. These houses have giant back yards. On my other side there's nothing but woods. As I walk I can see the giant gray coils rising up over the giant chain-link fence from the back end of the power plant. I come to the bend in the road and my heart stops. This can't be true. No way. I can't have this bad of timing. I take another quick glimpse. It's true. Heading my way, walking with their motorcycles, are Dean Magnumson and Bruce Rutter. I put my head down. I walk slowly forward. Everyone's getting closer. My heart's pounding in fear. I can hear their motorcycle tires against the dirt road. I can see their feet. Then I hear a snap of a finger and, "Birdsall? Right?"

I look up and with my heart pounding away and as calmly as I can, I say, "Ah, yeah. Hey Dean, hey Bruce."

Dean looks and points at my mower. "You got gas in that thing?"

I look at my mower. "Yeah, I got gas in it. I'm on my way to do a job," I say.

Dean nods. "Think we can borrow a lil'?

I look at my mower again. I shrug my shoulders. "Ah, sure. I guess," I say, not knowing how Dean's gonna borrow gas.

"Cool," Dean says, kicking down the stand to his bike.

I watch as Dean unties a black pouch that's tied to the handlebars of his bike. He opens it and takes out a dingy clear glass jar and a dingy clear rubber hose. He takes off the gas cap to my mower and sticks the rubber hose into the tank and sucks the other end and seconds later golden gas is flowing into the jar. He fills it about half-way, dumps half the jar into his tank, hands the jar to Bruce who does the same to his tank. Bruce hands the jar back to Dean, then pumps his kick start twice and his motorcycle is revving. Dean puts the jar and hose back into the pouch and ties it, hops on his bike and kick starts his motorcycle in one kick. Over the revving engines of the motorcycles he says, "You wouldn't happen t'have an extra few bits on ya for some petrol, would ya Birdsall?"

"Yeah, I got a couple of quarters here if you guys need it," I say, reaching into my pocket and showing the coins.

Dean looks at the money and says, "Two's good."

I hand Dean the quarters.

"Cool, man," Dean says taking the quarters, turning and handing one to Bruce. "Hey. We owe ya one, Birdsall," Dean says, pocketing the coin and then extending his hand, waiting for me to slap him five. I do. Bruce gives me a thumbs up. They rev their engines again and seconds later they're down the utility road in a cloud of brown dust.

Only two quarters lost? No teeth? That turned out better than anticipated.

I make the little cut through at the power plant and push my mower onto Juniper Street and into the new neighborhood. My neighborhood still calls this one the new neighborhood even though it isn't so new anymore. A few years ago us kids used to play baseball in the empty lots and roller skate and skateboard and play street hockey on the freshly paved streets. But the lots filled up and the houses on them as well and pretty soon other kids were playing on the streets and in the leftover lots.

There's two distinctions about the new neighborhood. One is there's not nearly as many trees here as in my neighborhood or the old neighborhood and two, as I walk down Juniper Street, a long and bending street, all the houses look exactly alike except for what side of the house the front door is on. It's as if one side of the street is made for right-handed people and the other for left-handed. Golden Rod intersects with Juniper and I turn down the corner.

Azalea is the third street on the right and I stop, check the address on the note, and head for house 37.

37 Azalea Court ends up being the next to the last house on the block. It's a small brown house much like the ones next to it with no fence but a decent size yard. There's one of those old four door Rambler's in the driveway. I survey the yard. The grass definitely needs to be cut and there are some small branches and twigs down from the one tree in the front yard. There's a few kid's toys strewn about the yard also. I leave my mower and stuff on the sidewalk and walk along the side of the house and take a look at the back yard. It looks pretty much the same as the front except that there's two trees back there and a fence. I walk to the front of the house. As I get near the front door an overwhelming peppery scent mixed in with dirty diapers filters through the screened door. I knock. A girl that looks about Tammy's age comes to the front door, holding a fairly new-born baby. Another girl, maybe three or four, clings right behind her, shielding her face behind the girl's apron. "Ah, yes, ah, hi," I say. "I'm looking for Mrs. Medina." I show the girl the address written down on the slip of paper. "I'm here to cut her lawn," I add, pointing to my mower.

"Si, yes," the girl says. "Roberto, no?"

She sounds a little bit like the Necci's when she talks. "Yes," I say. "My dad said that she called for me to work on the yard," pointing to the yard now.

"Si, yes," the girl says. "I call."

I stand there for a few seconds before it sinks in that *this* is Mrs. Medina. And that's because she doesn't look like any of the Mrs. that I know. She's young and really pretty with dark eyes and mocha skin and jet black hair. "Oh," I say, looking at this pretty young Mrs. Medina. "Oh." I say again. "Ah, so, ah, what do you want, what would you like to be done?" I ask.

Mrs. Medina says to the young girl clinging to her apron, "Espera, Espera," then walks out onto the front steps, infant in hand. "Si, yes, todos yard," she says, sweeping her free hand over the entire yard. She looks at me. I nod. "Alli," she says, pointing to the toys and twigs, "no mas," she says, making a stop sign with her hand.

I get it. She wants the whole yard cut and the twigs and branches and toys picked up. Okay. "Where do you want me to put the toys?" I ask.

"Alli," she says, pointing to the front of the house.

I nod. "And the same for the backyard?" I ask.

Mrs. Medina looks at me again with her black pearl eyes and shakes her head and says, "Yes, si, la misma."

I got yes and si. So now, unlike at Mr. Lampman's, I think about how much to charge. I guess it's about the same size yard as Mr. Lampman's so I say, "Ah, well, do you think two dollars is fair?"

"Dos dolares?" she says, holding up two fingers. I nod affirmative. She thinks for a few seconds and I'm wondering if she's thinking that that's too much. Then she nods her head and looks at me with her black pearl eyes again and says, "Si, yes. Eso es justo. Fair," she says. Then as she walks back into the house she adds, "Hazlo," and waves me into the yard with her free arm.

I take my time doing the work. First I go around and pick up the twigs and branches and break them up and put them in my green bag. Then I pick up the toys that include a rusting red wagon and a few bouncing balls and a plastic bike and a kid's jump rope and hula-hoop and put them in the front of the house. I start with the yard by cutting the front lawn first and then go to the side yard and then to the backyard. There's a picnic table and a grill and I move both to cut the grass there. Back by the fence the grass is thicker and higher and I have to tilt the mower upward and slowly lower the blade over the grass. When I'm all finished I walk the mower back to the front yard with the motor running just in case I missed a spot. Everything's good. I remember what Mr. Lampman said about young grass getting raked so I give the yard a light raking and put the clippings in my green bag. I sweep the grass off the driveway and the walkway. I look around. I did a good job, I think. I walk to the front door and knock. Mrs. Medina comes to the door this time unadorned with children. She walks out onto the steps and looks at the front yard. She walks to the side yard and looks and continues to the back yard, "Si, yes, muy bien," she says. Then she turns to me and says, "Very good." She reaches into the pocket of her apron and takes two dollars out and hands it to me. "Gracias," she says.

"Thank you," I say, taking the money. As we're walking to the front of the house I say, "Ah, Mrs. Medina. Can I ask you something?"

"Si," she says.

"How did you get my number and stuff?"

We've reached the front steps. "Su numero?" she says, pointing to me.

"Yes," I say.

"Iglesia," she says. I stare at her. "The church," she says. "On the…." Mrs. Medina stops, then motions like she's reading something in front of her and taking it down. "Annucio. In church."

"Oh," I say, having forgotten that I gave Tup one of my flyers to put on the church bulletin board. Well how about that.

"Si," Mrs. Medina says. "I see annucio, pero no Roberto."

I guess that means she saw my slip but not me. "Oh," I say. "Well, I'm kinda busy Sunday mornings. School work and lawn cutting and everything."

Mrs. Medina smiles and frowns at the same time and says, "Shame."

I nod with a tad of remorse. "If you need me again, you can call?" I ask.

"Si," she says as she starts for the door. "Gracias," she says again.

・・・

When I get home Mom and Dad are sitting on the front steps. I push the mower up the driveway and when I get to the garage dad says, "So how'd you make out there kid?"

I take the two dollars out of my pocket and show it to Mom and Dad. I put the mower in the garage.

"Feels pretty good, doesn't it," Dad says, Mom sitting proud next to him.

I shake my head that yes it does when I come out of the garage. "And I'm hoping I'll have Mr. Lampman again next week," I say as I walk to and past Mom and dad on my way into the house.

Before I get in the door dad says, "I guess pretty soon you won't be needing any more allowance, eh?"

That statement kind of freezes my mind. I don't know what to say, so I say nothing and continue heading for my room. Once there, I put my records back on. I put the two dollars I just earned into the Sucrets tin. Then I cut a picture of the Clydes I'm saving for from my *Street and Smith's* magazine and paste it onto the top of the tin can and put it back in my top desk drawer. Then I get my markers out and put the finishing touches on the Knick championship banner I started. When I finish I get two pieces of string and two pieces of tape and hang the banner dead center from my ceiling of my room. It looks really cool. Just as authentic as the Knick pennants I have on the backboard of my bed. I look at the clock on my desk. It says three thirty and too late to go to River End and get a game up. So I grab my basketball and head for the driveway and my hoop. Mom and Dad have left the front steps. I play a game of 21. Clyde against the Big O. As I play the score is 16-11 Big O. But Clyde's on the line. If he sinks ten straight points he'll win. Clyde takes the shot and the ball bounds off the rim harshly and heads toward the street. Clyde runs and grabs the ball before the second bounce and flings it toward the basket, missing everything this time. The ball rolls toward the garage. It's still 16-11 Big O.

It's Big O's turn. He's lining up his free throw. But before he can take a shot Tammy's coming up the driveway. I wait to shoot until she nears me. "Ah, Tam," I say, as she gets within earshot of me. "I heard somethin' I think you should know 'bout."

She stops. "Oh? And what's that?"

I stop lining up the Big O's free throw. I turn to her and say, "Well, I heard Mom tell Dad she has a good mind to not let you take your driving test at all if you keep pesterin' her about the car thing. With you know who."

"Oh really," Tammy says defiantly. "Well, we'll just have to see about that now, won't we lil' brother," she says confidently that she'll win the battle.

Hmph, I think. This could get interesting.

Chapter Thirteen

Monday morning I'm on my way to pick up Tommy at the bus stop. As I go to knock on the front door I hear Tommy's mother grilling him on how he came upon so much money. I see her standing by the television holding Tommy's money. If this was his dad I'd take off but since its Mrs. Hulse I knock. "Yes, Robby. Come in," she says.

I walk in the house.

"Robby, tell me the truth," Mrs. Hulse says to me. "Does my son play ping pong at school against his classmates for money?"

"Well," I slyly say. "I know better than to play 'em, that's for sure, Mrs. Hulse." Then I add, innocently, "But sometimes I play my classmates in basketball for money. Just the other day I won five bucks from Sikora," I say, looking at Tommy. "But the kid welched on me," I add, turning to Mrs. Hulse.

"Sikora," Tommy scoffs. "Sucker owes me two bucks."

Mrs. Hulse just shakes her head. "Thirteen dollars playing ping pong," she says. "And what would you do if you'd lost?" she asks Tommy.

"Fat chance of that," Tommy says.

"He is the best player in our school, Mrs. Hulse," I add.

Again Mrs. Hulse shakes her head. "Thirteen dollars, betting on ping pong," she mumbles to herself, handing Tommy his money back.

Tommy takes the money and puts it back in his room. He walks out of his room, looks at me, we both shrug our shoulders and head for the bus stop.

"Think she believes you," I say once we're out of the house and heading toward the corner of Truman and Constitution Streets.

"Doesn't matter," Tommy says. "'Long as Dad don't know."

The bus arrives and me and Tommy get on, We take our customary seats near the back of the bus. Next stop Broccoli gets on. He sits down across from me and Tommy. He leans over. "Did you guys hear?" he secretly whispers.

"Hear what?" I say.

"There's gonna be a walkout or somethin' today in the high school."

"There is?" I say surprised. "Where'd ya hear that?"

"My brother."

"Huh," I say.

"Did he say why?" Tommy asks.

"No, not really. I mean, I didn't ask him 'cause he didn't tell me. I overheard 'em when he was talkin' outside with his friend. He said somethin' about showin' up Monday morning out by the field."

"Huh," I say again.

"Did you hear anything from your sis?" Brock asks me.

"Not a word," I say. "I mean, she had her usual gatherin' of the Watt's clan Saturday, but I didn't hear anything."

Lloyd Rogers, sitting in front of us turns and says, "You guys talkin' 'bout the walkout?"

"Yeah," Brock says. "What did you hear?"

"Just that there's gonna be some kind of walkout or somethin' today. Supposedly out in the football field."

"Your sister tell ya that?" I ask. Lloyd's older sister is a sophomore.

"She didn't tell me," Lloyd says, "but I overheard somethin' like that."

"But she said the field, right?" Brock says.

"Yeah, somethin' about the football field," Lloyd says.

"Huh," I say for the third time, leaning back into my seat, wondering if Tammy and Brother Davis and the Watt's gang are involved in this walkout thing.

. . .

Before the bell rings on my way to class I ask Vinnie DeStella if he heard anything since his brother is a senior this year. He said he hadn't heard anything. When the bell does ring it's hard to sit in class and concentrate on this modular math stuff. It's gotten to be completely insane by now and my mind is wandering and wondering anyway if Tammy and Brother Davis and their band of bandits are involved with whatever's going on at the high school. So who cares about these binary codes and metric measurements and divisibility and clocks that don't tell the right time. I act like I'm paying attention and try and survive the class unscathed. I do because Ol' Kazoo never calls my name to answer any questions. He probably knows I don't know any answers anyway given I got a **D** on last week's mini quiz. My time-tested procedure failed me this time. The bell rings and I head for C wing and social studies. I meet up with Tommy on my way. "Hear anything more?" I ask.

"Only from Pritchard. He said that his brother said that there might be some kind of somethin' goin' on, but he wasn't real specific."

"Hmph." I say. "I asked DeStella if he heard anything and he said no."

"Well, I guess we'll find out soon 'nuff," Tommy says. "But ya know what would be real cool Birdboy?" Tommy asks.

I'm afraid to ask.

"If we had our own walk out right here. Maybe get up and walkout in Kilcommins class and get the entire C wing to join in!"

That would be cool, I think as we head into the room. But probably not too smart.

. . .

We end up not pulling any stunts on Mr. Kilcommins during social studies class. So there's no C-wing uprising. Not today. But I know Tommy will cook something up pretty soon. We had finished the world language thing last week and I got a sixty-seven on my second quiz but my combined quiz grade is sixty-nine, so I passed. Since then we've been learning about the countries in Europe that sent the most people to live here in the New World. It was the English, Mr. Kilcommins says. And the French and the Spanish and the Portuguese and the Netherlands, wherever that is. He's been explaining how the Portuguese mostly settled in Brazil and Uruguay in South America and the French up in Canada and down by Louisiana and the English here in North America and the West Indies and the Spanish in Mexico and Peru and the Dutch, the Netherlands people, well, they seemed to be everywhere. I don't see why this really matters anymore, but apparently it does. Anyway, at least it's not who speaks how and why.

When class ends I head for my locker to change my math and social studies books for history and English. I'm still thinking about whatever went on over at the high school until I see Diane Lindsay at her locker. She has on a light grayish skirt with a pink top with three buttons near the neck all buttoned. I don't know anything about shoe styles but today hers are heeled with and open toe with pink and white stripes coloring the straps. Her long blond hair is parted in the middle and his tight around her face and pulled back to a cute pony tail. As I pass her locker she turns and sees me. I smile. She doesn't smile back.

I walk into my history room. Before class starts I ask Curt if heard anything about a walkout over at the high school. "We'll," he says, "You're about the third or fourth person to ask me that, but no, I didn't hear anything," he says. "What did you hear?"

"I only heard it from Kenebrocki, who heard it from his brother," I say. But also this kid Lloyd Rogers who I ride with on my bus heard somethin' too."

"Like what?"

"Nobody's sure," I say.

Mrs. Stanton walks in with her pretty smile and before she begins class she hands us back our tests. As she does this she tells us she was pleased with the grades. So am I when I get mine back. A seventy-nine. Pretty good. Then she says we're going to begin studying an overview of the Roman Republic. She tells us we will be studying this for the next three weeks. She says there's going to be a test in the middle and then another one at the end. And we're to write an essay at least a one page long one on an approved Roman Republic topic. She tells us this is twenty-five percent of our last quarter grade. For some, she says, it can make the difference between passing and failing. She tells us we can hand our essay in whenever we feel we're finished with it, but it has to be in by the last day. And she says it will be half the grade. Mrs. Stanton goes on to say that the Roman Republic lasted a thousand years. She tells us they were the strongest nation on the face of the earth for eight centuries. She tells us they excelled in every aspect of human knowledge. She tells us the Romans excelled in engineering, primarily making aqueducts that provided daily fresh water and paved roads that allowed better travel. She tells us their system of law and governance was so advanced that many of the procedures and legal terms are still being used and applied today. In architecture, literature, civil law, all were well advanced thinking for that time she says. Then she tells us about the decline of the Roman Republic. That for over two centuries this great empire slowly crumbled apart. She tells us that there were various reasons for the decline. Dividing the empire in two, she says. A deepening division between the rich and poor. Over taxation due to excessive royal spending, she says. Too many wars, she says. She adds that near the end, in the last century of the republic, there were twenty different rulers leading to utter chaos and the loss of *civil trust*. I'm not sure what all that means but Mrs. Stanton tell us that our society, our form of government, the one we live with here, most resembles that empire. Oh, she says light heartedly, there's some Athenian thinking sprinkled in here and there, but by and large, our model is the Roman one. And we're not yet two hundred years old, she says with her pretty smile. I didn't know all that.

And then it's down the yellow brick road and a visit with the Witch Whitaker. I walk into the room and before I can sit down, before any of us can sit down, we have to hand in our weekend assignment, which is another thing that should be outlawed. Not only did we have to write a thesis statement on the topic we were handed Friday afternoon, but we had to explain what *style* thesis statement we are making. Mine is on the nineteenth amendment, which apparently gave women the right to vote. I never knew that they didn't have the right to vote. I did my best.

Minutes pass by and the bell rings and the Witch walks in and parks her broomstick. She picks up our essay papers, making sure they're all there, and starts class. And oddly, there's no Fig. This is strange because I know I saw 'em earlier in the hallway. I was going to ask him if he heard anything about this walkout.

On the blackboard the Witch is writing sentences that look like this: ___ is ___ because, ___, ___ and ___ ___ ___. And then things like this: T + P + A1+ A2+ A3. I can't even imagine what's coming from all that. As she's scribbling all this out Fig walks in. He puts his essay on the Witch's desk. Without turning around the Witch says, "So glad you could join us, Mr. Figaro."

"Sorry I'm late," Fig says. "I had trouble with my locker."

"That's one troublesome locker you have there, Mr. Figaro," the Witch says, still writing. "This must be the third time."

"It's quirky," Fig says, sitting down at his desk. "And I had to get my homework out of it to hand in," he says.

After Fig sits down and opens up his English book and settles in, I take out a sheet of paper and write, "Walkout?" and show it to Fig.

He looks at what I wrote and on takes out a sheet of paper and writes out, "football field?"

I shake my head and write, "Yes."

Fig starts to write something when we hear, "So, Mr. Figaro, Mr. Birdsall, Since you're both so busy scribbling back there how about one of you come up to the blackboard and fill in the blanks to either one of these thesis statements." She holds out a piece of chalk.

I look at Fig and nod that I'll be the one to go. I take a deep breath and heavily rise from my seat and slowly walk to the blackboard. I take the chalk and stare at the blackboard. I stare at the blanks and the few words between them. All the style of thesis statements I've been told exist are flashing through my mind. Argumentative. Analytical. Explanatory. Expository. Whatever else. I feel frozen. And then the miraculous happens. As I look at the blanks, I can see it. I get it. This is so easy. So I write, Clyde Frazier is a great basketball player because he plays good defense and has a good jump shot and because of his skills the Knicks always have a chance to win. I read what I wrote twice and triumphantly put the chalk down.

The Witch reads my statement. "That's actually a very good thesis statement, surprisingly, Mr. Birdsall," she says. "You used an explanatory and analytical style statement. What made you think of those two styles from let's say an expository one?"

Now I had no idea what the style of thesis statement I just put down on the blackboard was. I was just making a statement. As if I was telling Sasso the Buck fan or Driscoll the Celtic fan or Sikora the welcher in a basketball debate. And further more I still don't get what an expository thesis statement is. So my best response is, nonchalantly, "It just seemed to be the right one."

I sit back down. "Well, with hope, Mr. Birdsall, you can find more of the right ones as we move along. Mr. Figaro…."

Fig gets grilled next on the T + P + A1+ A2 + A3 thing. Let's just say it doesn't go very well. So the Witch tells Fig to study more and be here on time because the next time he's late he loses a point on is grade and he's too close to the line to be giving any points away. Then the Witch asks if anyone in the class can answer the question. A few hands go up.

Lunch period in the cafeteria. If any news is to be found out, or been found out, this is where we'll hear it. As Fig and me are waiting in line by the double doors to sit, some kids say they heard something about a walkout at the high school, others say they heard nothing. The bell rings and my lunch line files into the cafeteria while the last lunch period files out.

I brought my lunch as usual. Mom packed a bologna and cheese sandwich with a bag of pretzels and Snack Pack chocolate pudding. I stand in line to buy a milk. Figgy has everything in his lunchbox so he heads for our table. When I get to our table Cairnsy's already sitting there with his two pieces of bread and whatever is in between them and a Jungle Juice fruit punch. Broccoli joins us and from his brown bag lunch takes out a thick roast beef sandwich and a bag of Wise potato chips and a Hi-C.

"Any more news?" I ask Broccoli.

"Nothin' concrete," Brock says. "Just supposedly some kind of demonstration out by the football field."

"That's kinda what I heard," Fig says.

"Whadda you guys talkin' 'bout?" Cairnsy asks.

"Supposedly there's a walkout, or somethin', goin' on over at the high school," Brock tells Cairnsy.

"Really?" Cairnsy says with a shocked face. "How come?"

"Nobody's really sure," Brock says.

"You know what Tommy suggested?" I say. "That we have our own walkout right here,"

Broccoli looks at me. "You know, that's not a bad idea."

"I like it," Fig says.

"What do we walkout…on, for," Cairnsy says.

"Well. How 'bout horrible school lunches," I say.

"Yeah, and teacher abuse," Fig adds.

"And too short of a lunch period," Cairnsy says.

So for the next few minutes me, Fig, Broccoli, Cairnsy, start coming up with different reasons to stage our own walkout right here. Steve Dunn slides down and asks what we're doing. When we tell him he joins in. By the time lunch is over we have a good list of reasons.

• • •

When I get home from school Davis's ratty Beetle is parked in front of the house. I walk in and look out the back picture window and spot Tammy and Brother Davis out in the garden. I put my books down on the dining room table and walk out the back door, heading for Tammy's prized garden.

"Hey there lil' brother," Davis says. "Gonna smoke us out today?"

"No," I say.

"What do you want twerp?" Tammy demands.

I get right to the point. "We heard there was a walkout today at your school?" I say.

Tammy looks surprised. "What? The idiot jocks out on the football field? How'd you twerps hear about that?"

"What we heard was most of the senior class walked out," I say.

Tammy shakes her head and dismisses what I just said. "Robby, it was ten jerks from the football team that challenged ten jerks from the Deep Creek football team to some stupid game. Sorry to disappoint you."

I stand there. "Huh," I say. And that ends the great walkout of 1971 at Three Brooks High School.

. . .

Well almost. Next day, jarringly after first bell, me, Fig, Brock, Cairnsy, and Steve Dunn all get called down to Principal Pagano's office. One by one we walk into his office where he's sitting behind his huge principal's desk with all his principal stuff on it. When the last of us arrive, which would be me, Principal Pagano stands up and asks, "Can anyone explain this?" In his hand is the crumpled up paper that has all our reasons for staging a walkout. "Mrs. Darnold says she found this near the trash can where you all were sitting yesterday."

None of us say a word. Then bravely Steve Dunn says, "Well, that doesn't mean it's ours."

Principal Pagano looks at Steve and says, "You're correct, Mr. Dunn. It doesn't. But being an educator for twenty two years, the last fourteen of them here, gives me a good sense as to where this came from."

Again we're silent.

Principal Pagano crumples the paper and throws it in his trash. "I just want you all to know that this is duly noted." He looks at directly at us. "You boys can go to first period now," he says. "Quiet down those hallways."

And so *that* ends the great Three Brooks High School walkout, and probably ours too.

. . .

The week passes rather quickly. I didn't do as well with my nineteenth amendment thesis statement as I did with my Clyde Frazier one. Mrs. Whitaker wrote how could I understand one day and not the next? Mrs. Stanton gave us a quiz on the Roman stuff and I'm pretty sure I did good on that. Today, Friday, is presentation day for our science class projects. We're all sitting at our combined desks as pairs with our projects. Mr. Molnar has pulled our names out of the shoebox again to arrange the order we're going to present in. Linda and me are fifth. I have to admit I'm a little nervous.

Vicky Carlson and Stephanie Fabbri go first and what they did was make a jewelry line using materials one could get from the moon. They made different necklaces and bracelets and anklets and ear rings of all different moon shapes in all the shades of the moon. Blue, pink, orange, yellow, red. They told us what kind of rock was used and what stage or lunar event was happening in the image. I have to say it was pretty good and both Vicky and Stephanie looked very good doing the modeling.

Ty MacIntrye and Alex Grebel are next and they made a pretty cool solar system with moving parts and a bright light for a sun that shows how the moon is lit during different times of a year. It's pretty good but it's not like we haven't seen that before.

Jack Helmstetter and Steven Lerner are next and they made different size race cars and a drag race style racetrack with moon dust on the track. They demonstrate how the different cars would perform on the moon's surface. It's okay I guess.

Rick Varley and Lori Brunson are next and in an odd way, their project is a little like Vicky's and Stephanie's and a little like mine and Linda's. They made a clothes line of varsity teams from high schools on the moon. They picked a part of the moon where there is a valley and a mountain and a mountain ridge and a lake and a crater and gave each one a different color and a name and motto. On poster board they showed the jackets with the colors and the name and described the area from where that team came from. It's pretty good I guess.

It's Linda and mines turn. We bring our project up to the front. We begin describing the Oceanus Procellarum. We tell everyone it's the really large gray area of the moon. In moon talk it's a Lunar Mare that early astronomers thought were seas. We gathered as many pictures of the area as we could and pasted them on white poster paper. We have a dozen posters made. We made headlines of where and what the area is and we kept with Mr. Molnar's early suggestion of people taking vacations to the moon and applied that to this. When we begin, it's then that Linda, Linda Orken, who never says a word in class, but who I've gotten to know, and like, mesmerizes the class with her characterizations of the people on the moon. In one of the little bays that are near the bigger seas we decided to bring older couples for a stay in an area we named "The Golden Years." As I tell about the area, Linda acts out a grumpy old couple who aren't happy with the temperature of their coffee or the texture of their towels or the condition of the beach or anything else for that matter, and she acts out the unassuming bellhop trying to help them. In the end the older couple snicker to the bellhop that they didn't travel 238,000 miles to hear excuses from the local youth. In the area of the Carpathian Mountains we called it a place "For the Honeymooners" and as I explain about the area, Linda is acting out this over-the-top, lovey-dovey couple who don't notice anything because they're *so in love*, and the guide trying to point out the things that I'm saying that they're missing. In the area of the Sea of Clouds we called it "Moonstock," a place where all the hippies could go. As nervous as I am, watching Linda act out these people who think everything I'm saying and showing is a "stone cold groove" and "totally righteous" and "that's so right on" that even I have hard time not laughing. When I tell about this crater that's one of the brightest on the moon Linda puts her hand on her forehead and feigns fainting and says, "Oh wow, man. Like, wow." The class erupts in laughter. When we're finished the class actually gives us a rousing applause.

Linda and me return to our desks. She smiles at me when we sit down. We watch the last pairs and after the last presentation, Mr. Molnar hands out mimeographs with the names of the pairs of students on them. He tells us to circle the one we think was best. The sheet that we're given does not have our own names on it, so nobody can vote for themselves, and we don't have to sign them. It's a secret ballot, he says. Mr. Molnar gives us a few minutes to decide. I vote for Stephanie and Vicky. Mr. Molnar then collects the mimeographs, calculates them and says that Robert Birdsall and Linda Orken won with the most votes, nine.

At first it doesn't sink in what Mr. Molnar just said. But then I see Linda's smiling face looking at me as she mouths "WOW!" and she grabs and hugs me. Mr. Molnar congratulates us and tells us we've both won a five dollar certificate for the book fair next fall. And that our project will be on display with the other class winners in the main entrance area by the trophy case. Linda looks at me again and again mouths "WOW!"

After class Linda and I receive congratulations and everyone tells Linda she was really funny. And for the first time I walk with Linda as we leave the room and head for the back door and the buses. "I can't believe we won," she says.

"Me neither," I say, adding, "except that you were terrific up there."

"Well, that just came to me," she says.

"Really?" I say astonished. "You were so funny."

Linda smiles. "It was a lot of fun," she says.

"The book certificate thing is okay," I say. "But I'd rather have won cash."

Linda laughs. "Yes, cash might've been better, but I'll take the certificate."

"Me too," I say.

We walk out the double back doors. "I wonder if we'll win first place," I say.

Linda smiles and shrugs her shoulders and says, "Well, either way, it was just wonderful to have had you as my partner, Robert," Linda says.

"Yeah, me too Linda" I say, truly melancholy that our project is over with.

"So, see you Monday, I guess," Linda says.

I smile and nod. "See ya Monday."

Chapter Fourteen

Breakfast Saturday morning and I can tell Tammy's very nervous. This is the day of her driver's test. I'm munching on my Cocoa Puffs as loud as I can and it doesn't even get a mention. And she's actually listening to Dad as he explains for the hundredth time about the proper safety rules of the road. And what to expect on her test. And also there's no sign of Brother Davis or his ratty orange Beetle. So after all the huffing and puffing, yelling and arguing, Tammy's taking her test in the car that dad has fixed up for her and taught her how to drive in.

After breakfast I'm watching the *Harlem Globetrotters* when Dad and Tammy meet in the parlor. "Ready?" Dad asks. Tammy nods. "We're leaving now, Nance," Dad shouts out to Mom.

Mom emerges from the kitchen. She gives Tammy a hug and says, "Good luck. Just remember what you're father taught you and you'll do fine." Again Tammy nods. I watch as she and dad walk out the front door. They're not even out of the driveway when Mom is telling me to get off the couch and do my chores. "Five minutes, Mom," I say. "My show's almost over."

It's actually ten more minutes but after the show ends I'm in the front yard raking up the curly Q's and helicopters that fell during the week. As I'm working I'm wondering if the Lampman's need any yard work done this weekend. I could earn another two dollars and add it to my Puma Clyde collection. After lunch I think I'll go to their house and find out.

I walk into the garage to get a green bag to pick up the raking when Tommy comes barreling up the driveway on his bicycle with a brown paper bag in his hand. "Here, hold this," he says, out of breath, flipping me the bag.

I catch the bag. I don't even get a chance to ask Tommy what's going on because he's furiously pedaling his bike across the front lawn on his way back home. I open the bag and there's a *Playboy* magazine and his money and the reefer cigarettes he found. I better hide all this quickly. So I climb up the ladder that leads to the attic, crawl a little ways down and lift up a floor board and hide Tommy's contraband there.

I go back to the yard and finish with the curly Q's and helicopters and get the shears and trim the hedges. I do a good job and when I'm finished I sweep up the debris, put it all in the green bag, grab my basketball from the garage, and play a game of OUT. Clyde versus Pearl Monroe. Clyde's about to get T on Pearl when I see dad and Tammy coming down the street. I stand there as Tammy pulls the car into the driveway. I can tell she passed her test because she's smiling from ear to ear. And then she obviously forgets who I am because when she leaps out of the car she gives me a big hug as she runs into the house.

"I guess she passed, huh?" I say to Dad.

"She did good," Dad says.

I'm expecting dad to ask me if I finished my chores, but he doesn't. In fact, he asks for the ball, takes a shot, misses, shrugs, keeps walking into the house.

I finish my game and Clyde puts T on Pearl with a left-to-right-right-to-left behind the back dribble and then a one headed called bank shot from the middle of the key. As I'm waving to the Garden crowd with the victory, mom calls me in for lunch.

Lunch is set at the dining table. Mom's made triple-decker sandwiches with pickles on the side and those potato chips that are dark and crunchy. There's also a can of RC soda for me. I guess we're finally off the no cola regiment. When I sit down and look at Tammy there's this indescribable look on her face. Like it's the very last day of school. Forever. As we eat Dad's telling her that a license doesn't mean you forget the rules of the road. She says she knows. Dad then reminds her that just because someone has their turn signal on doesn't mean they're turning. They might have forgotten it's on. She says she knows. He tells her to be careful about cars waiting to get on the highway. He tells her many times they'll dart in because they've been waiting there a while and ae aggravated. She says she knows. And just like that she's done eating and gets up and goes to her room and gets her work shirt and pops back in the kitchen and tells Mom and Dad she's on her way to work. Mom and Dad follow her to the front door. I hear the car door open and close and hear the engine start. Mom and Dad return to the kitchen, look at each other, take a breath, then sit back down at the table. I finish eating. "I think I'm gonna see if Mr. Lampman needs any yard work done," I say. "He said maybe in a couple weeks."

"Give it a try," Dad says.

. . .

I walk in to the garage and pull the mower out to give it a test start. I set the choke and prime the pump and pull the cord and it snaps in half, throwing me into the just trimmed hedges. I must say "Son of a bitch!" too loud because a few seconds later dad's standing at the front door. I'm picking myself up and off the hedges with the broken cord in my hand. Dad opens the door and I'm expecting a lecture about taking care of the mower but instead he asks, "You okay?"

"Yeah," I say in an aggravated and exasperated tone.

"Do you know how to change one of those?"

"I think so," I say, knowing I've never changed one before.

"They can be tricky," dad says.

I don't say anything. Dad walks out of the house and into the garage. I hear him rummaging around. He emerges saying, "I thought I had an extra cord." He shrugs his shoulders. "Go for a ride to Durrea's?"

I shrug my shoulders. "Sure."

Dad walks to the front door and yells through the screen to mom that we're taking a ride up to Durrea's, Dad and me get in the car. Halfway there, he turns and says, "You have some money, right?" I don't say anything. It's my best option. He smirks. "I got it, kid."

Durrea's is a few miles down Heron Pond Road in the older section of town. There's a larger hardware store further down the highway past the Shop Rite, but dad likes Durrea's. And I do have to say that Durrea's is definitely a neater looking store than the square box looking one. Durrea's parking lot has a post and rail fence painted rustic red all along the front of the store which is set back some distance from the fence. There's the big box delivery truck on the side of the building near the big aluminum roll up doors with DURREA'S HARDWARE 310 Heron Pond Road Lower Brook spelled out on both. I can smell the hot dogs and sauerkraut from Frankie's Frank's cooking at the end of the store under the bright red and white awning. There's benches and chairs to sit on down there. There's even a popcorn machine like at the movies. And always when l walk into Durrea's there's that barn smell. I don't know why, but Durrea's always smells like the inside of a barn.

The store is halfway busy and I follow Dad down to the next to the last aisle. We turn down the aisle and near the end there's various lawn equipment stuff and a pegboard on the back wall. Dad walks up to the pegboard. There's chain saws blades of various sizes and engine belts of various sizes and hoses of various sizes and gaskets of various sizes and what Dad's looking for: A lawn mower pull cord replacement kit. He studies the choices, reaches for one, takes it, studies it again, turns and says, "This'll do it."

I follow Dad back down the aisle and to the front of the store and over to one of the registers. He puts the kit down, takes two dollars out of his wallet, hands it over the counter to what looks like a high school kid on a weekend job with a tan smock on that has **DURREA"S** spelled in red across the front. The kid takes Dad's two dollars, rings up the register, and hands Dad back some change and the kit, now in a small paper bag.

Once back home, I'm kneeling beside the mower watching Dad change the pull cord. He shows me how to remove what's still left from the old cord from the pulley. He shows me how to measure the correct length for the new cord. He shows me how to thread the new cord through the old handle and then onto the pulley. He shows me how to recoil it. When he's done, he stands up, sets the choke, primes the pump. pulls the cord and the engine turns over. He shuts the engine off, and starts it again. He turns it off again. "She's good," he says.

⋯

I leave the mower where it is and start for Mr. Lampman's house. When I pass Tommy's house and see his dad's car in the driveway, I know why Tommy's brown paper bag of ill-gotten gain is being hid away in my attic. His dad must be on one of his tirades. And then when I get to the Lampman's, unfortunately dad's good will in repairing the lawn mower goes for nothing. They're not even home.

I'm on way back home when I see Tommy's dad turn the corner of our street, heading my way. He passes me without any acknowledgement. I turn and walk backwards and watch him turn onto Constitution Street. I turn back around and head for Tommy's. When I get to his house, instead of knocking on the door, I rap on his window. No response. "Tommy," I whisper in the slightly open window. Nothing. I peer in. No Tommy. I crawl down to the ground and peer into the small basement window. No Tommy. I start to walk around to the back of the house and when I get there there's Tommy coming out of the cellar stairs. "Birdman," he says, gently closing the cellar door. "My stash good?"

"In my attic," I say, "under the floor board."

"'Preciate it Birdyboy."

"No sweat."

Tommy and me walk to my house. He tells me his dad was on one of his "everyone's hiding money from him" jags. I know from the past that when he does that he rummages through, no, it's more like a shakedown, of dressers and drawers and cabinets and closets. When we get to my house we can't retrieve the brown bag just yet because Dad's in the garage rearranging his tools and stuff. That didn't seem to need doing, but he's doing it anyway. I get my basketball and play 21 with Tommy until dad goes back in the house. When he does I wait a few minutes more and then go into the garage and climb up the attic stairs and get Tommy's brown paper bag.

. . .

Just as this is one of those years that Easter was "late," it's also one of those years that Memorial Day is "early." I don't get any of that, but the latter is just fine with me because that means that this school week, when it ends, will lead right into the three day Memorial Day weekend. And Memorial Day is really the last bridge to cross between school and beautiful wonderful fantastical incredible summer vacation.

As I'm sitting at my desk in the Great Kazoo's class Monday morning, listening to the morning announcements, I hear that Greg Manino and Diane Lindsay won the overall Lower Brook Middle School science class project. I heard that they won a ten dollar certificate to the New Learning Store. That's actually not a bad prize. There's actually some cool stuff in that store. Chemical kits and wood carving kits and cool models to build and just a lot of things. Pete looks at me and shrugs his shoulders and says, "Sorry."

I act like it's no big deal but I am a little disappointed. I hadn't seen the other class winners so when Kazoo's done squeaking and squawking and class is over I dash down to where the projects are on display. They're all on a cafeteria table in front of the trophy case with our names and classes next to them. Some kids stop and look at them but most just pass on by. I look at Greg's and Diane's and it's really not that much different than mine and Linda's. What they did was they designed this big city built on the moon where people lived and then took trips from there to other planets. The third one, by Jennifer Kaitling and Kevin McReynolds, is all about the orbits the moon takes around the earth every year. And they have cool pictures and the reasoning for what's called the thirteenth moon or the "blue moon," That doesn't happen every year, apparently. On a placard on the table there's commendations for all three class winners. And the reasoning for Greg's and Diane's project winning the overall, according to the staff, is because they took the initial video's slogan that we watched of "How far can we go?" and applied that. So what, I think. The warning bell rings for second period. I start down the hallway heading for C wing.

I have to hustle into class as the second bell rings and Mr. Kilcommins is shutting the door right behind me. I'm barely in my seat with my book out when Mr. Kilcommins starts class. He tells us we have a lot of material to cover. He tells us we're going to have a short overview of the five colonizing nations in the New World with a ten question quiz on each. He then says we're going to begin with the British. He tells us that though the British were nearly a century behind their counterparts in settling the New World, once they did, they outpaced the Spanish and Portuguese and French and Dutch considerably. He says that even though the first settlement in Jamestown was in 1607, Englanders really started coming over in masse during the second half of the seventeenth century. He tells us this was because England in the 1640's was turned upside down with at first, the beheading of some King and then like twenty years later the restoration of the British Crown. He tells us that most of the people coming to the New World were Puritans looking to expand their Protestant beliefs. I'm not sure I get all that but I do get crystal clear when Tommy says, "Say it ain't so Joe." Mr. Kilcommins doesn't respond. He just goes on with the lecture.

After class I take my time heading to B-wing and history, hoping I'll see Diane Lindsay at her locker. I'll congratulate her on winning the science projects. I wait around until the warning bell. She doesn't show. I head for history class.

Again I walk in right at the bell. Mrs. Stanton, standing at the door, gives me a stern look, but with her pretty face. I nod to Curt as I walk to my desk. I sit down and open my history book. On the blackboard Mrs. Stanton has two dates written down. On the upper part of the left side of the blackboard it reads 753 BC and at the bottom of the right side blackboard it reads 476 AD. She tells us to write these numbers down the same way on two sheets of paper in our notebooks. She starts class by telling us we will be filling in important dates to this ledger over the next two-and-a-half weeks. She tells us that our essays will be based on one of these dates, and that we can choose any one we like, at any time, it just has to be handed in one time. No exceptions. She reminds us that we're going to have a mid-study test next week and then a final the following Friday. Again she reminds us this is very important to our last semester grade. I'm not too worried. I'll use my almost always proven method.

When I get to English class I get the same condolences from Figgy that I got from Pete for not winning first place in the science projects. And I tell Figgy the same thing I told Pete. That's it's no big deal. We open our notebooks and the bell rings and the Witch walks in and grabs a stack of papers from her desk. She walks to each desk and hands out a small booklet of mimeographed papers. I look at mine when it lands on my desk. Are you kidding me! This Steinbeck clown again! *Of Mice And Men* it says on the heading. By John Steinbeck. Now what the hell is this gonna be about? When the Witch is done handing out the booklets, she tells us we're going to read these excerpts from the book. She tells us that they'll be no test, which gets a quick exaltation from the class, but there will be an essay on the character of our choice, either George or Lennie, both of which we'll be getting to know over the next five days, due next Monday, which gets an collective groan from the class. When class ends, Fig and me head for the cafeteria.

"Can you believe all this work we're still doin'?" I say exasperated. "Mrs. Stanton's got us studying the whole Roman Empire, Kilcommins has us studying the entire settling of the New World, The Ol' Kazoo still has us on the new math stuff. Now this."

"Yeah, ya think they'd let off a lil' bit near the end," Fig says.

Fig and me walk along the bustle of kids down the corridor from E-wing that leads to the cafeteria down by A-wing. When I don't stop to go to my locker Fig says, "You're buyin'?"

"It's peanut butter and jelly," I say, shrugging. "With a brownie and fruit cup. Add a milk and even the school can't mess that up." Actually, I don't know why they don't serve it more often.

Once we're in the cafeteria, I ask Fig, "So, whadda you got?"

Fig opens up his lunch box. I see he has a mom-made ham and cheese sandwich with the lettuce neatly trimmed around the edges. He has an apple cut up into quarters, a thermos of chocolate milk, and a bag of Cheez-its from one of those variety packs.

During lunch period, me, Fig, Broccoli, Cairsny, and Steve Dunn are still contemplating the best way to get revenge on Mrs. Darnold for rattin' on us last week. We've already come up with some good schemes. Like pushing the cafeteria table legs in just enough so that the slightest touch will knock it down. Or taping a tuna fish sandwich in a baggie with the flap open under the table. Whatever we decide to do, we've decided to wait a bit. And to NOT write any of this down.

In gym class we're on our second week of track and field. Today we have a choice to either participate in the long jump or the mile run. I choose the mile run 'cause when I get out of view I can walk it. What I'm really looking forward to is the end of the week when the softball games begin. Goddard says he'll make up the teams during the week and he'll let us know on Thursday and by Friday we'll have the first games. He tells us they'll be four teams, that we'll play each other twice, and after the six games the top two will play a one game playoff for first place, and the bottom two will play for third place. Just like the Olympics, he tells us.

When I finally get to the end of the day and science class, Mr. Molnar starts class by telling the class, and then me and Linda more specifically, that it was a really hard choice for the staff to pick a winner between the three finalists. And then he reminds everyone that we all did a terrific job. I look over at Linda and she smiles. Then Mr. Molnar starts class. And it's back to boring science class stuff. The Thursday before presentations we started to study the function of cells. And when I open my science notebook there are those awful words that I had to write down from the blackboard. They sound like terrible stuff. Mitochondria and cytoplasm and cell wall and cell membrane. Multicellular and unicellular. Cell function. I like Mr. Molnar and he's always fair, but I can tell that this is going to be awful.

When class finally ends, I motion to Linda if she'll wait up. She nods. Then like Friday, we walk to the school buses together.

"So what did you think of Greg and Diane's project?" I ask.

"I thought it was good," Linda says. "And so was the other one, with all the moon orbits."

"That's a pretty good prize they won," I say. "The ten dollar certificate to the New Learning Store."

"I've actually never been there," Linda says.

"Really? Never?"

"No, never," Linda says.

"Huh," I say. "So I guess it would have been doubly good if we won."

Linda smiles and looks to the ground and nods.

"Well, I'm thinkin' that the only reason why Greg and Diane won is because they're the most popular kids in the school," I add.

"Well, I don't know if the teachers care about that," Linda says.

Linda's bus comes up. "I guess maybe you're right. Well, anyway, see ya tomorrow," I say.

Lind smiles and nods.

. . .

For the next three days after science class I wanted to walk with Linda to her bus, but I didn't. I wasn't sure if I should. I wasn't sure if she wanted me to. Every day I told myself that I would, that I'd just ask her if I could walk with her to her bus, but then every day I didn't. And I'm not sure as to why I'm unsure. I'd wave and smile to her at the end of class, and she do the same to me, but then I dally at my desk and she'd get up and leave and then I stay in the room until it was empty. And I'm not even sure as to why I did that.

Otherwise, school wise, it turned out to be a better week than I thought it would. By Friday, on the cusp of a three day weekend, in math, we're starting something called ratios and proportional values. I don't know what it is yet, but I couldn't bear to see one more equation like 8 (mod 3) or N is divisible by three if and only if Ao + A1+ and Am is divisible by 3. So whatever this ratio and values thing turn out to be, it's got to be better than that. And the British colony thing hasn't been as bad as I thought it would be either. It's almost interesting to hear about why and where the British settled. In New England, and Virginia, here in the Mid-Atlantic. The West Indies. They settled in some place called the Falkland Islands. When Mr. Kilcommins showed us on a map where these islands are, it's hard to believe anyone would care about them. They're just these two little islands in the middle of the South Pacific Ocean, almost a thousand miles from the coast of South America and more than two thousand miles from what's called the Antarctic Peninsula. It's really nowhere land. The Roman stuff in Mrs. Stanton's class is okay, just a lot of dates and emperors to remember. I'll use my formula to get by. And believe it or not, this *Mice and Men* story from Steinbeck in the Witch's class is actually pretty good. It's about these two farm hands walking around California trying to get jobs. One of them, George, is smart and cares a lot about this guy Lennie, who is kind of slow in the brain. And this Lennie likes to pet soft things. George once had to yell at him for carrying a dead mouse around in his pocket. We just read where George, hoping to get hired, tells the guy who's hiring that he and Lennie are cousins and Lennie's a little slow 'cause he got kicked in the head by a horse when he was a kid. That made me laugh. They get hired and meet this old farmhand named Candy, who is missing a hand and has an old dog. And then there's this other guy Curly, who's the boss's son and kinda of mean and nasty. And is very jealous of his new wife. George and Lennie talk about one day having a farm of their own where they can tend to rabbits. I'm actually looking forward to see what happens.

And even gym today turns out good. I had no clue what we would be doing 'cause it rained pretty good last night and the fields are all muddy so I knew there'd be no softball games today. But it turns out O.K because Goddard has got the basketball nets lowered and the volleyball nets up. He tells us we can choose either game, but everyone has to do something. Of course I choose basketball.

It's me, Blair, Johnny Walsh against Sikora, Driscoll, and Lardier in a rematch of the championship, first one to seven, best two out of three. We won the first game 7-4, they won the second, 7-3, and right now it's all tied up at 5 in game three with class time running out. I pass the ball to Blair who passes it to Johnny who dribbles the ball toward the net then swings it my way and I take my famous Clyde pull up jumper and as the ball goes through the net I say. "6-5, series point." Then Goddard blows the whistle that ends gym class. As we're heading for the locker room, me, Blair and Johnny are saying we won 'cause we were up in the last game and Sikora, Driscoll, and Lardier argue back that the overall score was 16-16. And they won the real championship, anyway. In the middle of the argument we hear Goddard yell over to us, "Hey, any of you bums want to retrieve the basketball!"

I tell everyone to wait up and I turn to get the ball that's resting against the back wall. As I pick the ball up suddenly the back double doors are kicked open and I see a person and then something being thrown into the gym. I follow it in flight to where it lands and watch as it twists and turns across the gym floor like a snake, spewing out a putrid white smoke. A stink bomb. Whoever is left in the gym stops in their tracks. I'm standing like a statue with the basketball as Goddard comes sprinting across the gym floor with a white towel in hand. He throws the towel over the smoldering mess and stamps it out with his foot. He picks up the refuge and there's a small burn mark in the floor where the stink bomb settled. "Did you see who did this?" Goddard asks me, walking my way.

Instinct takes over. "No," I say. "I was picking up the ball when whoever it was kicked the door open."

"So you saw the door getting kicked open?" Goddard asks, now standing next me, looking at my view to the door, holding the towel of rubble. "But you didn't see who it was?" he says in a disbelieving tone.

I stutter and stammer. "Well…no…like I said…I was picking up the ball… and I heard the door getting kicked…." That's all I say.

Goddard takes a deep breath and purses his face. He looks at me and says, "You can get changed, Mr. Birdsall."

I hand him the ball and walk away.

When I get to the locker room it's quiet. Everyone knows the number one rule here: Though shall not fink on thy fellow student. And besides, when Goddard walks into the locker room and goes into his office, he leaves the door W   I   D   E open.

As I'm getting changed Blair and Johnny silently ask if I saw who did it. I shake my head no. I say that because I know that if one person finds out, the whole school finds out. Even Sikora and Driscoll and Lardier come over and ask if I saw who it was. They get the same answer I gave Blair and Johnny. When I start to leave, I try to shield myself between Blair and Johnny past Goddard's open office door and sneak out of the locker room but I don't make it. "Can you please come in here, Mr. Birdsall," is the request I hear. Blair and Johnny turn to me on their way out and wish me good luck.

I walk into Goddard's office where he's sitting behind his desk that's not only too big for the office, but is also always cluttered with note pads and magazines and books and papers. I sit down in the chair by the glass window opposite the desk, holding my duffel bag against my body like a shield. Goddard's busy writing something down and when he stops he looks at me and says. "Do you know what this is, Mr. Birdsall?" He shows me some kind of form he just filled out. I shake my head no. "This is a vandalism on school property form." I bite my lower lip and nod. I keep quiet. "I have to hand this in to Principal Pagano. On this form, along with what happened, I have to say that you were in the proximity of the act, possibly seeing who it was." I bite my lower lip a bit more profusely, but remain silent. "I have to, as of yet," Goddard says, "say that your statement is you didn't see who it was." He pauses. "So…is there anything…is there something you'd like to change on this form before I turn it in?" I know what he's getting at. With a small inhale and light shrug of shoulders, I nervously shake my head no. Goddard looks at me and takes a deep breath of his own and says, "Don't think that I don't…." He stops, then starts again, "I understand your dilemma, Robert. Believe me, I do. But…but what if that projectile landed on somebody, or started a fire? An act like that needs to be punished. Not rewarded." I breathe steady and stay quiet. Goddard stares at me for a few seconds, then takes another deep breath and shakes his head and says, "Okay. Maybe you're telling the truth. Or maybe you're just not ready yet to say anything. So I guess you can leave for your next class, Robert. But after I hand this in, I suspect Principal Pagano, and maybe even the police or fire chief might want a word with you after. So I'd think about that."

As I get up to leave, I have to say that last statement is very unnerving. The police? The fire chief? As I leave Goddard's office some of the kids coming in for their gym class are asking what that smell is.

After school on the way home I expected this on the bus ride: As soon as I get on and get to my seat, I'm bombarded by the question of if I saw who threw the stink bomb. I tell everyone no. Tommy and Brock try a different tact. They start throwing out names of all the known criminals at Lower Brook Middle School. Past and present. I listen and shake my head and in frustration. Then in exasperation, I say, "I don't know how many times I can say this guys. I didn't see who it was. Really. I was pickin' up the basketball, the door got kicked open and in came this thing. That's what I saw. Then Goddard came rushin' over."

Once off the bus and walking home, Tommy tries one more time. "C'mon now, Birdyboy. It's me an' you. Who did it?"

"Tommy," I say, "I tell ya if I knew. But all I saw was the thing gettin' tossed into the gym. Then I watched it snake across the floor. And then Goddard. That's it."

"Okay, Birdyboy," Tommy says, in almost the same disbelieving tone as Goddard. "Have it your way.

Through the rest of the afternoon, then through supper, and into the early evening, I haven't been able to shake from my mind what Goddard said about Principal Pagano and the police and fire chiefs wanting to talk to me. What if they make out some kind of line up and I have to pick out the culprit? What if they say I'm some kind of accomplice? What if they make me take a lie detector test? I obviously can't talk to any of my friends about this. And I know I don't want to discuss it with Mom and Dad. I really want to ask someone who might know what can happen so I guess that leaves Tammy. She just got home from work and it being Friday, I'm sure she's going to be quickly on her way out. So I walk down the hallway and knock on her door. "Who is it?"

"It's me," I say.

"Whadda ya want, twerp?"

"Ah, I...I need t'ask ya somethin'."

"If it's a car ride for you and your twerpy friends, forget it."

I pause. "No. It's not that."

A pause. "So what is it?"

I don't answer. I stand quietly outside Tammy's door. A few more seconds pass. "It's...it's just somethin'. Somethin' important."

I hear Tammy coming to her door. She opens it. "Okay, twerp, what is it?"

I look around and make sure mom and dad are nowhere in sight. I get right to the point. "Ah. Someone threw a stink bomb into the gymnasium today during my gym class."

She stares at me. "Okay. So? And?"

"And Mr. Goddard thinks...."

"Goddard," Tammy bellows, "that creep's still there?" She gasps. I nod that unfortunately he is. "Oh my God," she says incredulously. "Does he still always wear that stupid whistle around his neck?" I nod in a relinquishing way that he does. "Does he still reek of Vitalis?" I nod yes once more. Tammy smirks and shakes her head. "I hated that creep," she says "Okay. And so what? He thinks it was you?"

"No," I say, "but he thinks… he wants me to tell him who did it. He tol' me he has to hand in some vandalism form saying I was near the incident when it happened."

"So?" Tammy says.

"So what do I do?"

She shrugs her shoulders. "I'm guessing you already told him you didn't see who it was?"

"Yeah, of course," I say. "You know the rule."

"Then you have nothing to worry about, Robby."

I pause for a second. "Well, he told me I'm gonna get called down to Pagano's office and I might get questioned by the police chief. Or the fire chief."

Tammy smirks and says, "Robby. They're not going to do that. And even if they did, they know you didn't do it, and if you choose not to say who it was, that's up to you. They can't do anything to you," she says matter-of-factly. "You already told them you didn't see who it was, right?" she asks. I nod yes. "So leave it at that and stop worrying."

Summer

Chapter Fifteen

Mid-day Thursday on the first full week of summer vacation and I'm sitting at the kitchen table having lunch. In the morning I was over at Branch Park at the utility road end of Roosevelt Street trying out for the eleven to thirteen year olds basketball team, which in trying out and making the Branch Park eleven to thirteen year old basketball team consists of showing up wearing a pair of shorts, a shirt, sneakers, and socks. There's only seven of us to begin with and one of them is Vinnie Ryba, who stinks. But on the team this summer is me, John Powner, who's okay, Kevin Landry who lives just down the block from the park and who's actually pretty good, Pete Mancuso who lives two houses down from Mark Reimer's house on Constitution Street, the house of the stolen and then stolen again *Playboy Magazines*, Mark Cecere who's not too good either but tall, and this kid Quentin Prince, who technically does not live in Branch Manor, but stays at his Aunt's on Buchanan Street a lot once school lets out. And Ryba. Our coach is Pat McCullough who was a starter on both the Three Brooks High School varsity basketball team and baseball team this past year. We all like him as our coach and it's a cool league as we play the other five neighborhood parks in our section of Lower Brook one game each, and then the top four teams make the two rounds of playoffs. A semi-final game and then a championship game. Last year we finished 1-4 and in fifth place so we missed out on the playoffs. Cedar Lake Park won the championship. They even got trophies. I'm hoping to at least finish in the top four this year and make the playoffs. As soon as I'm finished with lunch I'm heading back to the park to meet up with Quentin and Kevin and get some practice in.

As I take my last bite, Mom walks in from the backyard with a basket full of laundry. I can smell the fresh air on the dried clothes. "Put your dishes in the sink when you're finished," she says. "And did you read the note I left you on the kitchen table?"

"Note? What note?" I say, even though I stared right at it during lunch. I've long ago stopped reading any notes left anywhere in the house for me to read because they always include something for me to do that I don't want to. I get up and put my plate and glass in the sink.

"The note right in front of you with your name on it," she says, walking into the dining room and putting the basket down on the table.

"Oh. That note," I say as I cringe and pick the note up from the table. I read it. I'm puzzled. It says in Mom's handwriting: Mrs. Hill. 109 Wren Street. And it has a phone number. Wren Street is in the old neighborhood. "What's this?" I ask.

"She called about an hour ago," Mom says. "She asked if you were available today to take care of her yard."

"Really?" I say, half in a state of shock. I remember getting energetic one Sunday afternoon and riding around the old neighborhood with some newly made lawn business slips, but that weeks ago. "Huh," I say. With the note in hand I walk over to the phone.

"Isn't that house in the old neighborhood?" Mom asks as I pick up the phone.

"Yeah," I say, dialing the number.

"So how are you going to get there with the lawn mower?"

"Mom, I'll....Hello, Mrs. Hill?"

I talk to Mrs. Hill for a minute or two and make arrangements to cut her lawn. She tells me where her street is and the color of her house. She sounds like a very nice old lady. I did plan on going back to the park to practice, but other than cutting Mr. Lampman's yard one more time, Mrs. Medina's one more time, and ol' man Martin's yard across the street once, and that was only because he ran over the electric cord with the mower, my lawn business and Puma Clyde collection has been at a standstill. I've put some of the earned money in my tin can, but it's still way short of the twenty two dollars needed. Right now, the can holds eight dollars.

"Robby," Mom says sternly after I hang up the phone. "How do you plan on getting the lawn mower over there?"

"Mom," I say in an annoyed tone. "I'm gonna push it there. How else do you think I'll get there?"

"What?" Mom says. "You're going to push it all the way to the light at the end of Roosevelt Street? And then back down the highway? Those are busy roads, Robby. I don't think so."

"Mom," I gasp. "I'm gonna cut through the new neighborhood and cross over right by Heron Pond Road. She said Wren Street in down off Willets Point, way before the bend. It's not that far."

"But there's no light there and people come flying over that bridge."

"Mom," I say, now exasperated. "I just told the lady I'd be there in about a half hour. I think I'm fully capable of pushing a lawn mower across a highway."

Mom starts to say something more about safety and my arms drop like anchors and I stare at the ceiling in defiance. She stops what she's saying. "Fine, have it your way, Robby. Since you're so determined to defy me."

"Mom," I say in a softer tone. "Nobody's defying anybody. I'll be fine. I'm more than capable of crossing a street with the lawn mower. And I already said I'd be there."

Fifteen minutes later I cross said dreaded highway, which by the way, if I lost a race with a turtle to get across, I still would've been okay. Once I'm on Heron Pond Road, Willets Point Road is the second street away from the highway. I come upon it and turn down and it's a long and bending road just like Heron Pond. And if it was ever finished it would, or could, meet up again with Heron Pond Road after the bend. But it just stops. The neat thing about Willets Point Road and actually most of the old neighborhood is that hardly any of the houses look the same. Unlike my neighborhood and certainly unlike the new neighborhood. And the houses here are abstractly set back off the road, unlike my neighborhood and the new one. Some houses have long driveways and huge front yards and are turned sideways on the property. Some houses are right up on the road with lots of back yard.

There are three cross streets on Willets Point before the bend starts and mine is Sanderling Avenue, the second one in. I get there and walk a few blocks down Sanderling where I make a left on to Plover Street and then another left on to Wren Street two streets down. I looking for number 109 and I remember the house as soon as I see it. The little yellow house near the end of the block. I remember seeing the leaves against the fence that are still there and the creeping vines on the cement foundation. I remember leaving my slip in the slats of the front door.

I've gotten into the habit of leaving my mower and rake and broom and shears and green garbage bag directly in view of the front door before I knock. That way anyone answering the door will know why I'm here. But I don't even get to the front door when I'm sure it's Mrs. Hill standing behind it. I wave and she acknowledges and steps out onto the steps. She's pretty much how I pictured she'd be. Pretty old with a shock of white hair. She has on one of those typical old lady type blouses on, light yellow with a string of either real or fake pearls around her neck, and even though it's late June, a light sweater, beige in color, buttoned at the top button with the arms falling over her shoulders. She has on a pair of those stretchy old lady pants in a very light green color. And those typical old-lady shoes. All black, hers, like grandmas, without any frill and the thick short heel.

"Robert," Mrs. Hill says. "Or do you prefer Robby?"

"Robert, Robby. Doesn't matter," I say.

"Did you find the house all right?"

"Sure. They were easy directions," I say. "And I actually kinda remembered the house once I saw it."

"Oh, that's good," she says.

Mrs. Hill wants to get to know me a little so she asks me where I go to school. I tell her. She asks me what grade I'm in. I tell her. She asks me if I like it. I tell her it's tolerable. She smiles. She asks me if I have any brothers or sisters. I tell her a sister. Older. She asks me how we get along. I tell her we fight like cats and dogs. She smiles at that too. The questions stop so I say, "Well, about the yard. I guess I can start over by the fence with the leaves. I'll rake them up and go around the yard and pick up any branches and twigs. I'll give the yard a good cut and I'll cut down those vines growing on the foundation." Mrs. Hill listens. "And when I'm finished I'll sweep the debris from the driveway, walkway and the sidewalk."

"Well that's sounds wonderful," Mrs. Hill says. "And how much do you charge?"

It's a lot of work and I should ask for three dollars but Mrs. Hill seems like a real nice old lady so I say, "Two dollars."

"Well, that's very fair. Should I get my purse?"

I shake my head no. "No," I say. "Not until I'm done."

"All right," Mrs. Hill says. "That couldn't be any fairer. So I'll let you go to work then."

And I go to work and I do, I think, a very good job. I start with the leaves like I said and rake them up and then pick up the branches and twigs all around the yard and then cut the grass and rake up the spots where it's needed. I cut the vines down clinging to the foundation. I rake them up into a pile. I get my broom and start sweeping off the walkway. As I'm doing this a car rambles into the driveway and parks behind the car already in the driveway. An older man about grandpa's age gets out of the car. He looks at me and then at the yard. I can't tell by his look if he's glad or mad that I'm here, which makes me a little nervous as he walks my way. I've heard that old guys can be kinda dangerous if they get riled. Especially if they're World War I or World War II old guys. I stop sweeping when he gets a few feet away.

"Hello, young man," he says.

"Hi," I say.

"Are you the young man that left the flyer at the house?"

I nod. "Yes," I say. "I'm Robert. Robert Birdsall."

"Edgar," he says, offering his hand. I shake his hand and he's pretty strong for an old guy. "Well, I see that you did a fine job here," he says.

I nod. "Thank you," I say. "I'm almost done," I add.

Edgar looks panoramically at the yard. "A fine job," he says again. He then starts to walk toward the front door. I go back to sweeping the walkway and then the driveway. I pick up the cut vines and put them in my green bag. I walk to my mower and tie the green bag to the push bar. I leave my rake and broom and shears next to the mower and head for the front door. I knock. Mrs. Hill answers and invites me in and even though mom and dad have told me never to go into stranger's homes, I feel comfortable here.

"I have a nice glass of iced tea fixed for you," Mrs. Hill says as we walk toward the kitchen. Now I just presumed that Edgar was Mrs. Hill's husband but I can see by the pictures on the parlor walls and the end tables that he isn't. Because whoever that man is, it's not Edgar. The next thing I notice is all the trophies and ribbons in an open glass case against the far parlor wall. As we pass the glass case I scan some of the trophies. **2nd Place. Charleston Dance Contest. Sleepy Owl Room. May, 1924. Babylon, New York.** Another says,

3rd Place. Dance Marathon. February, 1923. The Red Rug. West Islip, Long Island. I quickly do the math. Wow! That's almost fifty years ago.

I walk into the kitchen with Mrs. Hill and there's my glass of iced tea and opposite the glass of tea is Edgar, sitting and reading a newspaper. He's sipping on a cup of coffee. Between my seat and Edgar's seat is another steaming cup of coffee. "How about a brownie or an oatmeal cookie?" Mrs. Hill asks me. "They're homemade," she adds.

Edgar lets his paper fold over so I can see his face. "My sister's homemade oatmeal cookies and brownies are the best in town, Robert," he says like a salesman.

It doesn't take much to sell me. "Sure," I say. "I'll try the oatmeal cookie."

As Mrs. Hill sits in front of the steaming coffee, a good sized oatmeal cookie is placed in front of me on a small plate. I take a bite of the cookie and it is very good. Soft and chewy in the center with just the right amount of crunch on the edges.

Edgar puts down his paper and picks up his cup. "Baseball fan, Robert?" he asks.

"More basketball," I say, taking another bite of the cookie and sipping the iced tea.

"Oh? ABA or NBA?" he asks.

"NBA," I say. "Definitely NBA."

"ABA's got some real good players," Edgar says. "Have you ever seen that kid Rick Barry from the Nets? The way he shoots free throws? Underhanded?" I shake my head no so Edgar gets up and shows me how he does it.

"Oh. We call that the granny shot," I say, then feel bad with Mrs. Hill sitting right next to me. Quickly I add, "And he makes them in?"

"Ninety percent," Edgar says. "That was the way we were taught," he adds, sitting back down. "So who's your team?" he asks me.

"Knicks," I say.

Edgar gives me a wry smile and points to himself and says, "Celtics. Loved K.C Jones."

"I don't know him," I say.

"Well, he retired a few years ago, so, I guess you wouldn't. But I have to say, I like watching the New York Nets when they're on. It's very exciting basketball."

I nod but have nothing to say. I don't follow the Nets.

"Robert goes to the new middle school," Mrs. Hill says to Edgar.

"Oh? How do you like it there?" Edgar asks.

I shrug my shoulders with indifference.

"Well, I'm sure it's a lot better than where Sally and me went to school," he says. "You know that small blue house down by the pond?" he asks me.

"What? The one all boarded up?"

"That's the one. That was our school. Remember our old school room, Sally?" Edgar asks.

"Sure," Mrs. Hill says. "Remember Sister Jean?" she asks Edgar.

"Mean Sister Jean the paddling machine," Edgar says with a fond remembrance. "I bet you kids don't get paddled anymore, huh?" Edgar asks me.

"No," I say. "Not that I know of. Usually we just get sent down to the principal's office."

"Well, there were no principal's in our day," Edgar says. "Mean Sister Jean was teacher, principal, paddler, all rolled up in one."

"So how old is your sister, Robby" Mrs. Hill asks.

"Seventeen," I say.

"Ah, seventeen," Mrs. Hill says. "Such a sweet age.

I almost choke on my last bite of the oatmeal cookie. Sweet! Tammy?

"Probably still fightin' like cats and dogs, right?" Edgar asks.

I nod yes in an acknowledging breath. "Most times," I say. "But not always," I add.

Edgar lets out a short, quick laugh. "Sally and me used to go at it like a couple of tornado's," he says, "but soon enough it'll be the other way around, you'll see," he adds.

In a startling tone, Mrs. Hill says, "Dear me, I have to pay this young man."

Edgar leans back and reaches into his pocket. "I got it, Sally," he says. "How much do you charge, Robert?"

"Ah, we thought two dollars would be fair," I say, turning to Mrs. Hill.

Edgar thumbs through money that's held together by one of those big gold clips. Dad always keeps his money in his wallet. Edgar reaches across the table and hands me two dollars. "A job well done," he says.

I glance at the clock on the wall. "Well, I guess I should start heading home," I say, getting up from the table. "Thank you for the cookie and iced tea," I say to Mrs. Hill. I slip the two dollars into my pocket.

"Do you live here in Willet's Point?" Edgar asks me as we all head for the front door.

"No," I say. "Right across the highway. Branch Manor. Not that far."

"Well, you certainly be careful on your way home," Mrs. Hill says as I'm walking out onto the front steps.

"I will be. I found a real good short cut," I say.

"All right then. Well, thank you," she says.

"Anytime," I say. "And please, keep my number and call me again, if you need me," I add and head on my way.

. . .

Now one would think that going out and earning another two dollars on my own would be considered a commendable achievement. I know I felt good putting another two dollars in my tin can. But apparently not so. At supper time Mom calls me to the table and before I can even get out of my room there's Dad in the doorway demanding why I defied Mom earlier in the day. I say I didn't defy anyone and that I had already committed myself to going to Mrs. Hill's house. So he tells me that I should have just uncommitted myself and he doesn't care if it's in the next neighborhood or around the block, the next time I defy either her or him any money I earn will be taken away. I stand there and listen in a steely silence. I don't say so, but I'm pretty sure that's against the law.

Chapter Sixteen

Wednesday next week we have our first basketball game and it couldn't come on a better day. For various reasons. For one it was a "home" game, on our court, against Pine Grove Park. Secondly, the weather is beautiful early summer warm and perfect for basketball, and thirdly it's the day mom decided to shellac the parlor floor and the hallway. Which means I can't go back in my room until the floor dries, which means at least until lunch time.

I'm on the front steps wearing the maroon tee shirt with **SPARTANS** spelled out in white across the front that coach McCullough made for us. I'm lacing up my sneakers. Apparently the timing of the floor shellacking doesn't affect Tammy either because she's out on the sidewalk with her blue work shirt and on her way to work and arguing, again, with Brother Davis. That's all they seem to do anymore. He's sitting in his ratty orange Beetle with the engine running and she's standing on the sidewalk with her arms crossed in front of her. I take my time lacing up my sneakers, trying to listen to what they're saying and all I can hear is "ever since" from him and "not being able to handle" from her and "that's not it at all" from him and a throw of hands in the air from her and a "fine then" from him and a "good" from her and then a bucking of the car and a revving of the engine and I watch as he angrily drives off. I watch Tammy as she walks toward her car. I can't tell if she's mad or sad. She seems to be neither.

Our game is at eleven but coach McCullough wants us at the park by ten thirty for some warm-ups and drills so I have almost an hour to kill. I figure I'll stop by Tommy's and see what he's doing. I hop on my bike and get halfway down the block when I realize I forgot my basketball. It's not that I need it, 'cause everyone who has one brings their own, but I like practicing with mine. So I turn around and go back to the house and stick my face against the screen door. I find Mom rolling the television set across the parlor floor. She puts it in the porch room and when she walks back in the parlor she sees my face at the door. Annoyed, she asks, "Robby. What is it?"

"I forgot my basketball. Can I get it?"

A harsh breath, then, "Go ahead, Robby," she says with a wave of her hand. I walk in my room and hurriedly retrieve my ball. "Back door at lunch time," she reminds me as I walk back out.

I ride down to Tommy's house and glide my bike under the carport. I maneuver myself past Tommy's bike and then the old Impala and when I stop my bike I see Mrs. Hulse out in the backyard hanging laundry. I get off my bike and walk a few feet into the yard and yell over, "Hey Mrs. Hulse."

She turns and sees me and smiles and nods. "Hello, Robby."

"Tommy's bike's here, so I'm guessin' he's home?"

"Somewhere," she says.

I hold the basketball toward her. "We have our first game today," I say. "We're playin' Pine Grove Park."

"Oh. I see you still call the team the Spartans," she says.

"Yeah. I don't think that'll ever change. Just like Pine Grove will always be the Wildcats, I suppose. But this year we have shirts!" Usually its shirts versus skins.

Mrs. Hulse smiles at that and says, "Well, good luck."

I nod and head for the front door. When I walk in the house I yell out for Tommy but hear no response. The door to his room is open and I peek in and there's no Tommy so he's has to be down in the basement. I walk down the creaky steps into the musty smelling basement and find Tommy at his dad's workbench. As I get closer I see that he has one, two, three ping pong balls painted red, white, and blue with a string or something sticking out of the center of them on the workbench. He has more unpainted ping pong balls on the workbench. He has pieces of string that look like fuses. He has a few cotton balls. He has a dispenser of tape. He has small paint jars from an old paint by number set. And he's making some kind of powder, from matches, I'm presuming, because he has two dozen or more match books in front of him. "Hey Tommy," I say.

"Birdbrain," Tommy says, not turning from what he's doing.

"What'cha makin' there?"

"What's it look like?"

"I don't know. It looks like a miniature bomb or somethin'," I say.

"Pretty close," Tommy says. "Not so much a bomb. More like a big firecracker."

I don't want to disturb the mad scientist so I stand and watch as he takes the powder he just ground up and carefully slide it down a piece of foil into an opening at the top of the ping pong ball he's holding. Then he takes one of the fuses and slides it into the ping pong ball, leaving enough on the outside to be able to light it and get away. He takes one of the cotton balls and pulls it apart into strings and using a thin nail pushes the cotton into the ping pong ball, surrounding the fuse. He then takes a piece of tape and gently seals the top shut. He shows it to me. "Now all I have to do is paint it."

"Pretty neat," I say. "What'cha gonna do with them?" I ask.

"Keep a few," Tommy says. "Sell the rest for whoever wants them for the fourth."

"Oh yeah," I say with an air of excitement. "For how much?"

Tommy thinks for a second, then says, "Fifty cents each. Maybe three for a dollar."

I'm thinking three for a dollar is a good price. "I'll take three," I say.

"You want those three?" Tommy says. "They're a first edition. I'll even sign 'em."

"Well, actually," I say, "can I take two of those and paint that one myself?"

Tommy hands me the unpainted ping pong ball. "Be my guest, Birdyboy," he says.

I sit down on the empty stool and unlike Tommy's red, white, and blue motif, I'm gonna paint this one in Knick colors. The whole ball will be blue with NEW YORK spelled out in orange. I'm even going to paint black lines to make it look just like on a NBA ball. I get the paints and the brushes. Tommy's busy taking matches from the match books and cutting the tips off and grinding them into his explosive powder.

"So how'd you do on your final report card?" I ask Tommy.

"I passed," he says indifferently, like it doesn't matter either way.

"Well, it's better than failin'," I say. Tommy doesn't say anything. "I did all right. Got a C- from the Witch, but, so what. All my other classes were higher."

Tommy continues grinding the match tips into powder. "So what did Kilcommin's end up givin' ya?" Tommy asks.

"B-," I say, putting the finishes touches on the blue part of the ping pong ball and setting it down to dry. "I'll take a B-. How 'bout you?"

"D+" Tommy says, sliding the ground powder into the opening at the top of the ball.

"D+?" I say, quizzically. "So…what does that mean? Is that passin'?"

Again Tommy responds indifferently. "I guess," he says. "Means nothin' t' me," he adds, pulling the cotton ball into shreds. "What do I care what Ol' Say It Ain't So Joe Kilcommins, middle grade school teacher, thinks of me?"

I nod in quiet, understated approval because I can understand what Tommy's saying. Because that's kinda how I feel about Witch Whitaker.

"So who's that creepy guy your sis is with?" Tommy asks, slipping the fuse into the ping pong ball.

"What creepy guy?" I ask, "Davis?"

"No, Birdcage, I know him," Tommy says. "The other guy. I see her with 'em in her car. She picks him up down here at the corner of the street."

"Huh," I say. "She does?"

"I guess you didn't know, eh?"

"No, I didn't."

"Probably doesn't want your mom and dad t'know 'bout it. And I do mean *it*," Tommy says, tearing at a cotton ball.

"What's that mean?" I ask.

"You gotta see this guy Birdhead," Tommy says shaking his head. "If Cousin It has a cousin, he's it."

"Huh," I say again, now knowing why there's all the fighting between Tammy and Brother Davis. With the ping pong ball now dry, I start to paint the black lines to make the ball look like an NBA ball. "So what did you ever do with the rest of the reefer cigarettes ya found?" I ask.

"I got 'rm in a good spot, like Mark suggested," Tommy says, surrounding the fuse with the shredded cotton. "Safe an' dry."

"So what'cha gonna do with them?" I ask, finishing the black lines.

"Dunno," Tommy says, inspecting his almost finished ping pong ball bomb. "Ain't decided yet. Might just keep 'em and smoke 'em one day."

I don't know if Tommy really means that or not so I say, "Well, I've heard that someone can get addicted to reefer from the first time they try it."

"Don't believe everything ya hear," Tommy says, inspecting his near finished masterpiece.

I paint NEW YOK in orange on the ping pong ball. "We got our first game today," I say.

"Yeah, I kinda figured that out by the shirt, Birdbrain," Tommy says, carefully taping shut the small opening at the top of the ball.

"Yeah, I guess," I say, now finished painting the ping pong ball. I show it to Tommy. He nods that it's pretty good. I put it aside and pick out the other two that I want. I tell Tommy I'll come back later to get them. "Three for a dollar, right?" I say, making sure.

"That's the deal," Tommy says.

"Deal," I say, heading for the stairs.

. . .

Over at Branch Manor Park we win our first game against Pine Grove Park 15-9 and are 1-0 on the season. And the game wasn't as close as the score suggests. We were leading 8-1 at one point. Last year we lost our first two games so this is a good start. Kevin Landry scored six of our fifteen points. Quentin and me both scored three each. Quentin's much better than last year. Mancuso scored two and even Mark CeCere got a basket. On a really nice pick and roll play that coach McCullough set up for him. Our next game should be a tough one 'cause we're playing Midstream Park, on their court. Last year Midstream played for the championship against Cedar Lake Park and really gave them a run for their money. The game was pretty close. On game day coach McCullough wants us all to meet up right here at ten, get some practice in, then get on the playground bus and head over to Midstream and show them who we are this year.

When I get home it must be neighborhood laundry day 'cause mom is out by the clothes line hanging and folding laundry just like Tommy's mom was earlier. I walk over and tell her we won our game 15-9. She congratulates me and tells me lunch is waiting on the kitchen table and not to walk into the parlor or the hallway. I walk in the back door and the whole house smells of shellac. I step to the edge of the kitchen's entrance and peer down the hallway. At the end of the now glistening hardwood floor, mom has one of the big fans blowing at high speed. I look into the parlor. Another glistening hardwood floor and another big fan at high speed. I put my basketball down on an empty chair and sit down at the table and have lunch. A big, fat peanut butter and jelly sandwich, half an apple, a bag of potato chips, and cherry Kool-Aid. I quickly eat lunch, put my dishes in the sink, and decide to take a ride up to Necci's to see if the new *Pro Basketball* magazine has come in and if they have any cinnamon sticks.

Going to Necci's anytime around lunch time means that from way down the block you can smell what's being cooked. Sweet sausage and tangy meatballs and marinara sauce. Peppers and onions and garlic bread. When I near the front of the store I can smell small waves of rich coffee. I ride my bike onto the front porch and leave it at the end. When I near the screened door, I can smell chocolate. I open the door. The cowbell clangs out. I don't see Mr. or Mrs. Necci, but I see their grand kids are working. I don't remember their names but I remember them being here last summer. They're both behind the kitchen area. I walk over to the magazine rack and scan the sports section. *Sport Magazine* has Yaz on the cover. *Baseball Digest* has Willie Mays on the cover. The *Sports Illustrated* cover catches my eye. It says, "New Champion in from the Outback. Evonne Goolagong wins at Wimbledon." Evonne Goolagong I say to myself. What a strange name. She's kinda cute, but a real strange name. I flip to the article. I glance over the headline that says Evonne Goolagong beat last year's champion Margaret Court in two straight sets. And then I read that John Newcombe, another Australian, won the men's Wimbledon title. Australians are good at tennis, I guess. I flip the pages and see an article about a two and a half mile race track being built at the Pocono Racetrack. I've heard Dale and Brett mention that. They say when it's done it's going to be the Indy of the East. As I read the article the Necci's granddaughter walks over and tells me that the aisle is not a library. Either buy the magazine or put it back, she says. I frown like I shouldn't have to do that, but I put the magazine back in the rack. I look behind and between magazines for the *Pro Basketball*, but Necci's doesn't have it. So I walk up to the front counter and start to look for the red box of cinnamon fire sticks. I don't see them. I move things around searching. The Necci's grandson walks over and asks me what I'm doing. I tell him I'm looking for the cinnamon sticks. He quickly glances at the counter and says "Well, I guess we don't have any," rearranging what I just moved around. I frown again and head for the front door. On my way out I check the phone booths for dimes, but come up with nothing.

I figure I'll try the 7-Eleven across the highway. I could try Krauszer's, but 7-Eleven has a bigger newspaper and magazine section. And they have larger snack aisles, with more choices. And bigger soda cases, with more choices. A bigger coffee area for the grown-ups. And I'm halfway there anyway. So I ride out to Roosevelt Street and cross the highway at the light and pedal across and ride into the 7-Eleven parking lot. I leave my bike by the phone booths, check the slots for dimes, coming up empty again, and walk into the store.

The newspaper and magazine racks are right by the big glass window at the front of the store. As I walk toward the wooden racks holding the magazines, I can already see the *Pro Basketball* magazine right on top. I get to the rack and pick the magazine out of its slot and look over the cover. It has an in-game photo of Alcindor's famous sky hook shot, right over number 41 Wes Unseld of the Bullets. The headline says "Lew Alcindor. The Man and the Dynasty." The magazine also has next year's predictions. It also has articles on my man, Willis Reed, Pistol Pete Maravich, and incredibly, Rick Barry, of the famous granny foul shot that I was recently told about. I take the magazine and walk down the candy and cakes aisle and scan all the choices. I choose a Lemon Flip and head for the soda cases. I choose a Penguin lemon flavored soda. I bring everything to the counter. I give the person behind the counter a dollar and get a quarter and some pennies back. I take everything outside and sit by my bike and eat the Lemon Flip and drink the soda and read the article on Willis Reed. It's really interesting. It tells me everything that Willis has to do to get ready for every game. So much preparation. I finish the cake and the soda, fold the magazine in half and put it in my back pocket. I get on my bike and start heading for home.

I cross the highway at the light at Roosevelt Street and ride up to Constitution Street. I turn and start heading for my block. I'm slowly crossing Harding Street when all of a sudden I hear running footsteps and then my bike is being grabbed onto and pushed to the other side of the street where I'm then pushed off it. Landing on my feet I see that it's Luther Cobalt and two other kids I never saw before. "And jes where in the hell do you think your goin', jerk?" Luther snarls out.

Staying brave, "Home," I say, reaching for my handlebars.

Luther throws my bike to the ground. "Oh no you're not," Luther says. "Not for free ya ain't."

The two other kids walk behind me. Then I feel my new magazine being ripped out of my back pocket. I try to grab it back but the kid tosses it over to Luther before I can get hold of it. "Give it back," I demand.

Luther nonchalantly thumbs through the pages, says, "Oh, you're interested in this here magazine?" He turns to the cover, see it costs fifty-cents. "Well, that'll be fifty-cents," he says with his crooked smile.

"I already bought it," I say.

"Not from me ya didn't," Luther says. "And it seems that it's in my hands now."

I don't know what to say. I know that Luther will probably beat the hell out of me in a fight but I don't want to relinquish it so easy either. "I don't have to give you any money for somethin' I already paid for," I say.

"Who says we're askin'?" Luther says, with an even more crooked smile. He nods to the two kids behind me and quickly one of them pulls my arms behind my back and Luther tosses the magazine to the other kid and lunges at me.

I pull one arm free and swing at the kid me holding my arm but miss and we both fall to the ground. Luther stomps on my back with his foot and pins me down while the other kid rolls away and gets up. Luther's still pinning me to the ground with his foot and grabs at my arms and holds them back and tells the kid who I swung at to check my pockets. I'm screaming for Luther to get off me and I feel the kid trying to reach in my pockets and I'm squirming and screaming and then I hear somebody yell out, "Hey! What the hell's going on over there?"

Startled, the kid stops searching my pockets and Luther lessens his grip on my arms enough that I can pull away and get up off the ground. When I turn around I see Dean Magnumson bounding across the street. Bruce Rutter is also there, standing at the edge of the driveway. Dean briskly walks to where we are, looks at me, then looks at the two kids, then at Luther. "What the hell's goin' on here, Cobalt?" Dean demands.

Luther nods at me and says, "Jerk here think's he's crossin' our street for free."

Again Dean looks at me, the two kids, and Luther. "He is, Cobalt," Dean calmly says. "Birdman here's okay."

"Oh?" Luther questions. "Says who?" he asks.

Standing a few feet away from Luther, Dean closes the gap in one step and stands face to face with Luther and says very evenly, "Says me, Cobalt." He nods to Bruce still standing at the driveway. Bruce starts to cross the street. "Unless you," Dean then steps sideways, looks at the two kids, says grim faced, "and you're two sorry lookin' amigos here want t'make somethin' more of it."

Luther, trying to still sound tough, looks at me and spits on the ground. He frowns and says, "Jerk's not worth it."

Dean looks at the kid with my magazine. "That yours Birdman?" he turns and asks me. I nod that it is. "Give it," Dean says. The kid tosses me my magazine. Then adds, "I hear of any of you's givin' Birdman here any more trouble," looking at the three of them, "I won't hesitate to beat the livin' crap outta all of ya. Birdman here's okay," he says again with emphasis. "Come on, Birdman, I want t'show ya somethin' anyway."

I put my magazine back into my pocket. I pick my bike up off the ground. Luther and his cohorts slink back to where they came from. I follow Dean across the street. I know better than to look Luther's way.

• • •

We cross the street and walk up a driveway and then into a backyard that's hidden behind a six-foot stockade fence. When I step into the backyard it looks like I've entered a miniature motorcycle track. There's a hardened oval path the entire length of the yard that at the each end looks like it comes perilously close to the fence. Inside the track there's small hills for jumping. And like a junkyard there's spare motorcycle parts strewn all about. Wheels left listlessly against the fence. Bashed in fenders in one corner of the yard, an old handlebar in the other. Looks like an old motorcycle engine off in the far corner. There's an awning off the back of the house that hangs over two picnic tables with tools and motorcycle necessities on them. The tables are on an oil-stained patio. And where Bruce has walked to, I'm presuming it's his bike, there's some kind of contraption that's holding up a bike while he works on it. The entire front wheel is dissembled from the bike. As I take all this in

Dean comes walking toward me with his bike. "So Birdman. Whadda ya think of these?" he asks, pointing to bright red shocks on his bike. "These Red Wings really trick the pony, eh?"

Not knowing one thing about motorcycle shocks but seeing that they are real cool looking, fire engine red with black coil springs, I say, "Yeah. They're definitely cool."

"I put some lacquer on the cylinders to protect the paint and painted the coils gloss black myself," Dean says. "I think they stand out more. And," Dean says, lifting the front wheel of his bike off the ground and bouncing it a few times, "I readjusted the height and got 'em just right." He looks over to Bruce. "You copacetic Rutman?"

Bruce, having reattached the front wheel of his bike, gives a thumbs up.

"We're headin' to Pearls. Up for a ride?" Deans asks me.

Never having been on a motorcycle before, without hesitation I say, "Sure."

Dean and Bruce walk their bikes to the front gate and onto the driveway. I follow them. As Dean gets on his bike, he asks me, "Ever ride before?"

"No," I say.

"Well," Dean says, "hop on, hold on to the back bars, lean with the turns, and enjoy the ride."

And with that, we're slowly sputtering down the driveway.

We ride down the street and get to the utility road. As soon as we make the turn Dean and Bruce pick up speed and I instantly know why people love these motorcycles. Watching the ground pass below my feet, there's a feeling of exhilaration, a feeling of being in a state of accelerated liberation. We turn down the utility road. The backyards and houses of Garfield Avenue pass by in postcard pictures of mixed colors and sizes. Before we get to the power plant Bruce and Dean turn onto a good sized path that cuts through the woods. The path sort of does a double back up the utility road. The woods are deep at first but then begin to thin out and I can see the approaching highway through the trees. We run out of path and then out of woods and onto the grass embankment and there's no cars in sight and Bruce crosses over the highway and seconds later when Dean and I cross over I swear his bike gets airborne.

We pick up a trail on the other side that runs diagonally away from the highway and towards Old Branch Road. Pearl's is a bit down Old Branch Road. There's a few streets right off the highway that constitute a small neighborhood.

Everyone calls the neighborhood bungalow alley because almost all the houses are these small, two room houses with a small screened in front porch. All the way at the very end of Old Branch Road there's a patch of woods then a guardrail with Heron Pond Road on the other side.

The trail ends and we're on Old Branch Road and then turning into Pearl's Cycle Shop. Supposedly, *a long time ago*, the building was a General Store where one bought anything they needed, sold anything they needed, and ordered anything they needed. Apparently there was this giant catalog book that everyone ordered from, and since the store was also the mail depot, it was at the store that they picked the stuff up. Other than the old Willet's Point Methodist Church, if anyone wanted to find out what was going on in the town, they went to the General Store to find out.

We don't park in the lot but instead ride around to the back of the store where there's a small workshop. There's somebody working in the bay area and when he hears the approaching motorcycles he turns around. I can't tell how old he is but he's definitely not dad's age yet. Dean pulls right in front of the bay. The man walks over to Dean's motorcycle. "So how they workin' for ya?" the man asks Dean.

"Silky smooth," Dean says.

"You stay stock?" the man asks, bending down and looking at the shocks on Dean's bike.

"No," Dean says. "Adjusted 'em just a lil'. T'give a lil' more bounce. How d'ya like the black coils?"

"Nice touch," the man says.

The man stands back up and says to Bruce "You molly those bearings?"

Bruce gives the man a thumbs up.

"It'll keep 'em from getting' scorched. Take my word." The man turns back to Dean. "When you're ready for those tires you let me know. I'll get Carl t'work a deal for ya."

"Cool City," Dean says, extending his hand to let the man slap him five.

The man slaps Dean five and gives another thumbs up to Bruce and turns to go back to work. "Take care of your bikes boys, and they'll take care of you," he says.

We ride back around to the front of the store. Dean and Bruce park the bikes in a spot made just for motorcycles. We hop off the bikes and walk up the ramp, heading for the front door. Once we're on the porch heading for the front doors I see at the other end of the porch there's motorcycles on stands for sale under a maroon awning that says **Pearl's** in gold. Bruce walks toward the bikes. Dean and me walk into the store.

An overwhelming smell of rubber fills the air as soon as we walk into the store. There's a man about dad's age behind a counter. There's all kinds of colorful motorcycle stickers with motorcycle brands and slogans on a brick wall behind him. There's a door opening without a door that leads to somewhere.

"Hey Carl," Dean says.

"Dean," Carl says. "Where's your sidekick?"

"Lookin' at the bikes on the porch," Dean says.

"Still got his eyes on that Honda?" Carl asks.

"Probably," Dean says as he heads toward the back of the store, me following.

We walk down an aisle that has paints and waxes and small motorcycle accessories on the shelves. "So Birdman," Dean says. "What's goin' on with you an' that lawn mower of yours? I saw ya pushin' it down Heron Pond Road the other day."

"Oh," I say, "Well, I sort of started my own lawn care business."

"No kiddin'?" Dean says as we get to the end of the aisle. "How'd ya do that?"

"Just made up some flyers and put them around the neighborhood."

"Oh yeah? How's it workin' out?"

"Well," I say as we turn from the aisle. "I've gotten some yards. I did the Lampman's yard on Truman twice. The house you saw me going to, over in Willet's Point. I had some real pretty lady's yard in the new neighborhood before school ended. But I ain't heard from her since. A couple weeks ago I cut th'ol' guy across the street yard. He has an electric mower and the Ol' coot ran over the cord," I say.

Dean laughs at that. "So what'cha gonna do with all the lute?" he asks as we're passing a pegboard on my right with all kinds of motorcycle gloves and goggles and packages of motorcycle parts on it. On shelves to my left there's motorcycle seats and mirrors and lights and helmets and at the very end of the aisle those shield-like things I see on police motorcycles.

"I'm saving for Puma Clyde sneakers," I say as the store expands and we walk to where there's different style and sized wheels neatly placed on very large shelves. Just past that there's two large racks of two levels each holding a myriad of different sized and style tires.

Dean walks to the middle of the first rack and stops and from the second level pulls a tire off the rack. "This is what I'm savin' for," he says, holding the tire. "Firestone Dual Deluxe. Look at this tread," Dean says, showing me the tire. "Now that's got some bite," he says.

All I can do is nod and ask, "How much are they?"

"Well, I'm hopin', like Kenny said outside, that Carl will give me a deal on 'em. But still," he says, showing me the price tag.

Astonished, I ask, "Is that for just one?"

Dean nods that it is. "But when I get thirty bucks saved, I'll make an offer," he says. "Still," Dean adds, "amazin' how much they get for rubber these days, eh?" He puts the tire back in its place.

"Yeah," I say, as we head back to the front of the store. "The Clyde's I'm savin' for cost twenty two bucks."

"Oo ee," Dean says. "For a pair of kicks? That's some serious coin. How much ya got saved so far?"

"Ten."

Dean nods. "Yeah, I'm almost up to twenty. Maybe I should cut some lawns, too" he says. "But don't worry, I'll keep out of your territory," he adds.

We're back at the front counter. "I think I'm gonna try those additives," Dean tells Carl. "That Kenny recommended."

"The STP?" Carl asks.

"Yeah," Dean says. "I'll give 'em a try."

Carl walks through the door-less doorway. Dean takes a magazine from a small rack near the counter and hands it to me. "Take a look at her, Birdman."

I look and I'm stunned. The girl on the cover of this *EasyRider* magazine looks a lot like one of the girls on a *Playboy* magazine. She's a dark-haired beauty sitting on a motorcycle. And even though her back is turned to me, I can almost see her knockers. Almost.

"Not bad, eh," Dean says.

"And how," I say.

Carl returns with a red and white can that says NEW at the top of it and has the **S T P** logo in the center and says fuel treatment. He also has a blue and white can with the **S T P** logo in the center that says oil treatment. I give the magazine back to Dean who puts it back in the rack. "Did you install the shocks yet?" Carl asks Dean, ringing up the amount and putting the cans and a flyer into a small bag that says **Pearl's.**

"Just had their maiden run," Dean says. "Silky smooth." Dean counts his money, frowns, says, "Ya wouldn't happen t'have an extra mercury head, would ya Birdman?"

"Think so," I say, reaching into my pocket and handing Dean a dime, who then hands it to Carl.

Carl takes the money and puts it in the register. "Stay with the directions," Carl says. "Measure and use exactly what is recommended," he adds, handing Dean a few pennies change.

"Will do," Dean says, then hands me the pennies. "'Preciate that, Birdman," Dean says.

We leave the store and walk to where Bruce is still looking at the motorcycles at the end of the porch. "Rutman's been eyeing that Honda CT90 for months now," Dean says.

"An' a beauty she is," Bruce says. "A '68."

"Ooo eee," Dean says. "That's eighty-nine cubic inches of power comin' right at'cha Birdman."

"Four stroke engine, four speed trans," Bruce says, mesmerized with the bike. "Stamped steel frame, drum brakes front and rear. Jus' solid."

"'Magine the brake dive at max speed," Dean says.

"Like ridin' a buckin' bronco," Bruce says.

"Ooo eee. I hear flat lined they hit sixty," Dean says.

"And street legal in Cali, the left coast," Bruce says, tilting his body to the left. "Got t'get me there someday," he adds as we head back to the parking lot.

I have no idea of what all that means but I have to say it's a real cool looking motorcycle. It's got an orange frame with a chrome, honeycombed exhaust pipe that runs the length of the frame. There's a good sized area for storage behind the driver's seat and it just looks like it would be a real comfortable ride.

Back at the bikes Bruce jumps on his and kicks the engine over. Dean puts the bag of additives into the pouch tied to the back bars of his bike and we hop on. Dean kicks the engine over. "An' just for the record, Birdman," Dean says.

"I meant what I said to Cobalt back there. 'Bout you bein' okay an' all. An' it ain't got nothin' t'do with any coin," he adds. "Lots of people can give coin. You know how to keep your mouth shut."

And Dean's right about that. That's because I never told anyone it was Bruce who threw the stink bomb into the gymnasium.

Chapter Seventeen

We lost our second game yesterday to Midstream Park, but it was a close score, 15-11. And we were only down 12-11 before some kid they called "Sleepy" woke up and hit three straight long range jumpers. And I do mean long range. He had missed those shots the whole game and then suddenly they started going in. Apparently this Sleepy loves watching the ABA where they take long range shots that count as three points. Me, Kevin, and Quentin all scored three points and Mancuso scored two. So we're 1-1 and play Heron Pond Park Friday on our court. If we win that game we should have a good shot at making the playoffs.

Today, I wake up really excited because it's the Fourth of July, one of my favorite holidays. Which is odd because it's a holiday that I don't get any presents, money, candy, or anything else, but it's still a favorite. I think it's the freedom of the day that I like the most. Mom and dad are occupied most of the day with their "open backyard party" they have every year, so I kind of have a free rein. Their open backyard party is where anyone who wants to stroll over to our backyard is invited. Broccoli and Tommy are showing up and they're going to have a small fireworks display. Tammy and Debbie are usually here for a while. Aunt Lorraine and Mario and Maria will be here. Uncle Steve and Aunt Mary with Richard and Jeffrey always show up. The Scott's up the street who have boys about Richard and Jeffrey's age I know are coming. Ray, one of dad's co-workers will show up. Mom invited her friend Cynthia from down the street, who apparently is a divorced person, in hopes of her "hitting it off" with Ray, from what I heard. Our backyard neighbors the Cutro's usually stroll over. Dad fires up two grills so there's plenty of hamburgers and hot dogs and chicken wings. There's different kinds of salads and there's potato chips galore and all kinds of sodas and different flavored ice pops and later, red, white, and blue cupcakes. Uncle Steve brings the beer and wine for the adults.

And I also don't mind in helping setting things up. From their hibernation in the garage I break out the horseshoes and the jarts and the badminton net and the Frisbees and the wiffle ball and bat. I also help with the red, white, and blue pinwheels we put around the yard, and the red, white, and blue streamers we hang from tree branches. Mom always decks the picnic table out in a red, white, and blue tablecloth with red, white, and blue napkins and paper plates. She also brings out our two card tables and decks them up in red, white, and blue.

Uncle Steve and Aunt Mary are always the first to arrive. The car is barely stopped when the front door opens and Richard and Jeffrey bound out of the car, running for the backyard screaming like wild Indians. Aunt Mary gives me a hug on her way to the backyard and I help Uncle Steve take the cooler full of beer and wine and ice from the back of their station wagon. I help him carry it into the backyard. When we park the cooler by the big oak in the yard, the first whiffs of cooked food have filled the air. From inside the house the kitchen radio, propped up on the kitchen windowsill, blares music into the yard.

The yard begins to fill up. Aunt Lorraine and Mario and Maria show up. Then the Scotts are at the back gate with their two boys. Tommy's right behind them. I think they must have smelled the cooking. Tommy has the fireworks display he and Broccoli are gonna set off in a brown shopping bag. He shows them to me. He tells me what should happen when it goes off. If it works, it should be pretty cool. Mom's friend Cynthia walks in the yard and not much after that, the hopeful groom, dad's co-worker friend Ray, shows up. The first wave of food is cooked and me and Tommy each grab a hamburger and a hot dog and a chicken wing and a handful of chips and he chooses root beer soda while I choose a RC and we sit at one of the card tables. Before I take my first bite, Broccoli's walking into the back yard. He sees me and Tommy and points our way and we point back and minutes later he's sitting at our table munching away. All the adults are seated at the picnic table, with the kids seated at the other card table right next them. The radio is blaring and everyone is eating and talking. After making sure everyone has had firsts, me, Tommy, and Broccoli take seconds.

When everyone seems to be done eating, I ask dad if Tommy and Broccoli can set off their fireworks display. "Sure," Dad says. "Just set up far enough away from here."

Tommy grabs the bag with the fireworks and he and Broccoli walk to the middle of the yard and start to set up. I follow them. First Tommy takes a piece of cardboard that was folded into threes and he spreads it out on the ground. Broccoli proceeds to stick two sparklers into each corner of the cardboard, one sparkler being shorter than the other. Then they both spread these things they call black snakes away from the sparklers toward the center of the cardboard. They spread three snakes from each sparkler. Then Tommy aligns half a dozen firecracker mats to where the black snakes should burn to, and at the end of the mats in the center of the cardboard there's four canister looking things, each with the fuses sticking out the bottom from one of Tommy's ping pong ball bombs. After they're all set they inspect their display. They nod to me they're ready, and I turn and call everyone over.

Everyone walks over and gets into position to watch. Uncle Steve makes sure the twins and the Scott boys are in a safe spot. Aunt Lorraine has stayed by the picnic table with Maria. Tommy and Brock, one on each side of the cardboard, synchronize lighting the taller sparklers. They wait about thirty seconds, then they light the smaller sparklers. When the smaller sparklers burn to the end they light the ends of the black snakes that then twist and turn and hiss along the cardboard right toward the mats of firecrackers. The mats ignite, bursting out in loud snaps and crackles and seconds later light the fuses emanating from the canisters. The fuses light the ping pong balls and they go off in a loud boom. The canisters are blown apart and colorful streamers go into the air. They land on the charred board in a heap of aashes from the firecracker mats and black snakes. The larger sparklers then burn out. When it's all over Tommy and Broccoli actually get an applause. They take their bows.

After the fireworks the Cutros who live behind us have strolled over. They're sitting at the picnic table eating and watching as some of the games are being played. Mario and Mom are playing Aunt Mary and Dad in a game of jarts. Cynthia and Aunt Lorraine are playing Uncle Steve and Ray in a game of horseshoes. Maria is inside taking her nap. The kids are playing tag and hide and go seek and whatever else that they're young minds keep attention to. Me, Tommy, and Brock are playing wiffle ball. Mom announces she's going inside to bring out the cupcakes. Aunt Mary says she'll help. Everyone stops their games and heads to the tables. I throw a few more pitches to Tommy when…

Tammy walks into the backyard with…well somebody, or something. Tommy notions that this is the person he was telling me about the other day. Cousin It. And Tommy's description of this…person, is completely correct. I'm sure there's a face somewhere there but I can't see it behind all that hair and the John Lennon sun glasses he's wearing. His pants look like something a wizard would wear. They're purple-ish and very baggy. He has on a long sleeved dress shirt even though its summer and it looks as if it's been patched all together. It also looks like an old piece of rope is holding everything on. And he's walking barefoot.

Mom and Aunt Mary, cupcakes in hand, temporarily stop halfway back to the picnic table when they see what's walking their way. Then they continue on and mom says something to dad who turns around from his place at the picnic table. Mom places the plates of cupcakes down on the tables. Aunt Mary puts cupcakes on the kids table and mine, Tommy's, and Broccoli's table, then sits down at the picnic table. Tammy's proceeding across the yard with whatever. I slowly follow behind them when they pass. I really want to hear *this* introduction.

"Dad, Mom," Tammy says when they get to the picnic table. "I'd like you to meet Karl Maier."

Now I have to say I'm a little more than shocked when this Karl Maier takes his John Lennon glasses off and pulls his hair back behind his ears and vigorously shakes dad's hand and in perfectly enunciated, well-mannered English says, "Mr. Birdsall. It's such a pleasure to meet you."

Dad shakes Karl Maier's hand and says a friendly hello but I can see he really doesn't know what to make of him.

Then Karl Maier turns to mom and in a much softer way and tone he shakes Mom's hand and says, "And a real pleasure to meet you, Mrs. Birdsall." Mom smiles back.

"Mom, Dad," Tammy beams. "Karl is beginning his second year of college this fall. He's working toward a double B.A. One in environmental studies and one in Eastern Religions. His spiritual name is Baharupa."

That enunciates from me, a slight, condescending giggle. I can see it aggravates Tammy, but she doesn't respond.

"Well, let me introduce you to everyone," Dad says, getting up. "My brother Steve," Dad says, pointing to Uncle Steve.

Staying seated, Uncle Steve gets a vigorous handshake. "Glad to meet you, sir," Karl Baharupa Maier says.

"His wife Mary."

Aunt Mary also stays seated and gets the softer hello and handshake.

My son Robby there," dad says, nodding my way. Karl Baharupa Maier looks at me and smiles. I sort of frown back. "His friends Tommy and Andy." More smiles from the Baharupa. "Over there is Mario and his wife Lorraine." Hello's go all about. "That's Ray, and that's Cynthia over there." The Baharupa nods. "Our neighbors the Scotts," dad says motioning to them, "and the Cutros." More hellos. "Those are the kids," dad says, motioning toward the table with the four kids who are face first in the cupcakes, not paying a bit of attention.

After the introductions are over there's an eerie silence for a few seconds before I say, "So, Barracuda. Why no shoes?" Smirks and quick guffaws spill out behind me from Broccoli and Tommy.

"That's Baharupa, twerp," Tammy seethes out with as much controlled venom as she can muster.

I feign for forgiveness. Mom and Dad are giving me their "I shouldn't be asking that question" look. Karl Baharupa Maier looks at me, then at everyone, and says, "That's perfectly all right. It's actually a very logical question," he adds. He turns to me. "The reason, really Robert, or do you prefer Robby?"

I shrug my shoulders in indifference. I just want to know the answer.

"Well, the first reason I go barefoot is when the earth allows me to. Which obviously is mostly on her terms. But I always have sandals," he says, pulling a pair of sandals from his wizard-like pants. "And these," he adds, showing pairs of those things you put on your feet when trying shoes on in the store. Baharupa turns back to me. "And the second reason is it makes me think, and appreciate, every step I'm taking. I feel…," Baharupa says, hesitates, closes his eyes, "I feel it puts my mind into a simpler, and slower frame." He opens his eyes back up and is looking at me and smiling. I just blankly stare back. "And as for the clothes," he says, turning back to the adults, "they're all made from discarded, but still wearable items. These pants were actually curtains at one time."

Me: (Not hard to believe)

"The shirt's mended together from other shirts."

Me: (Knew that)

"And the sandals are made from old pieces of foam and leathers and twine."

Me: (Didn't need to know that)

"It's all part of a college thesis I'll be working on next year. On the necessary needs for living."

A thesis? Did he just mention a thesis? On July 4th? A thesis? I shake my head in disbelief and drop the wiffle ball and motion for Tommy and Brock to head for our table where the plate of cupcakes are waiting for us.

"But, please," the Baharupa tells everyone as me, Tommy, and Broccoli walk to the ice chest and pull out cans of soda. "Don't let me interfere with your holiday."

"Nonsense," Dad says. "Please, sit and join us," he adds. "Are you guys hungry? I'll fire the grill back up."

"No, but," Tammy says, looking at the Baharupa. "Would you like some homemade spearmint tea? It comes from my garden."

"Sure," Baharupa says, smiling at her.

"I'll be right back with it," Tammy says, smiling back.

Tammy brings out two glasses of her homemade spearmint tea and in the time it takes me to eat two cupcakes and finish another can of RC soda, I hear that the Baharupa comes from a small town in Pennsylvania and he's staying with a friend of his in nearby Green Harbor. Mom asks why he decided on taking on courses for two B.A's instead on one and then earn a master's degree. Baharupa says that his two B.A degrees will overlap each other, and give him multiple options right away, instead of just one, whatever that means. Dad asks him which B.A he thinks will be his most desired pursuit.

"I'd have to say at this point Eastern Religions, Mr. Birdsall."

"Oh? And why is that?" dad asks.

"Well," Baharupa says, "I'm very interested in religions. The history of them. The organization of them. Their ideals, and their words. I've read, and still read the Bible, old and new Testaments. I was actually raised as a devote Lutheran," he says. "I've read and still read Muhammad and the Koran. And I've also read and reread the Vedas of Hinduism. And I find the breakdowns to…to understanding life is just more fluid in the Vedas. I find them to be much less…violent. I find their total elements to be more grounded toward…

toward a more, connected and natural life. And that's why I'm also interested in environmental studies."

I look over to the grown-ups table. Mom and dad are shaking their heads approvingly, but I bet they don't get any of this either. I get up from my table. Broccoli and Tommy follow suit. I look at the Baharupa on my way and shake my head. Does he even know it's the Fourth of July?

. . .

The afternoon wanes and the open back yard party winds down. Afternoon turns into early evening and the yard starts to empty out. Fortunately, Tammy and the Baharupa are the first to go. I watch from my game of horseshoes with Tommy and Broccoli as the Baharupa smiles and shakes dad's and mom's hand and Uncle Steve's and Aunt Mary's hand again on his way out. As he walks toward the back yard gate he puts his John Lennon sunglasses back on and his hair is once again shrouding his face. It's like watching a scary movie in reverse. Except now, he's holding Tammy's hand. Then, one by one, everyone except Aunt Mary and Uncle Steve leave. They're always the last to leave. As Aunt Mary helps mom bring things into the house, Uncle Steve helps Dad clean the grills. Jeffrey and Richard are inside watching television. I help out by putting all the games back into the garage. When everything's done, I play some records in my room and then Jeffrey and Richard are whisked to the dining room table with coloring books while Mom, Dad, Aunt Mary, and Uncle Steve watch *All in the Family*, a new television show they all like. Then it's "Robby come out here" and hugs and handshakes and kisses and goodbyes. And then an hour later Tommy's back over and we're hopping into the back seat of dad's car on our way to the fireworks display over in Heron Pond Park. I've brought the three ping pong ball bombs I bought from Tommy and he has a few more mats of firecrackers and two canister bombs and we're gonna meet up with Broccoli whose bringing some black snakes.

When we get to the park the entrance is all lit up and the sign out in front of the guard rail says FIREWORKS TONIGHT! Along with a real cop on one side of the park's entrance, Dave, who all us kids call the parking lot cop, is on the other side of the entrance waiving people either in or commanding them to halt. I never understood what kind of cop Dave is until dad told me he's in the auxiliary police force and is like a volunteer. To me, he seems to take that volunteering very seriously. His uniform looks darn close to a real cops and just like Goddard in school, he's whistle happy.

We pull into the park and there's rows of cars parked like at a drive-in movie. Down the main stretch there's a few more figures with flashlights waving cars this way and that way. We get up pretty close to the front and when we turn down our lane I see the ice cream trucks lined up at the end of the lane against the fence like in a convoy.

The park is decked out in its usual Fourth of July regalia. The platform from which the fireworks are launched is moored out in the pond and its side is covered with red, white, and blue bunting. A string of white lights rap around the tops of the four mooring poles. On the side of the park near the playground area there's the banner suspended between two poles that reads **CELEBRATE THE FOURTH OF JULY! AMERICA'S 195th BIRTHDAY!** Everybody says that when the banner says "Celebrate America's 200th Birthday!" it's going to be a real doozy of a celebration.

Once we're parked me and Tommy hop out of the car. Through her rolled down window Mom tells me to be back at the car right after the fireworks end. I give no argument and Tommy and me make our way toward the pond. Brock's meeting us at the guard rail. When we all meet up the lights in the park flicker once, then twice. That's the sign that the festivities are about to start. Then a voice comes over the loudspeaker asking for everyone to turn their attention to the people on the platform. Then some of the important town officials gives the same schmiel speeches and then the same song they play every year comes out of the loudspeaker, *This land is your land, this land is my land*, that one, and when it ends everyone who has one waves little American flags in the air. Then all the people on the raft except for the ones who light the fireworks get into small boats and row back to shore like George Washington crossing the Delaware.

As the fireworks start me, Tommy, and Brock trek our way along the guard rail. We pass under the big banner and continue past the playground and out to the woods line. We walk a little way into the woods and then along a small path behind the first row of trees. About halfway back toward the park's entrance we find a nice clump of trees where we can set up our fireworks display.

Just like at the house, minus the sparklers, the black snakes are going to light the firecracker mats that are going to light my ping pong ball bombs and Tommy's canisters sending everything exploding into the air. I hand my stuff to Tommy and he takes Broccoli's black snakes and quietly sets everything up at the base of the trees. He's the expert. When he's finished he quickly scoots back behind the trees and hands me the book of matches and says, "Want to take the honors?"

Excitedly I take the book of matches. I creep out in front of the trees. Keeping an eye out to see if anyone's watching, I light a match. I hold the small flame to the fuse Tommy attached to the first snake. The fuse sizzles and I scoot back behind the trees. The fuse lights the snakes that slither to the firecracker mats that light up and burst out, attracting some people's attention. When the fuse to the ping pong ball bombs light, instead of them exploding into air, they screech along the ground and shoot out white smoke in three different directions. People turn look to see what's happening and a few start heading our way. Me, Tommy, and Broccoli quickly take off into the woods. Broccoli's quicker than me and Tommy and is ahead of us. I'm quicker than Tommy and I'm ahead of him. From the back of the pack, Tommy yells out to keep running until the bend in the road and then we'll double back to the park. I yell out to Tommy that I want my dollar back.

Chapter Eighteen

The Friday after the Fourth we beat Heron Pond Park rather easily, 15-7, to go 2-1 on the season. But then we got beat real bad two days ago on Tuesday to Cedar Lake Park 15-6. So we're now at 2-2. Mike Driscoll's on the Cedar Lake team and I have to say they are pretty good. But our problem Tuesday was Quentin couldn't play and all we had to replace him with was Ryba, which is like replacing a ten speed Schwinn Continental with Horsehead's beat-up one speed banana bike. So our game Friday against River End Park will be our make or break game for the season. Win and we are definitely in the play-offs, lose and Coach McCullough says we might get in and we might not. There's some strange kind of three-way tie thing that we could lose out on. So when Tuesday's game ended he told us to try and get some extra practice in as a team if we can. Thursday was the consensus so this morning I'm going to meet up with whoever can show up around ten at the park and get some practice in.

At least I thought so.

I know something is…different the second I walk into the kitchen for breakfast and dad's at the table and not in his work clothes. I grab my cereal bowl and milk from the 'fridge and today its Lucky Charms and as I sit down I say, "No work today, Dad?"

Dad, sipping the last of his morning coffee, recoils, looks at Mom who is at the kitchen sink, then back at me and in complete exasperation says, "Robby, I reminded you this very Monday that Gene and Mario will be over today to help dig the trench line. I've told you a million times that the week of the 16th township is coming to inspect our water line. Next week. What the hell do you think all that piping in the garage is for?"

In a complete state of incomprehension I say, "I thought you said we were *digging* that thing the week of the 16th."

Dad just shakes his head in bewilderment. "No, Robby," he says, getting up from the table. "Today. We're digging it today. You, me, Mario and Gene." He hands his dish and coffee cup to mom and walks out of the room.

Sitting down at the table to finish her coffee, Mom looks at me and says, "I wouldn't dwell too long there, if you know what's good for you."

So fifteen minutes later I'm lacing up my sneakers and watching Dad in the front yard. He's got the all pipes that we have to dig the line for spread out in their place in the yard. From the street the line starts off straight for about twenty feet, but then does this crazy out, up, back, then straight again configuration, going around the three trees in the center of the yard. I finish tying my sneakers and head for the yard, joining Dad. He's been all revved up about this water line thing for like two months now. I still really don't get it. All we seem to be getting out of this is something Dad keeps calling city water, which apparently is different from well water. Dad keeps saying that this does away with the septic tank and we'll have much better water pressure. He says that it will be a much better water system. When I've asked Dad why Tommy says that his Dad says it's just another way for the town to have their hands in your pockets, all Dad did was laugh a little and say, "Well kid, I guess somebody's gonna have their hands in there regardless, so, given the choice, I'll take the city water."

Mario shows up first, without Aunt Lorraine or Maria. He greets me and Dad standing in the yard. Dad thanks him for coming. Dad explains to Mario something about the diameter size of the piping and the angles of the line. He then tells Mario the reason for this is that him and Mom just didn't want to lose their maple trees. Then from up the street we hear a car coming our way, radio at full blast. I walk out to the street to see who it is, thinking that it might be Gene and his Road Runner. I'm pretty sure it's Gene so I walk further out in the street and see that it is, indeed, Gene. And his Road Runner. Moments later he parks the coolest car I've ever seen right in front of my house. A jet black two door Plymouth Road Runner convertible. The car and street goes silent as Gene turns off the engine. I walk around the car gasping in amazement. The interior is a dark red. There's a Jensen eight track player with an

AM/FM radio in the center of the dash. Two Pioneer speakers are mounted on the back deck panel. The wheels are chrome mags. The Road Runner insignia is on the quarter panels. Navy blue stripes run from both front doors all the way to the tail lights. The silver hemi emblem is mounted on the fenders. The hood has a slight scoop. "Cool car," I gush out.

"Yeah, she's a sweetheart for sure," Gene says, stepping out of the car.

"Think I can get a ride in 'er?" I ask with great hope in my voice.

"Well, let's see how long all this takes," Gene says, looking toward the yard and waving to Dad and Mario.

Gene walks in the front yard with me following, still gawking at the car. And then after more hellos and thanks for coming, we actually start the digging process. I can instantly tell that it's gonna be a lot harder than expected. For one thing, the trench line has to be three feet deep and eighteen inches wide and when I put my first shovel to the ground it skims off the hardened earth. So with my stronger leg I push down on the shovel with my foot, but still hardly make a dent in the ground. I keep at it, but it's a struggle. Sweating, I look and see I'm not the only one struggling. Gene's made more progress than me and Mario more than him, but still, there's a long way to go. Then where Dad is digging, where the line has to go around the maples, I hear him slam his shovel into the ground and say "son of a bitch." Everybody looks his way. "There's a lot of root here," he says to no one in particular.

"And the ground's like rock here," Gene says, further down the line.

"Here too," I add.

So Mario then comes up with an idea that helps with the hardness of the ground. He gets the hose out of the garage and wets the ground down really good where we have to dig. It does allow the shovels to dig into the ground, but it also makes the dirt twice as heavy. Dad's got his small saw from the garage and is cutting some of the roots that are intruding his progress. We're at it for a good hour or so and have made a little more progress, but I can see this is gonna take most of the day. So when Mom sticks her head out the front door and tells everyone to come in and take a break for some fresh iced tea, we all drop the shovels and head for the house.

I gulp down my iced tea and then ask Gene if I can sit in his car. "Yeah, sure, be my guest," he says.

"Can I play the radio?"

With a slight hesitation Gene looks at dad. I see him mouth to dad, asking, "He's okay?" questionably. Dad gives a subtle nodding approval. Gene turns to me. "Sure kid. The radio's hooked up direct to the battery, so all you have to do is turn it on."

"You make sure you don't touch anything else or break anything in that car, Robby," dad says. "Or you'll be cutting lawns for a long time to make up for it."

Almost tingling, I get up from my chair. "Thanks," I say.

"*Morrison Hotel* is in the player. I hope you like The Doors," Gene says. I shrug my shoulders as if having to listen to one of mom's or dad's records in the car wouldn't matter. "I've been listening to them a lot since Jim's death last week," I hear Gene say as I hurry out of the kitchen.

I walk out to the car and gently open the door. The invitation to the dark red seat and eight track player and sleek dash panel is intoxicating. I slip into the driver's seat and turn on the eight track player. I have no idea what the song is about but it's loud and rhythmic and cool. Jim Morrison is singing, *'There's blood in the street it's up to my ankles, blood in the streets it's up to my knee. Blood in the streets in the town of Chicago, blood on the rise it's following me.'* I stare down the hood of the car. I grip the steering wheel and pretend I'm driving the car around the neighborhood with the music blaring. I'm wishing that somebody I know will ride past my house and see me sitting in this cool car. No one does. The song that is playing ends and the next song comes on and it's a complete change of style. Instead of an upbeat rhythm, a sort on somber tone takes over. I listen to the first line. *'I found my own true love was on a blue Sunday.'* And the next thing I hear is, "Cool car lil' brother. That lawn care business of yours sure must be raking in the dough."

Startled, I look up. I see its Brother Davis and one of the Watt's gang. And they have shovels in their hands. "What are you guys doin' here?" I ask.

"You kiddin'?" Brother Davis says. "We're here to help launch the Birdsall's into the 21st century."

"Huh?"

"We're here to help dig," Davis says.

"Help dig? Why? Tam's not here."

"I'm not here for her lil' brother. I'm here, Kev's here, for your pops."

"Oh?" I say. "Well, how'd ya know we were diggin' today?"

"How?" Brother Davis asks as if that answer is on the lips of everybody in the neighborhood. "Your pops only mentioned it like a thousand times."

A million, according to what dad said earlier.

"So who's car?" Davis asks.

"My cuz there," I say, pointing to Gene as I see everyone walking out the front door. I turn the eight track player off. I get out of the car and walk to the front steps, leaving Davis and his sidekick at the sidewalk. I tell dad that Brother Davis said he's here to help out. Mom, standing behind Dad, says, "Ah, that might not be such a good idea, Bob. He and Tammy aren't dating anymore."

"Nan," dad says, "for two extra shovels, I wouldn't care if Tammy just broke up with one of the Manson clan."

So we're back to digging, digging, digging. Aunt Lorraine shows up after a while with Maria. The sun is now straight overhead and beating down mid-July heat. Mario keeps wetting down the ground where we're digging. There's piles of dirt everywhere. Every once in a while mom pops her head out of the house asking if anyone needs iced tea or water. We all say or nod not yet and keep digging. And digging. I feel as if I'm about to be liquefied when Aunt Lorraine steps out onto the steps and tells everyone that lunch is ready. Everyone but Brother Davis and his friend Kevin stop digging and starts walking toward the house. "Hey guys," Dad says to the both of them. "Come on, take a break. Have some lunch."

I look at the line on my way in to the house. I have to say that Brother Davis and his friend have been a big help. We're well more than halfway done.

And as we walk into the house, we can see that mom and Aunt Lorraine have made a spectacular lunch. Triple-decker sandwiches, macaroni and potato salads, pickles and potato chips, a fresh pitcher of iced tea, and another of cherry Kool-Aid. All waiting on the dining room table for us. One by one we walk into the kitchen and wash and dry our hands at the sink. We see a peach pie is waiting for us on the kitchen table, once all the food on the dining room table has been eaten. And mom tells us there's vanilla ice cream in the freezer to go with the pie. One by one, we find a place at the dining room table.

I'm next to Gene who is next to Kevin who is next to Brother Davis who is next to Dad who are having an actual conversation. In the almost year now that Brother Davis has been coming around, I can't recall anything coming out of Brother Davis' mouth other than Beatle lyrics or Watt's stuff. But now I hear Brother Davis saying to Dad that he's joining the school paper for his senior year and that he's going to apply to Allend College next year, which he says is one of the best journalism colleges around here. "Well, best of luck with that, Martin," Dad says.

I'm also listening to Gene telling Kevin how got his Road Runner for a "real steal." He says that he got the car for a G note and says something about putting in a new exhaust cam and resetting the timing and that was all the car needed. He says that the previous owner said he couldn't afford for a mechanic to do the work, and he couldn't do the work himself, so Gene says he made him an offer and the person took it. I'm listening to all this and it doesn't matter to me how Gene got the car, I'm still hoping that I'm gonna get my ride in it. I look around the table again and everyone is eating and talking and relaxing until….

The front door opens with such a force that a tremendous whoosh of air is picked up throughout the house and then is escorted out of the atmosphere. We all look up and there's Tammy, in the parlor, staring at Brother Davis like she's watching a horror movie. Our hellos are met with perfunctory response and a zombie-like, "I like your new car Gene" as she robotically makes her way through the parlor toward the hallway.

"Thanks," Gene says. By the look on his face I can tell that he's not sure Tammy comprehended.

To his credit, Brother Davis seems unnerved by any of this. A few seconds later music is coming out from behind Tammy's closed door.

Silently, Mom gets up from her chair and walks away from the table and down the hallway. I'm sitting at the end of the table so I can hear the light knock at Tammy's door and the announcement that its mom and then the music getting louder as Tammy's door opens. Then the hallway gets quiet again. I look around the table and other than Maria, I'm sure everyone realizes that there's some kind of situation here, but no one says a word.

The conversations at the table pick back up and a few minutes later mom's coming out of the kitchen with the peach pie and vanilla ice cream without the slightest bit of acknowledgement that anything happened. The pie is already cut into equal parts and the ice cream is passed around and put on top of the pie, or off to the side as is my choice. Then emotional tidal wave number two hits the house as Debbie is knocking at the door, then standing just inside the door, and looking at Davis with the same incalculable horror that Tammy exhibited. Thankfully a few seconds later Tammy walks out of room and down the hallway and into the parlor and then out the door with Debbie. And just like that, all the tension is gone.

As lunch ends Dad claps then rubs his hands together and says, "Well, what do you say everyone, just a little bit more to go?"

Chairs scrape against the hardwood floor with silent acknowledgements from everyone on their way to the shovels lying on the ground in the front yard. Mario asks Dad when he's going to put the pipes in the ground. Dad says he's going to let the thing settle and Saturday he'll put the piping in the ground. Township will be by on Monday for an inspection. Dad and Mario are first out the front door followed by Gene and Brother Davis and Kevin. I'm last and as I make my way down the steps and into the yard Brother Davis meets me. "So, lil' brother," he says. "Help me out some here. Has Tam been seein' anyone?"

"Seein' anyone?" I say, heading for my shovel.

"Yeah, you know what I mean lil' brother," Davis says. "Has anyone been…you know, hangin' around her?"

Standing over my shovel, scratching my head, I say. "So ya dug dirt all this mornin' just to come here and ask me that?"

"Well," Davis says with hesitation, "I did tell your pop I'd help out with this. It's not his fault that Tam decided…" Davis says, not finishing the sentence as his voice trails off.

I pick up my shovel. "Baharupa," I say.

"Huh?" Davis says.

I shrug my shoulders and sink my shovel into the ground and say, "Some… person that she calls, they call, whoever calls, Baharupa." I pick up a shovel full of dirt and throw it on the pile. Davis is staring at me. "Karl something's his name," I say, plunging the shovel into the ground again. "Maier. Karl Maier. Also known as the Baharupa."

· · ·

By mid-afternoon we're finished with the trench line. Dad thanks everyone for coming and helping and it's a good thing that Tam's not here because dad shakes hands with both Brother Davis and Kevin as they leave. Before Gene leaves, I ask, more beg, for the ride in his Road Runner I was sort of promised. Dad tells me not to pester him but Gene says it's okay. He's stopping for gas on the way home so he'll take me over to the Citgo and then back here.

Citgo's good. It's about a mile or so down the highway from my neighborhood. As we approach Tommy's house I ask Gene if he'll give a *meep meep* of the horn, hoping if Tommy's around it'll grab his attention. Gene obliges but as we pass Tommy's house there's no sign of Tommy. It doesn't matter. Here I am, riding through the neighborhood in a jet black Road Runner convertible. With *Morrison Hotel* playing at a loud decibel. "So what's up with your sis and that Davis dude?" Gene asks me. "Man, if looks could kill."

"Oh, him," I say. "Well, they were datin' a while back and I guess Tam broke up with 'em or somethin'."

"Yeah, I'd say so," Gene says. "By the looks of it. And what's up with that Debbie chick? She's a real looker."

"Debbie?" I say as we turn onto Constitution Street. "Yeah, she's okay. She's datin' some friend of Davis'. I think. I mean, I guess they're still datin'."

"Yeah, chicks can be funny that way," Gene says. "What about you?" he asks. "Whadda ya now? Going into eighth?" I nod that I am. "Got to be some real lookers in your world by now," he says. "Anybody smokin'?"

"A couple of 'em," I say as we're now on the down side of the crest on Hoover Street, approaching the traffic light. As we near the approaching highway the light turns orange and Gene floors the gas and I'm thrown back in the car. During the turbulence, Gene asks, "So, anyone ya got your eye on?" Turning and slowing the car at once onto the highway makes the tires shrill out against the pavement.

Once on the highway my body relaxes like at the end of a roller coaster ride as the car slows down. "Well, I kinda like this girl Linda Orken from school," I say.

"Oh?" Gene says. "Well, spill the beans."

"Well," I begin, and then proceed to tell Gene about the science class project and how Linda and I won and how she hugged me after when we did and how I started walking with her for a while to her bus and how we all use to call her Orken the Dorken, including me, because she looked scraggly and hardly ever spoke to anyone but then as I got to know her I found out that she is really cool and when I sat next to her and really looked at her I saw she was actually pretty.

"Yeah, chicks can be funny that way," Gene says as we pull into the Citgo.

"And she signed my yearbook," I say.

"Oh? And what did she write?"

"Just that she was glad to get to know me and is looking forward to seeing me next year."

"Huh. Well maybe you shouldn't wait that long," Gene says, pulling in front of the gas pumps.

"Whadd ya mean?"

"Call 'er up. See what's shakin'."

"I don't have her number," I say.

"They got phone books 'round here, don't they?" Gene says, getting out of the car, looking at me as if that should have been my obvious conclusion.

The attendant that walks over from the chair in front of the station is no older than Gene. He asks Gene how much gas he's getting and Gene tells him three dollars worth of premium but tells the attendant he likes to pump his own gas. The attendant nods and shrugs his shoulders. "Copacetic with me," he says. He sees the Hemi insignia on the fender. "She's a true 426?"

"All stock," Gene says, putting the nozzle into the tank, gas fumes instantly dominating the air.

"Bitchin' motor," the attendant says. "What year's she?"

"Early production '68."

The attendant nods. "That's my Gran Sport over there" he says, pointing to a really cool almost rust colored car at the far side of the station. "She's got a 455."

"Whew that's some serious power," Gene says. "What year?"

"'66."

"All stock?"

"Well I added some power valves and leaner jets, so she really purrs now."

The meter hits three dollars. Gene takes the nozzle from the tank and hands it back to the attendant. "Yeah, I didn't want to mess with the carb on this," Gene says, counting out three dollars and handing it over to the attendant. "Previous owner already spun a cam, so I put that in, set the timing, and let things be."

"Sometimes things are better left untouched," the attendant says. "Hey good luck with 'er," the attendant adds, starting back for his chair.

"Own the road," Gene says with a thumbs up.

Not turning around, the attendant also gives a thumbs up

Chapter Nineteen

I should be playing in the first semi-final playoff game for the 1971 Lower Brook Playground championship this morning, but instead I'm riding down the utility road with Tommy and Broccoli, heading for Jumper's Bridge. And that's because that crazy three-way tie thing that coach McCullough warned us about last week actually did us in. Well, losing to River End Friday 15-9 was the first thing that did us in, and because of that loss us, River End and Heron Pond all finished at 2-3. And in some crazy overall points scored equation, they're in and we're out.

At the power plant we walk our bikes through the short cut and then ride down Juniper Street. We make the right onto Goldenrod and when we get to Azalea Court I tell Tommy and Broccoli I want to take a look at something. So we ride down the block and when we get to Mrs. Medina's house I stop and peer about. "What are we stoppin' here for" Broccoli asks.

"I cut this lady's yard a few times," I say. "I just wanted to take a look."

"Well it looks like some party's goin' on," Tommy says.

I guess Tommy's right because we can hear music coming from the backyard and I'm guessing maybe it's a very belated Fourth of July party because there's an American Flag hanging from a tree and some variation of an American Flag right below that and then right below that there's another bright red flag with a globe in the center and a gold banner below the globe that says something I can't make out. In the front window of the house there's a handmade sign that says **Bienvenido a casa Papa!**

"Is this that hottie's house?" Tommy asks.

I shake my head that yes, it is. I look around at the now well-kept yard.

"Well, it looks like that well's run dry, Birdyboy," Tommy says.

"Guess so," I say, turning my bike around and heading back toward Goldenrod Street, Tommy and Brock on either side.

"So how's that whole yard cuttin' thing goin' anyway," Broccoli asks.

"Kinda slow," I say. "But I did cut the Lampman's yard again over the weekend. So I put another two dollars in my savings."

"Ask 'em what he's savin' for," Tommy says to Broccoli.

Broccoli looks at me and waits for an answer. "Puma Clydes," I say, with a confident shrug of shoulders.

Broccoli looks at Tommy and notions that it's of no concern to him. "Well, whatta ya think there, Horsehead," Broccoli says. "About that other thing? Think we should let ol' Birdfoot here in on it?"

"In on what?" I instantly say.

Broccoli looks at Tommy and then Tommy at me. "Naw. Wait till we get to the bridge," Tommy says. "Lil' suspense never hurt no one."

"In on what?" I ask again.

"To the bridge," Tommy says, standing up on the pedals of his banana bike, picking up speed.

Jumper's Bridge isn't so much a bridge as it is an overpass on Middle Brook Road. And the jump itself is nothing more than a five or six foot drop into the river below. We never tell our parents we're going here because they don't want us jumping into the river off the overpass, because they think it's dangerous. Yes, boats do go cruising through here, but one would have to be a complete spaz not to see that.

As we approach the overpass we see that so far, no one else is here. That's good because sometimes it can get very crowded. We leave our bikes on the side of the road along with our socks and sneakers and shirts and with some trepidation make our way toward the stone wall barrier. Walking barefoot like this makes me think about the Baharupa and his barefoot approach to traveling. "So," I say as we approach the stone wall barrier. "Am I gettin' in on this thing or what?"

"Jumps first," Broccoli says. "A lil' more suspense never hurt no one neither."

So we line up along the stone wall barrier. We look both ways to make sure no boats are coming. Then in almost synchronized succession, Tommy, then me, then Brock, cannonball into the waiting river below. And the water is that perfect summer temperature. It's not in the ice cold low sixties of June, nor in the unrefreshing low eighties of August.

For the next half hour or so me, Tommy, and Broccoli race each other from the middle of the river back to the shore line, time each other as to who can stay under water the longest, time who can touch the bottom of the river and then back up the quickest, and try to outdo each other's jumps from the overpass. Tommy, I guess being the most fearless, wins the last one with a backward somersault cannonball jump into the river.

After all the races and contests are done, we're sitting on the embankment letting the July sun dry us. "So." I say, "am I gonna hear about this…thing now, or what?"

Broccoli looks at Tommy who nods his approval. So Broccoli gets up, walks up the embankment to where his socks and sneakers are, returns with a sock, and pulls a folded piece of paper and a news clipping out from it. He unfolds the news clipping and hands it to me.

I read what it says. **COMING TO LOWER BROOK PLAZA TWIN THEATRES. FRIDAY, AUGUST 7TH. CARNAL KNOWLEDGE. STARRING JACK NICHOLSON, ANN MARGRET, ART GARFUNKEL, CANDICE BERGEN. FIRST SHOWING AT 7:05. SECOND SHOWING AT 9:30.** I read the clipping again. "Okay. What about it?" I say, handing the clipping back to Broccoli.

"We can be in the theatre," Broccoli says.

"We?" I say. "In the theatre?" I add, my voice dripping with incredulity. I look over at Tommy.

"I tol' ya that'd be his reaction," Tommy says.

"Well," Brock says with a deep breath and looking at Tommy. "If he's not interested…" he adds, beginning to fold the clipping back up.

"I'm interested," I say, my hand held in a halting position. "I'm just, ya know, wonderin' how we're gettin' into an R rated movie theatre. That's all."

Brock then unfolds the piece of paper he's been holding and hands that to me.

I take it and look at it. It looks like some rudimentary, hand drawn map of something. "Okay," I say again. "And just what is this?"

"THAT," Brock says, "is a sketch of the basement at the Twin Theatres."

"The basement?"

"The basement," Brock says. "'Member my brother worked there last year?" I nod that I do. "Well, he says that underneath the theatres there's these alley ways and walkways that connect them both. He says they're filled with all kinds of junk, old billboards and candy machines and cigarette machines and popcorn machines and stuff like that, so we have to be careful, BUT, he says if we follow along this path," Brock points out the arrows on the map, "he says we can go from one theatre to the other using the trap doors behind the screens, here and here," he says, pointing to the map. "If our movie in in the larger theatre, which it probably will be," he says, "there's also a stairwell that leads to the stage."

"Trap doors?" I say. "Stairwells?"

"Tol' ya he'd question everything Brockwurst," Tommy says.

"No, it's not that I'm questionin' everything," I say. "But, how are we gonna just disappear behind a movie screen and then down some trap door without being seen?"

"Well, we got that all figured out Birdfoot," Broccoli says. "Mark says that the other movie always starts earlier than the main attraction. So he says to wait a week or two and pick a weekday night, 'cause it won't be so crowded. We have to make sure we're absolutely the first ones in the theatre. Once in, don't waste time. Get in, get to the trap door behind the screen, follow the map, get to the other trap door, or stairwell, and into the empty theatre. We can hide in the janitor's closet. Mark says no one goes in there until after the first show."

I'm thinking that that sounds like a lot of things have to go right, but I guess that could work if they do. I take a deep, reflecting breath. "Sounds… possible," I say.

"Very possible," Broccoli says.

"Easy peasy, Japanesey," Tommy says.

"And Birdman," Broccoli adds, "rumor has it that this Ann Margret shows off a really nice pair of knockers right there on the big silver screen. Just shows 'em off! How's that sound?"

I nod approvingly. "Sounds like we need to pull this thing off," I say.

• • •

The last Thursday in July is always the day of my neighborhood's giant block party. It's held every year over in Branch Park and it's an all-day event. It's really one of the highlights of the summer 'cause it has something for everyone. There's puppet shows and clown acts and coloring contests for young kids and weaving and braiding and bead making contests along with fifty yard dash races and free throw contests for older ones. Last year was the first year I didn't participate in any of that and just came around the time of the huge cook-out and was allowed to stay until darkness started to fall. This year will be the first year I'm allowed to stay until the whole shindig ends, which is sometime after nine. So this will be the first year I can participate in the neighborhood wide capture the flag game.

So after Dad gets home from work and changes out of his work clothes, I'm following behind him and mom on my bike as we're heading over to the park. I'm making wide, looping turns to keep pace with their slow-paced walking. I have to do this because mom always says if we're going somewhere together as a family, it's very important for us to walk in as a family. And I guess that means even if it takes forever to get there.

We're about halfway down Roosevelt Street and I can see cars parked out in front of the park. As we get closer I hear a low din of music in the air and once the trees surrounding the park come into view, the first whiffs of cooking hot dogs and hamburgers and chicken wings tinge my nostrils and stomach. I see that the bike racks out front are pretty full. I see more bikes leaning against the fence that surrounds most of the entrance to the park. And of course, standing guard, just outside the gated fence leading into the park, in his full auxiliary police uniform is Dave the volunteer police man. I leave my bike against the fence.

Like Mom wanted, we walk past Dave the imposter cop and through the gate in near unison, and then past the banner that says **WELCOME TO BRANCH MANOR'S ANNUAL SUMMER JUBILEE**. As we enter the park there's kids playing on the swings and the monkey bars and the see-saws and people milling about or sitting on benches where there's a small line of trees before the fields. Past the softball field the basketball court is set up with the little stands where people bring stuff to either trade or sell. There all aligned in a big square around the edge of the court with a string of overhead lights running throughout. Between the softball field and the basketball is the record player with two giant speakers that's blasting the music. Right now it's the *Monkees*. Some fools are over there dancing. The entire softball field has been turned into one giant picnic area. There's rows of picnic tables filled with people and families. Over by the back stop I count, one, two, three…eight grills in all with what looks like about twenty volunteers working them. Past the grills there's a few more volunteers near the barrels full of ice and juices and sodas and the big boxes full of potato chips and Cheez-its and Bugles and a host of other goodies. We walk along the path through the kids play area and I point out an empty picnic bench to mom and dad and head towards it. I look around and see some people I know and more that I don't. I don't see Tommy yet. Broccoli always shows up a little later with his dad in his dad's old Packard. Everyone knows it's him 'cause he always honks that horn as he approaches the park. *Aooouuuggh! Aooouuuggh!* is what we hear as he makes his way down the street. And I have to say that he does let as many kids, and adults for that matter, that want to take a ride around the neighborhood in the car, take a ride. And he fits as many people in there as he can, too. Six, seven, sometimes eight people at a time. Last year I think he made a half a dozen trips, all of them with the car filled to the brim.

After we sit down Mom and Dad hold the bench while I walk up to the grills. I look around. This is better than the spread after Easter Sunday church services. This is even better than our back yard Fourth of July party. I ask for a hamburger and a hot dog, a cup of the macaroni salad over the potato salad, a bag of potato chips, a slice of watermelon, a vanilla frosted cupcake, and a Penguin cola. I return and mom and dad make their way to the grills. They return with a much simpler plate. A hamburger each, a pickle on the side, a cup of potato salad, and two cans of Lipton iced tea. About halfway through my plate, Tommy shows up at our table with enough food for three people. Dad looks at Tommy's plate. "Hungry, Tommy?"

"It's free, Mr. Birdsall," Tommy says, taking a big bite into hamburger number one.

Mom and Dad finish eating first. As they pick up their empty plates and empty iced tea cans, Mom says, "Robby, Dad and I are going to take a look at the stands and be on our way." Then sternly, she adds, "And be home as soon as this ends." I nod that I will be. "And be careful riding your bike through the neighborhood in the dark."

Once Mom and Dad leave the table, Tommy takes a Red Man chewing tobacco pouch out of his back pocket and places it on the picnic table. "Take a look," he says.

I unfold the top and in the empty pouch are the reefer cigarettes that Tommy found way back when in the kids Nova. I quickly refold the pouch shut. "Why'd ya bring this?"

"Gonna sell 'em," Tommy says.

"Here?" I ask questionably, looking around to see if anyone is watching us.

"Not here at this picnic bench, Birdegg," Tommy says, shaking his head. "But later, in the park when the older kids get here."

"Aren't you, won't you be…afraid of gettin' caught?"

"From who?" Tommy scoffs. "Dave the bicycle cop? I'm sure he'll be way occupied watchin' all the tricycles."

"How will ya know who…ya know, who t'try an' sell it to?"

"Birdhead," Tommy says in a frustrated tone, "whadda ya think? I can't tell who smokes or not? 'Sides. Brock says he might know somebody."

I finish eating and Tommy finishes his three helpings and we sit at our bench and eye the crowd. Some of the older kids are showing up now and the music being played changes from the *The Monkees* or *The Turtles* or *The Grass Roots* to *Uriah Heep* and *Rare Earth* and *Bob Dylan*. Some of the kids must have been at the beach because they're still in bathing suits and cover ups. I see Robin DuVall over by the record player and point her out to Tommy. Next to Diane Lindsay and Robyn Luft Robin Duvall is the prettiest girl I've ever seen. She has a Susan Dey face with the long blond-brown hair and blue eyes. She's wearing denim hip-hugger shorts with a top that's like a bikini top but has frilly arm coverings. Tommy stares her way. "Should be illegal for one chick to be that hot," he says.

"And how," I say.

Then from down the block we hear Brock's dad *Aooouuuggh!* his entrance to the park. Me and Tommy stand up on the picnic bench and wait to see Brock enter the park and when he does we flag him down. He acknowledges us and walks over to the grills and a few minutes later he's at our picnic bench with a hamburger, macaroni salad, can of soda, and multi-colored sprinkled cup cake.

"So'd ya bring 'em?" Broccoli asks Tommy, taking a bite from the hamburger.

Tommy takes the Red Man pouch from his pocket and shows it. "Right here."

"Good. Lemme finish this and we'll take a look around. I know Orcutt said he was interested."

Not wanting to be part of that endeavor, I say, "Well, why you guys are doin' that, I'm gonna take a look at the stands. We're still meetin' at the stage coash, right?" I say.

Silent nods of yes.

. . .

So as Tommy and Broccoli walk around the park looking for any perspective reefer buyers, I stroll around the basketball court and take a look at some of the stands. There's still daylight left in the sky but the overhead lights strung around the court are already on illuminating the stands into a festival like atmosphere. I stop at the Henderson's stand. Dale and Brett are sitting with their dad and selling stickers of different racing cars and racing car buttons and programs from past events. They also have old gas station signs and highway signs that they're selling. In the background of the stand they have a picture of Mr. Henderson when he was younger next to a racing car and being handed a trophy and the picture of Dale and Brett from our paper with their trophy. There's a few people here talking to them and I'm pretty sure that one of them is the kid from the gas station with the Gran Sport.

I walk on. The Hogans are here selling their usual fishing stuff. There must be seven Hogans in that family and every one of them likes to fish. Even the mom and the two girls. I pass the usual conglomeration of stands selling old clothes. They're always clumped together for some reason. This stand wasn't here last year. Or any year that I can remember. I stop. I watch as Anita Matisse, Artist, is sitting on an art chair in front of a drawing board with different sized and shaded pencils spread out on a small table next to the board. She's sketching the portrait of what I guess is a husband and wife sitting opposite her on a small bench. Hanging on a large, well-lit board behind her are other sketches of people. I have to say the drawings look pretty good, very detailed. Even the one she's doing now. Looks just like the couple only in black and white. I watch for a few seconds more as this Anita Matisse, Artist, sketches the faces of the couple sitting in front of her.

I walk further and see that Mrs. Bellatrix is here with her Ouija Board. I remember her from last year. She's got her stand set up away from the other stands and sitting in a high-back chair that's three sizes larger than a normal chair she looks like a creepy fortune teller from inside a slot machine game at a carnival. She's dressed all in black like at a funeral and her gray and white hair only adds to her corpse-like figure. Her stand is pretty creepy looking too. There's a dull, blue-colored orb with cracks in it on a table with a skeleton head next to that and an oversized open book that looks like some sort of Bible next to all that. There's flowers spread out all over the stand and behind her there's a picture of giant hand with marks and words written on the fingers and palm. Above the hand the word **PALMISTRY** is written out. And she's burning those incense sticks. As I get a little closer I'm pretty darn sure that's mom's friend from down the street sitting at Mrs. Bellatrix's stand. The one who came over on the Fourth of July. I could be wrong, but it looks like her.

Anyway, what Mrs. Bellatrix does is she has a person sit down in front of the Ouija Board and place two quarters on the table. Then she takes their hands in hers and closes her eyes and breathes deeply and sways about and inaudibly chants as she moves the hands and that thing around the board. When she comes to her conclusion, if the person is happy with the result, she keeps both quarters. If they're not she gives a quarter back. She holds the quarters in a jar next to the board. And Mrs. Bellatrix takes her Ouija very seriously. She'll warn people, even if they're just walking by, to never, never disbelieve the Ouija.

Ah! There's Mr. Jacobs. He's got a stand just for trading, selling, and buying baseball and basketball cards. He keeps the most prized cards in books that have slots where the card neatly slides into their own holder, and he has all those books labeled. He has other cards in shoe boxes, also all labeled. There's a couple of kids and a grown up man all ready at the stand. I walk over. I pick up one of Mr. Jacobs basketball card books and thumb through it and listen as the man tells Mr. Jacobs that he's looking for a '61 Roger Maris card.

"Aren't we all," Mr. Jacobs responds. "I don't have that but I do have a rookie Hank Aaron card," he says, reaching under the table and producing another book, opening it up to the page with the card, "if you're interested," he adds.

The man looks at the card. "A little steep," the man says.

I peer over and look at the card. I take a double look. The price on the sticker says ten dollars. Ten dollars! For one card! I get ten new cards for a dime in a *Topps* pack. With a piece of gum.

"Hammerin' Hank could be the one to break the Babe's record," Mr. Jacobs says. "Makes it a very valuable commodity. Looks like he's gonna catch Mays this year, anyway."

"Not if Willie can ever get the hell out of 'Frisco. That park's been eating up his home runs there since the move," the man says. "Unlike Fulton County in Atlanta."

"Won't be any asterisks next to the record though, if he does break it," Mr. Jacobs says. "Unlike Roger's 61." Then looking at the two kids, Mr. Jacobs says, "You two just looking or do you want something in particular?"

"No," the one kid says, closing a book and putting it down on the table. "Just lookin'." They go on their way.

"Let me think about it," the man says.

"I'll be here till the end," Mr. Jacobs says as the man walks away. "How 'bout you young man. Anything in particular you're looking for?"

As Mr. Jacobs says that my eyes bulge as I come across a rookie Walt Frazier card. It has a dollar fifty sticker price. "Maybe this," I say, showing Mr. Jacobs the card.

"Knick fan?" he asks. I nod that I am. "I also have a Willis Reed rookie card, if you want them both." Mr. Jacobs pulls out another book and shows me the card. That one has a two dollar price tag. "I'll give you both for three dollars," he says.

I frown because three dollars is a lot of money for just two cards. So I say, "Maybe I got something I can trade with?"

Mr. Jacobs takes a deep breath like he has to reach to the bottom of the ocean for that answer. "Do you have a rookie Wes Unseld?" he asks. I shrug my shoulders that I don't know. So Mr. Jacobs pulls out a magazine and shows me the card.

"That's the card?" I ask in shocked disbelief. I had that card. I ripped it up along with all my other Baltimore Bullets cards after they beat my Knicks in the playoffs. "Why's that card so valuable?"

"You kidding? Second player in NBA history to win rookie of the year and the most valuable player the same year," Mr. Jacobs says. "If he ever adds a championship to that resume, that's quite a feat. So it makes it quite a card."

"Huh. I'll have to take a look," is all I say.

. . .

With early darkness descending in the park, I look around all the stands for Tommy and Brock. There's no sign of them. I look over to the record player area where the older kids have now completely taken over. I don't see them there either. I scan the picnic area and there's no sign of them. I look around the park. I think I see them by the back fence by the utility road but as I make my way there I see it's not them. Then from down the utility road I see two headlights and the low sound of approaching motorcycles. I wait a few seconds and see that it's Dean and Bruce. They cut their engines and lights before they reach the fence. I walk over. "Birdman!" Dean says, kicking the stand down on his bike. Bruce does the same.

"Hey Dean, Bruce," I say.

Bruce nods and they both climb up the fence. Dean slaps me five. "How's the lawn empire goin'?"

"Lil' slow," I say. "Not much grass grows this time of year."

"No, guess not," Dean says. "Any grub left in there?"

"Think so," I say

"Dave the fake cop 'round?"

"Was out front by the bikes last I saw."

"Watch our bikes?" Dean says.

"Sure," I say.

"Let's go see what we can rustle up Rutman."

Dean and Bruce make their way to the grill area as I pray no one comes near their bikes. A few minutes later they return with some burnt hot dogs, a couple of flattened cupcakes, and two bent-up cans of soda. As they devour the food, Dean asks, "So Birdman. You see Knievel jump those thirteen cars las' week in the Dome?"

"I read about it in the paper," I say.

"Can you believe that! Two nights in a row!" Dean says. "100,000 eyes watchin' live. Millions more on the tube," he adds, shaking his head in amazement. "You know next year he's plannin' on jumpin' Snake River. In some kind of rocket! It's gonna be on *The Wide World Of Sports* and everything. Man, I can't wait for that."

"Where's Snake River?" I ask.

"Idaho, my man," Dean says, as he and Bruce finish the food they rustled up. "God's country. Hey, thanks for watchin' the bikes," he says. "And listen, Birdman," he adds as he and Bruce hop back over the fence, "This comin' Thursday, one o'clock sharp, out in the Zone. Me and Rutman here are gonna put on our own jump. Spread the word."

I nod that I will. They kick over their engines and down the darkening utility road they go. I make my way for the stage coach.

Chapter Twenty

Saturday comes with August and August heat. Every summer has its hottest spell and it looks like this week will be it for this summer. Luckily, I'm starting it out on the right foot because I've been invited over to Fig's today with Broccoli for Fig's belated thirteenth birthday party. His birthday was actually earlier the past week and he said he asked his parents if he could have a small pool party so today is it. And it took a little talking from me and Broccoli, but we also got Tommy invited. Well, actually we told Fig that we'd let him in on an upcoming caper we're planning to pull off, and one that he certainly did not want to miss out on. We just didn't tell him what it was. The suspense thing actually works.

Fig's pool party starts around eleven so after breakfast, with it being too hot to do anything other than think about swimming in Fig's pool, I'm sitting on the back porch in the shade of the house watching Tammy in full peasant worker regalia diligently working in her garden. She's got her gathering baskets in there and I can see one is full of spinach. More spinach! Popeye I'm not. Another basket has those purplish things that are tasteless mush. Eggplants, I think they are. Another basket has tomatoes and right now she's amongst the different colored peppers. There's red peppers and green peppers and yellow peppers and some peppers that are green and yellow. Other peppers have a bit of orange in them. And I don't know how she did it, but she actually grew strawberries. And they're really good. I see them near the tomatoes in one of those square strawberry boxes. She emerges from the peppers with her basket holding one of each color and then like a waiter at a restaurant, she picks up and dangles two baskets from each arm and gently holds the strawberry box in her hands and heads for the house. I open the back door as she comes up the steps and take a nice sized strawberry from the box as she passes by. I'm hardly done with the strawberry when Broccoli's at my back gate. Minutes later me, him, and Tommy are on our way over to Fig's.

"Do you think Fig's gonna want to come along with us," I ask Broccoli.

"If he has any sense he will," Broccoli says.

"Yeah, I suppose so," I say. "So, Horsehead. Did you ever sell those funny cigarettes?"

"I sold two, kept one."

"Still plannin' on smokin' it," I ask.

"Possibly," Tommy says mischievously. "Possibly."

Fig's house is on South Terrace Street near the end of Midstream Road which makes it a good hike from our neighborhood, but Midstream Road is a pretty straight and flat run with plenty of space on both sides of the road for riding a bike. We get to Fig's street and then Fig's house and when we ride our bikes up the driveway I see through the picture window Tup's mop of red hair and Fig sitting in a chair opposite him. I guess Fig invited Tup also. I stand up on my bike so Fig can see its us and he motions that he'll be out in a minute. Tup turns around and sees us and gives us that big-tooth smile. Then I'm almost knocked off my bike when Joni Iachello's face appears in the window. She sees us and then me and sneers and sits back down.

We leave our bikes on the side of the house and walk into the backyard, the smell of the chlorine pool very inviting. Fig's dad even built a big deck from the back door to the pool with posts to hang your clothes and sneakers on and chairs sit and relax in. In the pool is one of those in-water basketball hoops and I see in the yard that Fig's got his jart game out. I also see that the picnic table already has paper plates and cups and bowls on it. We all want to jump in the pool right now but we know we have to wait for Fig, who comes out the back door a few minutes later. "Hey guys," he says. "Glad ya came." He sits down and starts unlacing a sneaker.

We follow suit. "What's goin' on in there?" I ask. "Why's Joni here?"

Fig makes a defeated face and says, "Because of Mrs. Demerast. You know, the lady at church who does the Sunday school classes with the little kids?"

"Yeah, I know who she is," I say.

"Well, she had some family emergency, so, she's gonna be gone like, the whole month of August."

As I untie my other sneaker I look at Fig, waiting to hear what that means.

"So Joni's in there with Pastor Mark because my mom volunteered me for weeks two and three to fill in for her. Tup's takin' tomorrow and the last week."

"Really?" I say. "I would have figured Tup would do all of them."

"Well he probably would have but his family goes on vacation for two weeks in the middle of August, so…," Fig says in that defeated tone again.

"So you got volunteered?" I say. Fig nods like there's nothing he can do about it. "So what are you gonna have to do?" I ask.

"I have to meet up with Joni and Pastor Mark during the weeks it's my turn and go over the stuff the kids are gonna study that week."

"That kinda sucks," Broccoli says.

"It's really just one night each week," Fig says, but in another defeated tone.

"Well," Broccoli says, sinisterly looking around to make sure no one's listening as he takes the news clipping of the upcoming movie and his brother's map to the treasure chest from his back pocket. "We got somethin' here for ya Figster that doesn't suck." He huddles us all into the corner of the deck. He hands Fig the news clipping and the map. He unravels the grand plan, letting Fig know what we need to do to pull it off. Just as Brock finishes telling Fig the plot, and Fig tells us he's definitely in, the back door swings open and striding toward us is Pastor Mark and Joni. Broccoli snatches the map and the clipping from Fig and shoves it back into his pocket.

"Good afternoon, young men," Pastor Marks says in his Sunday morning sermon face as he reaches us. Looking up into the brilliant sunshine he adds, "Splendid day, today, is it not?" We all nod that it is. He extends his hand my way and says, "Master Birdsall, very nice to see you. Sorry to say it's been a while." I shake his hand and can't help but notice Joni's snickering I-told-you-so-look. "And you two young men, I don't believe we've ever met," he says, extending his hand Tommy's way, who looks like he's just seen a ghost. "What's your name, son?"

Tommy blinks and stammers out, "T, Tom, Thomas Hulse."

"Master Hulse, my pleasure. And you young man?" he says now to Brock, extending his hand his way, "Your name is?"

"Andy, Andrew. Kenebrocki."

"My pleasure. Do you all know Miss Iachello here?" he says, turning Joni's way.

We nod that we do. And even though Joni's always stern and serious about things, and for some reason hates my very existence, I still have to say she looks real pretty in her sleeveless yellow shirt and colorful shorts and tanned legs and arms and face and her dark hair pulled back into a neat pony tail. As I'm noticing Joni Tup comes barreling out of the back door in his bathing suit and opaque skin and fire engine hair all ready to jump in the pool.

"Well, I don't want to keep anyone from their recreation," Pastor Mark says. "But I did want to thank you again, Rich, for filling in for Mrs. Demarest and to wish you a belated happy birthday." Fig nods. "And I hope maybe to see the rest of you young men again," Pastor Mark says to a stony silence. He and Joni then turn and walk back into the house and the next sounds are five cannonball jump into the waiting water.

• • •

The morning of Dean's and Bruce's Evil Knievel stunt I do my chores around the house to earn my allowance that week. I plan on putting a dollar of it in my Sucrets tin. The grass doesn't need cutting but the hedges need some trimming and dad left me instructions to sweep out the garage, which requires taking almost everything out of it first. I'm also to make sure all the garbage is in the cans and out to the street. Seems like a lot for a dollar and a half but I don't say anything because I haven't hardly added anything to my Puma Clyde fund lately and it's already August. About halfway through the garage Tommy rides by and makes sure I'm still going at one to watch Dean and Bruce. "Of course I'm still goin'," I say.

"Get me when you're ready," he says.

I'm finished with everything and sitting at the kitchen table having lunch and I turn and look at the clock and see its half past twelve. I'm figuring on getting out to the zone in about a half hour. Mom left my allowance near my bologna sandwich and when I'm finished with lunch I walk in my room and take my Sucrets tin out and add the dollar to what's there. I count the money again. Thirteen dollars. Just nine more dollars and I'll have enough. I pick out some records to listen to and sit down at my desk and look at some of my old

Basketball Register's. A few records later, mom, walking past my open door, says, "Almost ready, Robby?"

My head snaps up from my magazine. Did I hear that right? Almost ready? Ready? Ready for what? I jump up and pop out of my room and stand at my doorway and ask, "Did you just ask if I was ready?"

Rummaging through her pocketbook mom says, "Ah, yes Robby. I told you that we were going to Two Guys today for your new suit."

"Yeah, I know, but, right now?"

"Yes, Robby. Right now."

"But…" I stop 'cause I can't say anything about going to the Zone, so I say, "I was plannin' on goin' to Fig's and go swimmin'."

"Well this won't take but an hour, so you can go swimming then."

"But by then it'll be too late."

Mom snaps her pocket book shut. "And why would it be too late?"

I think for a second. Because whatever happens in the Forbidden Zone will be over by then. "Well, I told Fig I'd be over 'round one."

"Well, call him and tell him you'll be over around two."

I want to say that the phones at Fig's house are all not working, but I'm gonna lose this argument one way or another, so I just relinquish with a long, drawn out breath.

On our way to Two Guys I strain looking out my window to see if I can get a glimpse of the Zone as we pass by, but I can't really see anything and it's gone in a blip anyway. I slink back down in my seat. "What do I even need a new suit for, anyway?" I say.

"Well for one," Mom says, "your old one hardly fits you anymore. And secondly, whatever you stuffed into the pocket of your jacket on Easter has permanently attached itself to the lining. And thirdly, dad wants everyone to look nice for our twentieth anniversary coming up. Is that too much, Robby, to ask?"

Another lost argument.

When we get to the Two Guys there's not a lot of cars in the parking lot. On our way into the store I ask, "And when is your and dad's anniversary thing?"

"We're celebrating on Sunday the sixteenth, Robby. For the hundredth time."

I want to say that it's really only the ninety ninth time, but think better of it.

Over in the young men's department Mom first picks out a white shirt. It looks extremely uncomfortable. She hands it to me and we walk over to where the suits are. There's a rack that turns that's full of them. She stops at a dark grey one. She takes it off the rack and inspects it. "Do you like this one?" she asks.

"Mom. I **really** don't care what kind of suit we buy."

Mom stops inspecting the suit and gives me a stern look. "Well for twelve dollars of your father's hard earned money, you better start caring young man." I scratch my neck. I don't respond. Mom goes back to turning the rack. She stops at a dark blue suit, takes it, inspects it, and says, "Let's try on these."

We walk over to the changing rooms and mom hands me the grey suit first. I walk in to the room, quickly change, and emerge saying that the suit is perfect and we can get going. But mom already has picked out another suit besides the blue one for me to try on. I see that any hope I had of getting out of here quickly and out to the Zone is squashed. So I try on all the suits and for each one Mom pulls at the arm of the jackets and tugs at the collar of the white shirt and pulls at the pant legs. The whole time I'm praying that nobody I know walks by and sees me getting dressed by my mommy. And when we're finished with all that, mom decides the best one is the grey one. The first one I tried on.

A new tie and a new pair of socks and a new belt accompany the suit and even though we're not buying them today, Mom walks over to the shoe department to look at the shoes. Since we're not buying them today, I politely ask Mom if I can go and look at the sneakers. I get my reprieve and walk to the sneaker section. And there they are. My Clydes. My beautiful Puma Clydes. I walk down the aisle. I pick up a box in my size. I'm mesmerized with the golden suede color and famous black Puma stripe. I can see them on my feet as I'm streaking down the court as the starting point guard for Lower Brook Middle School Golden Eagles. Mom's voice calling me breaks my reverie. I put the sneakers back.

• • •

On the way home mom drives over to the Shop Rite. She tells me she's only running in for a few things and for me to wait in the car, but I get out anyway and say I'll stay up front by the magazine racks. "Robby, if you're not there when I'm done, you'll walk the rest of the way home," mom threatens me.

"Fair enough," I say. As Mom walks away I yell out, "How 'bout some RC?" I want to say putting up with the suit thing merits it but that would be like me building my own stand and me tying my own noose and then asking for someone to give me a push. The magazine racks are right near the express checkout lanes so there's no chance of missing mom's return. I look around to see if the crazy old cigarette rancher is here but I don't see him. I pick up a magazine. *Teen Beat*. Today's stars show off tomorrow's fashions, the headline says. I turn to that section. I'm barely a few pages through when mom, true to her word, is already approaching the checkout lane. I see a 64oz RC soda bottle is in the cart. I get up and put the magazine back and wait at the end of the conveyor belt as mom puts the soda, a half-gallon of milk, two sticks of butter, a carton of eggs, a six pack of Fresca, three apples, and a loaf of bread on the belt. It starts to move my way. Carefully I bag the groceries, making sure the bread and eggs and apples will go on top. As I'm doing this I look down the checkout lanes. Is that…? My heart flutters. Is that who I think it is down at the other end of the checkout lanes? I put my head down and slowly turn and take another look. And again my heart flutters because I see that it is indeed her. Linda. Her hair is lighter, and shorter, and she's wearing a blue and white rugby shirt with cut-off jeans showing nicely tanned legs and a pair of flip-flops. I notice she's not wearing her thick, black framed glasses either. I must be taking too much time bagging the groceries and staring down to the end of the checkout lanes because mom's now next to me saying, "Robby, are you getting paid by the hour or something?"

I put the bread on top and pick up the bag and say, "That's the girl I won the science class project with."

Mom looks down to the end of the checkout lanes. "That girl?"

"Yeah," I say. "That's Linda Orken."

Mom nods her head. "She looks like a nice girl."

"She is," I say.

"Well, then why don't you be a nice young man and walk over and say hello?" she says to me. "Just be snappy about it."

As I start to walk Linda's way Mom takes the grocery bag from my hands. My heart is pounding. My legs feel like jelly. I'm nervous. What if Linda's putting something in the bag that's only for women when I get there? She's doesn't see me as I approach. I'm slightly behind her. I clear my throat. "Linda?" I say.

She quickly turns her head and when she sees that it's me she gives me a warm smile. "Robby," she says, "Hi."

She's definitely gotten prettier over the summer. "Ah…hi…I was…we were…" I robotically turn and point out my mom, "we were just checkin' out and I thought it was you."

"Well, it's me," Linda says. "Mom, this is the…my friend Robby from school. The one I won the science class contest with."

I smile at Linda's mom who smiles back at me in a not-too-overly-friendly way. I see that she has regular money in one hand and what looks like monopoly money in the other. I look back to Linda. "Well, I was surprised to see you so I really wanted to say hi," I say, heart still pounding. "I guess, I guess I'll see ya back in school."

Linda smiles at me and says it was nice to see me, too.

I'm quiet on the car ride home thinking about Linda. About how nice she looked. About how her lips now melted perfectly into her face. About how her hair now perfectly surrounded her face. About how nice she smelled. About the science class project when our hands and arms would touch or our legs would brush against each other. About how it felt when she grabbed and hugged me when we won. In the background, mom's warning me not to have another charade with my new suit like at Easter, but I'm thinking about Linda.

When we get home I carry the grocery bag into the kitchen and take a look at the clock. Its past two thirty and I had kind of forgotten about Dean and Bruce's Evil Knievel display, but I'm sure it's over now anyway. I start to take the groceries out of the bag when I see Tammy in the backyard with the Baharupa. They're sitting on the ground Indian style and facing each other and holding hands. And Baharupa looks like he's got another one of those home-made outfits on that come from the garbage can of necessary living. Mom is at the kitchen sink washing the apples. I've put everything on the kitchen table. As I'm folding the brown grocery bag the back door swings open and Tammy's jubilant face pops in and she looks at mom and exclaims, "Mom! Guess what! Baharupa's going to come to church with us for your anniversary! Isn't that great!" And just as quick Tammy's jubilant face disappears as the back door shuts.

I turn to mom who looks expressionless. "Tammy's goin' to church?" I ask.

Chapter Twenty One

Next day, Thursday morning, me, Tommy, and Brock are riding our bikes out to the Plaza. We want to see the marquee at the theatre. The billboard for the movie, our movie, should be up and the movie name should be on the big marquee since it opens tomorrow. As we make our way down the utility road heading toward the highway, I'm listening to what I missed out on yesterday. "It was just a mad dash, Bird-in-the-park." Tommy says.

"Dean damn near ran me over with his motorcycle gettin' the hell out of there," Brock adds. "Bruce too."

"How many cops were there?" I ask.

"Well just the one car," Brock says. "But who the hell was gonna wait for any more t'show up? Soon as we saw flashin' lights, we all took off."

"Ya had t'see it, Birdyboy," Tommy says. "Everyone scramblin' for their bikes, or just takin' off into the woods. Dean and Bruce were down the big trail quick as a flash."

"I think the cops were actually laughin' at us," Brock says. "But we weren't takin' no chances."

"Huh," I say. "So what happened before all that?" I ask.

"Now *that* ya had t'see," Tommy says. "Dean and Bruce had some launch thing set up and a bunch of beat up garbage cans they were jumpin' over."

"Ya had t'be there Birddog," Brock says. "One time Dean spread out all the cans, six of 'em, and started from the edge of the woods to pick up speed and hit the launch and cleared them all."

"Ya," Tommy says. "The back tire grazed the last can, making it wobble. His bike swerved this way and that way."

"He kept the bike up, though," Brock says.

"Should've been there, Birdbeak," Tommy says. "Should've been there," he says again as we pass the now silent Forbidden Zone.

When we get to the Plaza the movie, our movie, is now indeed spelled out on the marquee. **CARNAL KNOWLEDGE**. Me, Brock, and Tommy are sitting on our bikes underneath the marquee and staring up at the big letters like we're in a trance. We pedal over to the billboard. We read what it says. We look at the four faces on the poster. We can't really tell which girl is Ann Margaret because the names are all mixed up. "I think she's the one," I say, pointing to the girl to the right with auburn colored hair.

"Oh yeah? What makes you think so," Brock asks.

I look at the girl's face. "I don't know," I say. "I just think that's her."

"Guess we'll find out soon 'nuff," Tommy says, wearing a smirkish smile.

On our way back home we decide to stop off at the 7-Eleven. We check the phone booth coin slots for change but come up empty. I'm conserving money so I walk out of the store with only a small slurpee. Brock's got a cherry Italian ice and Tommy a Klondike. We're sitting on the curb by the phone booths wondering just when and for how long and how often Ann Margaret shows off her knockers during the movie. We're wondering how big they are. We're wondering if the girl I pointed out on the poster is actually her. We wonder until we're done eating what we bought and we hop back on our bikes. We ride to the light at Roosevelt Street and the highway. The light's red. As we're waiting to cross over, who other than Brother Davis pulls up to the light. He sees us and shouts out the open window to me, "Hey there lil' brother." I sort of nod but otherwise ignore him. "So how'd your pops make out with that trench line? Got approved and everything?" Again I nod, but continue to stare ahead. And then, Davis asks, "So how's your sis doin'?"

With that I turn and look at Brother Davis and just as the light turns green I say, "You didn't hear? She's gettin' married in a few weeks. Can you believe that? And to that Baharupa clown!" And with that I pedal away, following Tommy and Brock.

When I catch up to them Brock asks, "That's not true, is it? 'Bout your sis?"

"Nah," I say mischievously. "I just wanted to stir some things up there in Mr. Brother Davis' brain."

We stay on Roosevelt Street and as we get near the corner of Constitution Street we notice an old wooden canoe in somebody's front yard with a cardboard sign attached to it that says, **FREE**. Tommy skids to a halt. He looks at the canoe, then at me and Brock. "Whadda ya think there, guys?"

"'Bout the canoe?" I ask.

"No Birdbrain. About the Caddy in the driveway," Tommy says. "'Course about the canoe. Sign says it's free."

"Be cool t'have," Brock says. "But where can we keep it? I don't think my mom 'n dad would let me keep it at my house."

"Mine either," I say.

"I could probably keep it at my house. Or maybe we can stash it out in the big woods. Near the creek."

We all look at each other and silently nod that that sounds like a plan. So Tommy hops off his bike and walks to the front door and knocks. A woman about our mom's age answers the door and Brock and me watch and listen as Tommy asks if the canoe is indeed for free. The lady nods yes, it is. We listen as Tommy asks if there's anything wrong with it. The lady says there's nothing wrong with the canoe, they just don't use it anymore. So Tommy says that we'll take the canoe and the lady nods her head that that's okay but then warns Tommy that it's free to the first person who takes it away. So if we want it we better take it quick because somebody else had stopped in their car and was looking at it. So we take the free sign away. Then Brock comes up with a pretty ingenious idea on how to get the canoe over to Tommy's. So I'm left behind to guard the canoe while Tommy and Brock quickly pedal back to Tommy's house and drop off their bikes. Ten minutes later they come walking back. And what we do is I hold onto the front of my bike as Tommy and Brock lift the canoe up and rest as much of the front of it across the handlebars as possible. Then they gently set the rest down onto the seat. We slowly start making our way, me in front doing the steering and making sure the road is clear while Brock and Tommy walk on each side of the canoe balancing the rest. The only time we have any trouble is making the turns on to the streets. When we get to Tommy's house we bring the canoe to the backyard and lift it from the bike and put it near the old Impala in the carport.

"How we gonna get it to the creek?" I ask.

Tommy shrugs his shoulders and says, "Same way we got it here. Should be 'nuff room down the main path out to the creek. Whadda ya think, Brock?"

"Don't see why not. And maybe Mark can load it in his Camino and bring it to the end of Constitution Street. I'm sure we can find a good spot in the woods t'stash it."

"We should paint a cool design on 'er first, Tommy says, motioning to the front of the canoe. "Shark teeth or an Eagle or somethin' cool like that."

We all like the idea. Tommy's mom walks onto the back porch. "There you are," she says, looking at Tommy. "Hi boys," she says to me and Brock. Then she sees the canoe. "Where'd that come from?"

"Somebody was givin' it away. So we grabbed it," Tommy says.

"I'm not sure Dad will want it in the yard."

"Not keepin' it here," Tommy says. "We're gonna stash it out in the big woods. By the creek. Just gonna paint a cool design on 'er first."

Tommy's mom nods and says, "Are you boys staying for lunch?"

Brock and me both graciously decline.

. . .

I go home and have lunch and after I sit down on the couch to watch a little television. *That Girl* is on and it's a real stupid show but Marlo Thomas is gorgeous. As I watch I hear the phone ring. Mom picks it up and I hear her say I'm sure he'll be interested. Then I hear her say "I'll send him right over." She then walks out of the kitchen and says to me, "That was Mr. Lampman. He has a job for you if you want to earn a few dollars."

"Right now?"

"Well he didn't just call to say next week, Robby. Yes, right now."

"But my show just started."

Mom stares at me then says, "Okay Robby. I'll call Mr. Lampman back and tell him that you're not interested. And when your father gets home I'll let him know that you turned down work to watch television."

I stare at Mom for a few seconds. I huff and pull myself off the couch but I know she's right. I know I really don't need Dad hearing that I turned down work and I could definitely use the money. "Did he say what the job was?"

"Staining the back fence," Mom says. "That can't be too hard now."

Well those last six words from mom will ring in my ears for all eternity. Because when I get to Mr. Lampman's house and start staining the fence, it is exceptionally hard work. Extremely exceptional hard work. When I'm just halfway through my side of the fence my hands are sore from holding the brush and my shoulders and arms are tired from the constant motion. Plus my fingers and palms hurt because wood splinters jab into them as I have to wipe the fence down with a rag before I stain it to remove the debris and the imperfections. But Mrs. Lampman helps out some when she brings two cool glasses of iced tea with plenty of ice for me and Mr. Lampman and a few cookies to go along with the tea.

As we work Mr. Lampman asks me how my mom and dad are doing and I tell him fine and then he asks me about Tammy and I give him a sarcastic laugh and tell him about Tammy's spiritual stuff and the Baharupa. Mr. Lampman smiles and says in his day everyone was a flapper or a dandy. I don't ask.

I actually finish a half a section before Mr. Lampman and when we're both done we collect the empty cans and bring everything into the garage. As we're washing our hands and arms with Boraxo and turpentine, I notice Mr. Lampman has a can of stain still halfway full. I ask him if I can have it. I tell him about the old wooden canoe we found and the stain would make it look really cool. He taps the lid shut with a hammer and hands it to me. "You have a brush?"

"I'm sure my dad has some. Or Tommy's dad."

He nods and reaches into his pocket and hands me two dollars. "For a job well done," he says.

On the way home I stop at Tommy's. He's down in the basement searching through his dad's old paint cans. I show him the half-filled can of stain. I tell him we can stain the canoe with it.

"Where'd ya get that?" he asks.

"Mr. Lampman. I just helped him stain his fence and this was left over."

Tommy takes the can and swirls it. "How much is in here?"

"'Bout half."

"This'll work," he says.

And even though any more staining of any more wood structures is the last thing I want to do, me and Tommy grab two brushes and stain the canoe. When we're finished we stand back and look at our work. We're more than satisfied with the glistening shine emanating from our free canoe freely stained. So as soon as we get the stain off our hands we make plans to go up to Necci's and try their new root beer soda. It's served from a big silver barrel into a clear, thick mug and has just the slightest taste of vanilla to it. It's only ten cents per glass and goes really well with a Hostess apple pie.

So ten minutes later we're pedaling into Necci's parking lot. There's two cars parked in front of the store and one of them is a Lower Brook police car. We leave our bikes against the side of the building and walk up the ramp. The door is open and the big fan is on. We walk in and head straight for the silver barrel. Today Mr. Necci is behind the counter handing the cop in the store a cup of coffee. The cop turns and nods mine and Tommy's way when he sees us. I read the name on the badge. Jankowski, it says. Tommy and me take two mugs from a table near the silver barrel as the cop reaches into his pocket to pay. Mr. Necci holds up a hand to stop him. "Thank you," Mr. Jankowski the Lower Brook cop says, and then adds, "and don't worry Sal. You won't be seeing those two riding around these streets any longer. Their latest stunt was their last."

Tommy and me look at each other but keep quiet as we fill up our mugs with root beer.

Later, just after supper, I decide to ride over to Dean's and warn him about what I heard earlier at Necci's. So I hop on my bike and head over to Dean's house. I look very carefully as I approach Harding Street and don't see anyone lurking so I ride up Dean's driveway. The front door is closed and it looks like no one's home but I walk up to the door and knock anyway. I wait a few seconds, knock again, sense there's no one's home, and turn to leave.

When I do, instantly, my heart races. Standing next to my bike is Luther Cobalt. "Who ya lookin' for there, Birdcrap?"

Trying to keep my composure, walking timidly toward my bike, "Ah, Dean," I say. "I…I had, have, somethin' pretty important t'tell 'em," as I grab hold of my handlebars.

"Well, he ain't here," Luther says, holding on to the frame of my bike. "And, well, you 'n me, we have a lil' score t'settle," Luther says sinisterly.

I start to say that no we don't but Luther lunges at me and I take a quick step backward, letting go of my bike in the process, where Luther's feet then get all tangled up and he falls violently forward. I watch as my handlebars jam right into Luther's side and I hear his head hit the driveway in a resounding thud. Luther grimaces in pain and I already see a welt with some blood trickling down Luther's head as he rolls over. He tries to get up but he wobbles back down and finally just sits there, holding his head. I grab my bike and hop on. I look down at Luther. "You alright, Luther?"

From his prone position Luther nods he's okay. I pedal away. Quickly.

Chapter Twenty Two

I'm sitting in my room mid-Monday morning with my door half open listening to some records and counting the money in my Sucrets can. I just added another dollar from my allowance and I'm now only eight dollars away from my goal. I hear the phone ringing. I hear Tammy answer it and I hear her say, "Sorry, nobody here by that name." A pause. "Nope, no Robby cuts lawns from this number, sorry," she says and hangs up the phone.

I almost fall off my chair dashing out of my room and into the kitchen. I pick the phone up. "Hello! Hello! Hello!" Dead silence. I slam it down. "That's just great!" I wail out. "That was somebody who needed yard work, wasn't it?" I seethe out. "I really need…."

Before I can finish Tammy, with as much venom as I delivered, snarls back, "Serves you right, you little twerp. What the hell are you doing telling Martin I'm getting married! What's the hell wrong with you!"

"Hey, if your stupid boyfriend…."

"Ex-boyfriend!"

"I don't care who…." The phone rings. I look at it and then glare at Tammy.

"If that's Baharupa and you…."

I tepidly pick up the phone, ready to slam it back down…if needed. "Hello," I say. I sneer at Tammy. "Yes, this is Robby. No, yes, you have the right number."

It's Mrs. Hill from the old neighborhood asking if I can work in her yard today. I tell her sure. As I make the arrangements Tammy is standing right by the phone, smirking at me the whole time. When I hang up the phone I say, "Boy were you lucky."

"Yeah, sure, twerp."

I walk back in my room and turn off my record player. Mom appears at my door and asks what all the yelling was about. I tell mom how Mrs. Hill just called and needed yard work done and Tammy told her that I didn't live here. "That lady from across the highway?" Mom asks.

How does Mom always arrive at the wrong conclusion? "Yeah, but that's not the point."

"I thought we were supposed to discuss this with your father first?"

Oh my God. I have to stop this line of questioning and quick. "We did discuss it, that day, the first time," I say matter-of-factly.

"I don't remember Dad saying he was all right with anything," Mom says. "In fact, I remember his telling you to abide by my decision."

With as much of a controlled frustrated huff as I can muster, I say, "Fine. I'll just call Dad at work and get his approval." I start to walk toward the kitchen and the phone.

"Don't you dare bother your father at work over this," mom warns me. I stop and turn and stare at mom. She stares back for a few seconds and says, "Okay, Robby. Go ahead. But you best be careful crossing that highway."

"Mom," I say with a sense of relief, and victory. "I will. It's no big deal."

A half hour later I'm standing on the sidewalk in front of Mrs. Hill's house. As I scan the yard I can see that it does need some work. Grass has built up in some areas and in other areas it has wilted and died. So a good cutting will make it look at least even. The vines are once again crawling up the cement foundation and the shrubs by the picture window are also in need of a trimming. I leave my mower and rake and shears and broom and green bag on the sidewalk and stroll up the driveway. I knock on the door and Mrs. Hill answers and smiles and invites me in and thanks me for showing up on such short notice. She tells me that her grandson had taken care of the yard the last few times it needed work, but he's not available this time. Then she asks, "Is it still two dollars?"

"As long as you think that's fair," I say.

"Of course I think it's fair," Mrs. Hill says. She has her purse on a night table and she reaches for it and opens it and takes two dollars out. She hands it to me.

I put my hands up. "Not until the job's done and you're happy," I say. "Remember?"

"Nonsense," she says. "You're a hard worker," she adds, the money still extended my way.

Reluctantly I take the money and put it in my pocket. "You let me know, though, if you're not happy with something."

Mrs. Hill nods and I get to work.

I start with picking up any branches or twigs. Then I and run the mower over the entire yard. Even in the dead spots. When I'm done I rake the clippings up and put them into my green bag. I drag the bag over to where the vines are crawling up the foundation and cut them down and put them in the green bag. Then it's over to the shrubbery and I trim down the hedges and put all those clippings into the green bag. I sweep off the walkway and the driveway and leave everything once again on the sidewalk and I knock on the door. I tell Mrs. Hill that I'm all done and for her to take a look. Without stepping out of the house she looks around the yard and says it's a fine job and she invites me in for a glass of lemon water and the famous oatmeal cookies.

I sit at the kitchen table with two oatmeal cookies on a plate and a glass of lemon water setting before me. Mrs. Hill asks me how my summer is going and if I'm looking forward to school. I tell her that the summer's been good and no, I'm not looking forward to school. When I'm finished with the cookies and the lemon water I thank Mrs. Hill and stand up to leave. As we walk into the parlor and toward the front door, it opens and in walks Edgar. He sees me and smiles and says, "Hello, again, young man. I thought that was your stuff out there."

"Yes, it's my things," I say.

"Looks like you did another fine job," he says, standing by the door and looking out over the front yard.

I acknowledge the compliment as I head for the door.

"Oh dear," Mrs. Hill exclaims, "I forgot to pay you," she says, reaching for her purse still on the night table.

I stop where I am and look quizzically first at Mrs. Hill then at Edgar. "No you didn't," I say, reaching into my pocket and revealing the two dollars that she gave when I first got here. "Remember? You paid me first."

Mrs. Hill looks at the money and then at Edgar and I can see her mind racing and after a few seconds she sort of gives up. "Well, I guess I must have," she says.

I put the money back in my pocket. "Thank you," Edgar says, lightly slapping my back on my way out the door.

"Yes, thank you," Mrs. Hill says.

When I get home I put the two dollars into the tin can. It's at sixteen dollars now. I'm getting really close.

Next day I follow Tommy and Brock out to the big woods where they stashed the canoe. Tommy tells me he painted a real cool design of shark's teeth on one side of the canoe and Brock said he painted a setting sun on the other. They say they took it out and went south in the creek and found out it goes for about a mile or so then the creek splits in two. Another mile or so they said they came to a dead end near Jepson's Marina. So we're riding our bikes down Constitution Street and then down the big path as far as we can go and then jump off our bikes and leave them when the path becomes just a reed wide and the underbrush gets too thick to ride through. "You guys got the canoe out to here?" I ask. "How?" I say, high stepping over some of the underbrush.

"Well Mark brought it to the woods line in his Camino," Brock says. "We took it from there. Wasn't so bad."

"We came over t'get ya," Tommy says. "But your mom said you were cuttin' someone's lawn."

"Yeah, I was," I say. "Mrs. Hill's yard in the old neighborhood."

We continue to walk on and the trees are thinning out and then all of a sudden Brock darts to a thick clump of underbrush and pulls it away and turns with a haunted face and says, "What the...."

Tommy, eyes narrowing, slows his walk to a still-framed picture of angst.

"What?" I ask.

"It's gone," Tommy says almost in silence.

"The canoe?" I gasp.

Tommy looks at me as if I took the canoe. "You see any canoe there," he seethes.

No, I guess I don't. Well, that was short lived, I think.

Sunday morning. The morning of the day of Mom and Dad's twentieth anniversary celebration. I wake up and look over at the clock on my desk. A little after eight, it reads. I lay for a few minutes and let the cobwebs dissipate. Through my closed door I hear the low din of Tammy's and mom's voices coming down the hallway. I can smell percolated coffee and toast. I get up and slumber over to my window and look out. An ocean blue sky with white puffy clouds. And it's not as hot as it's been. All good signs for having to wear a suit and tie for much of the day.

I walk out of my room and across the hallway and into the kitchen. Tammy's sitting in her place and is already dressed in a long white dress with short sleeves and blue trim around the edges. There's baby's breath and colorful beads woven throughout her hair. Dad's in his Sunday suit and reading the Sunday paper and Mom has a new dress on sitting between Tammy and Dad, sipping on her coffee. I plop down in my chair. I reach for the orange juice and grab a piece of toast.

"I thought I was going to have to wake you," Mom says.

I shrug my shoulders and chew on the toast but otherwise have no response. I'm expecting some remark from Tammy about my hair or my pajamas or whatever else but instead she turns to mom and says, "Twenty years, guys. Wow." She shakes her head in disbelief. "Twenty years," she repeats.

Mom looks over to Dad and mimics Tammy. "Twenty years, Bob. Where'd they all go?"

Dad looks up from his paper. "Right here, Nan," he says, shaking his head, looking around the table. "Right here."

Mom finishes her coffee and says, "Hey Tam. Can you fix my hair up with some baby's breath?"

Tammy nods and pushes her cup away and says, "Sure. I still have some. I might even have a barrette to match your dress."

Tammy and Mom get up from the table and Mom looks at the plates and the glasses and the cups. "We got it, Nan," Dad says. Then he looks my way. "Don't we, Robby?"

I know what that tone means. I remain silent.

Actually there's not many dishes to do and when dad and me are done I go to my room and start getting dressed. Everything with my new suit is okay except for the new white shirt. It's got that annoying rigid new shirt feel to it. The tie Mom bought is a real one so Dad already has the knot tied. All I have to do is tighten it. But not too tight. As I'm straightening the tie, looking in the mirror that's on the back of my bedroom door, behind me I see something that looks like the van from the *Partridge Family* pull up in front of the house. And who else emerges from that van but the Baharupa himself, Karl Maier. And maybe I'm wrong, but it looks like he's wearing a bed sheet. Whatever it is its light blue in color and wrapped around him and tied at the center with a colorful scarf. He's got some crazy beads around his neck and a red shawl around his shoulders. He's wearing sandals that look like something the Romans I studied back in school would wear. And there's a thin braided piece of rope keeping the hair off his face. I quickly finish the tie. When dad gets a first look at this, that I gotta see.

When I get to the parlor dad has already opened the door and in walks the Baharupa. They exchange hellos and to dad's credit he doesn't show any signs of bewilderment. Baharupa sees me and says, "Good morning, Robby. How are we today?"

"Me? I'm fine," I say, thinking I'm not the one standing here dressed like I just got tumbled out of a dryer. "How are you?" I ask with that same thought on my tongue.

"I'm very well," Baharupa says. He turns to dad, "So, Mr. Birdsall. This is the big day," he says in a calm demeanor. "Tammy told me it's been twenty years for you and the Mrs. Many congratulations."

"Thank you," Dad says, still amazingly stoic.

There's a few seconds of eerie silence, then I break the ice. "Dad, uh." I say, stop, scratch my head, and continue. "Is he, are they…is he allowed to walk into church dressed like that?"

Now dad looks bewildered and he shoves his hands in his pockets and shrugs his shoulders and doesn't say anything. Then the Baharupa throws his head back and laughs and says, "I'm quite sure, Robby, that the church will hold no objections…to my clothing. The congregation? Well, that's another matter."

I don't even know what that means and before I can even begin to figure it out Tammy and mom come waltzing into the parlor. Tammy, wearing what looks like ballerina slippers seems to float on a cloud as she walks over to Baharupa. She slips her arm into his. With her long white dress and colorful hair, she and the Baharupa actually blend together. They both look at Mom and Dad and then Baharupa says, "*May your fountain be blessed, and may you rejoice in the wife of your youth. A loving doe-a graceful deer-may her breasts satisfy you always-may you ever be captivated by her love.* That's from the book of Proverbs," Baharupa says.

I stare at the Baharupa in frozen fascination. Did he just say breasts in front of Mom?

. . .

We all pile into the car and I get the misfortune of having Baharupa sit next to me. And by the smell of things, I'm really believing what the Baharupa's has said: He certainly seems to be living off the land. When we pull into the church parking lot, I see Pastor Mark's wishes of seeing more faces on Sundays has fallen on deaf ears. The lot is only half full. We park and get out of the car and I'm a fifth wheel in this walking caravan of love, trailing behind Mom and Dad who are holding hands as they walk into church, and behind Tammy and Baharupa who are arm-in-arm.

Once in the church we walk to our pew and I see some of the reactions of the congregation as Baharupa and Tammy walk by. I know that look. A person or two remembers Tammy and they say hello as she passes. Dad then Mom slide into our pew and I make sure that Tammy and Baharupa slide in next. That puts me two bodies away from the long arm of the law. I need that distance because when I get the chance, I'm gonna slip downstairs and see what's going on with Fig and Joni and that Sunday school thing with the kids.

I'm scanning the pews and the organist is playing and before I know it Pastor Mark and the lay leader are strolling down the center aisle. Pastor Mark is looking at the people sitting in the pews as he passes and smiling and when he passes us he sees Tammy and gives her a nod and a smile. As he walks on by I'm thinking Pastor Mark has to gives us Birdsall's some credit. We may not come here often, but when we do, we bring some of the real thing.

I sit quietly during the announcements and the call to worship and the opening hymn and the first prayer and the opening passage and the second hymn. It's when Pastor Mark's long sermon begins when I make my move. I lean forward and mouth to mom that I need to use the men's room. With pursed lips she tells me to wait but I act like its urgent and she sternly mouths two minutes, holding up two fingers. I nod with acquiescence. I can easily turn two minutes into four.

I'm down the center aisle as fast as I can be and out the chapel door. I then race down the hallway and bound the steps leading to the downstairs rooms two at a time. The classrooms on both sides of the hallway and daylight streams through the windows at the end of the hall. There's three rooms on each side and I find Fig and Joni in the last one to my right. I peer through the small window on the door. All the kids are sitting in a circle with Fig and Joni sitting in the center and Fig's got some kind of lion's mask on. Joni's dressed like a Sheppard. She's holding Fig's hand and pretending to pull something out of it, to Fig's great relief. Then she's wiping pretend tears from Fig's lion face and she gently kisses Fig's hand and wraps it in a bandage. Then she turns to the kids and says something. If that was my hand, I'm thinking, Joni would have just as well chopped it off.

I get back to the service and I know I wasn't gone all that long because I don't get any looks from mom. And there's still a good portion of Pastor Mark's sermon yet to endure. He goes on and on about something and then finally I hear Pastor Mark say, "Glory be to God." That's the cue. The ushers move forward and everybody stands up and sings whatever that song is we sing at the end of every service. *Praise God from all who blessings flow, praise Him*....and then rest of it and then it's over. Standing in line to greet Pastor Mark, I'm searching through the church for Fig. There's no sign of him. We gather together as we greet pastor Mark who tells us it was wonderful to see the family again and he shakes Baharupa's hand and says he was happy he could join today's service. Then we're out the chapel doors and I see Fig standing near the entrance of the rec room with Joni. We nod to each other. I motion that I'm gonna give him a call. And even though I'm here in church, Joni still sneers at me.

Unlike Easter, we don't stay for the breakfast after the service. We pile back into the car and head over to the Silver Stream Diner for brunch. Once there, I have a plate of French toast with the white powdered sugar and I take one of those pre-packaged maple syrup containers sitting on the table for dipping. Two pieces of bacon accompany the French toast and a side dish of home fries that are burnt just right around the edges. A small dish of vanilla ice cream with crushed graham crackers on top and a large glass of chocolate milk finishes my order. Mom and Dad both have an omelet with vegetables and ham stuffed inside and fruit cups. Coffee and orange juice, like always. Tammy and the Baharupa both order eggs but without the yolks, which to me erases the reason to eat an egg. They ask to have any kind of green vegetable off to the side and rye bread, unbuttered, if they have that. They have no meat at all and two cups of chamomile tea. I find it terribly hard to understand that that's what they *chose* to eat, given their options.

I'm eating and half listening as Baharupa tells Dad that he goes to a two year college upstate and next spring he'll have his Associate's Degree.

"Can you matriculate all those credits to a four year school?" I hear Dad ask, not knowing at all what that means.

"Yes, Mr. Birdsall," Baharupa says, "I can. Because it's a two year state county college, as long as I get my degree, I can transfer anywhere." Baharupa smiles, then adds, "Well, anywhere that will have me."

That'll be a major stumbling block, I think, dipping my French toast into the maple syrup.

"But I'm thinking on spending a year in the Peace Corp first."

"The Peace Corp," Mom says in a tone as to why would anyone want to do that. "Why the Peace Corp?"

"Well, Mrs. Birdsall, I truly believe it would enhance, even balance the thesis I'm working on."

There's that word again.

"It would give me a better…a truer, reasoning as to what necessary living is. Seeing it, for real. What the *need* is and *where* the need is, and not just the waste."

Mom nods.

"So, Karl," I interrupt. "What made ya," I look and motion at his clothing, "ya know."

Baharupa looks straight at me and says, "What Robby? Think this way?" he asks. I nod that that's close enough. "Well, believe this or not Robby. A bird."

"A bird?" I ask in a jaw-dropping demeanor. "Like, a real bird? With feathers and a beak?"

"Yes," Baharupa says. "A real bird. With feathers and a beak."

So for the next few minutes I listen as the Baharupa tells everyone how he was raised in a devout Lutheran home. His family were weekly church goers, still are. So he believed, still believes, in a God and Jesus. But then one day, one miraculous day, when he was sixteen and walking down his street toward home, this bird started to follow him. Came right out of the bushes and started hopping right along with him. If he stopped, the bird stopped. When he got home he walked in the house and turn and looked out the front door as the bird stood and waited on the front steps. So he walked back out onto the steps and the bird jumped up and perched itself right on his shoulder. He says he looked at the bird who then lightly pecked him on the cheek, and then flew away. No one was there to see it, he says, but it happened. Then Baharupa looks squarely at me again and says, "So, since that day, my thoughts really started to evolve, Robby. Toward reincarnation. Toward yes, a God. But more than one God. I guess…I guess I found things, find things, too complex for the singularity of the Lutheran…Christian mind. Or the Jewish mind. Or the Muslim mind."

"Huh," is all I have to say. I'm sorry I asked.

. . .

When brunch ends it's over to Heron Pond Park for anniversary pictures. And I do mean anniversary pictures. Pictures of Mom. Pictures of Dad. Pictures of Mom and Dad. Pictures of me. Pictures of Tammy. Pictures of me and Tammy. Pictures of Tammy and the Baharupa. Pictures of me and the Baharupa. Pictures of me, Tammy, Mom, and Dad. And finally, as a complete stranger holds Dad's camera, a picture of everyone.

Chapter Twenty Three

Wednesday next week and it's the big day. The day we're going to see Ann Margaret bare everything on the big screen. We were going to give it one more week but something happened, or is going to happen, that we never took into consideration. And that's the movie we're telling everyone we're going to see. For the past few weeks it's been *Escape from the Planet of the Apes*, which, considering how everyone knows how much I liked the first two *Planet of the Apes* movies, I would definitely want to see this one. But come Friday the movie is changing to *Bedknobs and Broomsticks*, which, apparently, is some kid's musical. So Wednesday is the day, first show, when everyone can get together. So this is our plan.

The movie we're telling our parents that we're going to starts at 6:35. *Our* movie starts at 7:05. So we're all gonna be at the Plaza by quarter after six, if not before. The box office opens at 6:20 and we know we have to be first in line. Once we have the tickets its straight to the theatre, a quick look to make sure we're alone, and behind the screen and to the trap door and down. We say we're gonna ride our bikes there and we cover our tracks on the return trip because Mark's agreed to go along with us telling our parents he's going to pick us up and throw our bikes in the back of his Camino.

So right after supper Tommy and Brock are knocking on my front door. I go to my room and get the money for the ticket. A full week's allowance. Through my open bedroom window I hear Brock, standing on the front porch, flawlessly and convincingly affirming to mom that yes, his brother's gonna pick us up when the movie ends. A few seconds later I'm at the front door. I leave with wishes for safety and a good time.

Me, Tommy, and Brock pedal out to the Plaza in record time. We ride over to the theatre and find Fig already there looking at the billboard to the movie. We lock up our bikes and walk over. We say our greetings. "So which one is she?" Fig asks

I point to the girl to the right and say, "I think it's her."

Fig takes a step back from the billboard. Looks at the girl. "Why do you think it's her?"

"I don't know," I say. "I just do."

"I think Birdfeathers here might be right," Brock says. "She looks like she wants us to see her knockers. Which one do you think it is, Horsehead?"

"Either one's good for me," Tommy says.

We go over the plan once more. Brock reminds us to be careful and not to crash into anything. He reminds us to be careful when we get to the concession storage area. He says Mark says that workers pop down there at any time. He reminds us that....the box office lights suddenly flicker and then turn on. All at once we dash over, throwing our money down on the booth.

"Whoa!" the lady who's always behind the booth with the perpetual cigarette dangling from her mouth says. "You kids act like you're breakin' into the joint!" She separates and counts the money. She slides it off the booth and into the register and produces four tickets. We each grab one and dash toward the entrance.

With the first hurdle cleared we scurry into the theatre and head for the corridor that's playing *Return to the Planet of the Apes*. There's a kid by the doors about Mark's age sitting on a stool who takes our tickets, rips them in half, hands us half, and tells us to enjoy the show. Once in the theatre we head down the center aisle, scoping everything out to make sure no one's here. It's a clear coast. We bound up the steps leading to the screen. My heart's pounding. We're quickly behind the giant screen. There's a rug on the floor and we slide it away and there's the trap door. A brief second of excitement and congratulations. Brock opens the door and we look down and we see stairs and darkness. Brock gives us a giant grin and hands the door to Tommy and down he goes. As soon as Brock clears the stairs Tommy hands me the door and down the steps he hustles. I hand the door to Fig and just before I can take another step a back door opens and a rush of air and the smell of cigarette smoke fills the stage. Then, we hear, "Hey! What the hell are you kids doin'!" Me and Fig freeze. The person storms over. We gaze up. Harry, the nametag on his blue Twin Theaters blazer reads. "You kid's ain't supposed t'be up here," he growls at us.

Fig's still got the trap door in his hand. We both look down into the dark basement. Brock and Tommy are gone. Finally, I stammer out, "Ah…we…we was just lookin' 'round before the movie starts."

"Yeah, well," Harry says, taking the door and slamming it shut. "Take a look around for a seat. There's plenty of 'em." He kicks the rug back over the trap door. Fig and I walk back toward the seats. Harry walks behind us and then starts folding the seats up in the aisles. A few people have entered the theatre and Fig and me go and grab two center seats. We look at each other. "Well," I say to Fig in a disappointed voice, "at least we get to see *a* movie." Fig nods, also with disappointment. Then, a few minutes later, Brock and Tommy are rejoining me and Fig. Turns out Mark's underground stairwell door leads to the back alley, locked from the outside.

. . .

Summer wanes quickly. Already and unbelievably, school schedules arrive with Monday's mail. I take the perforated letter that says my name and Mr. and Mrs. Birdsall or guardian on it and toss the rest of the mail onto the kitchen table. I sit down and carefully bend and tear around the edges and pull out my 1971-72, and last, Lower Brook Middle School schedule. I read what it says. Math is first again but not with the Ol' Kazoo. I have Mr. Sellers who I've never had but hear is a lot easier than old iron grip. Oh my God. English is next and again with the Witch. Again! You've got to be kidding me! The Witch! Again? Science is third and I'm sorry to see I don't have Mr. Molnar this year but Mr. Foley, who I don't know other than seeing him in the hallway outside his door. He seems nice. Social Studies is fourth with Mr. Napier instead of Kilcommins and History is fifth with Mr. Kennedy. I'm going to miss looking at Mrs. Stanton. Lunch is next and then some class I've never heard of: Study Skills with some lady I never heard of, a Mrs. Abernathy. What the heck is a study skills class? Then lunch, and maybe a fitting finish to all this is, drumroll please, gym class, my very last class and not with Goddard this year but with Mr. Lowry. So I will not ever have to relive the great Lower Brook Middle School stink bomb incident of spring 1971.

I get up from the table and start to head out the door to see if Tommy got his schedule yet. Before I reach the door I'm startled with, "Robby. Where do you think you're going?"

I turn and look and find mom just outside the porch room door. "Jus' over to Tommy's. To compare schedules," I say, holding up my new school schedule.

"And didn't dad ask you to trim the bushes on the side of the house, along with taking out all the garbage that's still sitting around the house, by-the-way?"

"I'll get to it," I say.

"Yes, Robby, you will, Right now. You want your allowance later this week, don't you?"

A loaded question if ever I heard one. Either way I answer I'm defeated. And I do need my allowance. So I say nothing. I walk to my room and leave my schedule on my desk. I gather and take out all the garbage, putting it into the silver can. Then I walk out to the garage and get the shears.

I start with the lilac bush. Some of the stems have grown so tall that I have to pull them down to me to cut them. When I'm done with the lilac bush I continue with the bushes that I don't know what they're called but they sort of look like Christmas trees. There's two of them right next to each other. I start clipping and when I'm between the two trees I hear a car pull into the driveway. I peek out and see it's the van that dropped the Baharupa off for Mom and Dad's anniversary, still idling behind Tammy's car. From my angle I can't see who is driving but when I hear the sliding door open I do see Tammy and the Baharupa emerge. As they walk my way I can see Tammy's upset. They disappear from my view but I can still hear them.

"You'll forget all about me," Tammy whimpers.

"My Sona," Baharupa says, "that would be impossible. This summer, *our* summer, that can't be erased. And could never be forgotten."

"Oh, you'll forgot about me soon enough," Tammy says. "You'll be earning your degree and I'll just be the high school girl left behind."

"My Sona," Baharupa says. "You have to be kidding me. Like a piece of time I'll carry you. Always. And besides, this isn't good-bye for forever. Just for now."

"I know, I know," Tammy sniffles out. "But, I just, I wish, I hope…."

I hear Baharupa shush Tammy. "My Sona," he says. "Hope and tomorrow. Two of the most beautiful words in the English language. In any language."

"I'll miss you," Tammy says.

"And I you," Baharupa says.

It's quiet for a minute or two and then I hear Tammy and Baharupa walking back to the van. I peek out from between the bushes. I watch as they embrace. Then Baharupa opens the passenger door and steps into the van. Leaning out the open front window he grabs Tammy's face and kisses her and their hands clasp. They hold onto each other for a few seconds, then they let go. The van starts to back out of the driveway. Once in the street Tammy dashes to the van and she and the Baharupa kiss once more and as the van starts down the street, Tammy stands in the middle of the road watching it disappear. She stands there for a few minutes, then walks up the driveway with her arms crossed in front of her body. And she's crying. Really crying.

When I hear the front door open and shut I walk around into the front yard and see Tammy through the picture window. She nearly collapses into mom's arms. I watch as mom says something to Tammy and Tammy shakes her head no and mom says something else and again Tammy shakes her head no. Then mom hugs Tammy really tight and whispers something into her ear and Tammy finally shakes her head yes and mom lets go and Tammy, head in hands, walks out of the parlor. I walk back to the side of the house and start clipping again and a few minutes later, Tammy comes out of the house. I stop clipping and watch as she gets into her car with her blue work shirt on. Her eyes are red and welled up. She starts the car and slowly backs out of the driveway.

Later in the day, I catch up with Tommy and compare schedules. We don't have any classes together this year. He says he thinks Brock's in my history class. We take a ride up to the Krauszer's. When we glide into the parking lot there's Dean Magnumson, on a bicycle. I can't remember ever seeing Dean on a bicycle. He's sitting on his bike and leaning against the wall. He sees us. "Birdman, Hulse," he says.

"Hey Dean, what's up," I say.

"Grounded a while," Dean says.

"Yeah. We know," I say.

Dean looks strangely at me. "How do you guys know?"

"I was in Necci's when I heard some cop talk to Mr. Necci. He said the stunt out in the zone was the end of the road. I think it was Thursday, maybe Friday, a week ago. Jankowski is the cop's name," I say. "I rode over to your house to warn ya, but no one was home."

Dean scratches his neck, thinks. "Yeah, it was Friday when I got de-wheeled," he says.

"Helluva way to go out though," Tommy says.

"Yeah, I'm sorry I missed it," I say. "I had a job that day."

"Yeah, was real cool." Dean looks at me. "Jankowski, huh?" he says.

"Yeah," I say, "I read his name tag."

Early evening, a little after supper time, Tammy gets home from work. I'm in the parlor and she doesn't look as distressed as she did earlier, but I can see she's still sad. Mom saved her a plate and sits with her in the kitchen for a few minutes. Dad, who was reading his newspaper there, exits to the porch. Then Debbie Hutton shows up. Tammy finishes eating and they disappear into Tammy's room, where music soon after seeps through her closed door. After a little while Tammy and Debbie walk into the parlor and they embrace and Tammy says thank you and Debbie walks out the front door. Then Tammy looks at me and the television and says, "Is anybody watching this?"

I look around and I guess I'm anybody since I'm the only one in the room. "Well, not at the moment," I say. "But the *Mod Squad* comes on in a half hour."

Tammy walks to the television and changes the channel and then curls herself up in a corner of the couch. A minute later the television says, *"From the dating capital of the world, in color, this is The Dating Game."* And so for the next half hour I sit on the parlor floor and watch and listen as this pretty blonde girl from Pensacola, Florida asks the three possible dates hidden behind partitioned walls a bunch of questions. And in the end when the girl picks bachelor number one I'm surprised because I thought she'd pick bachelor number three. When the show ends Tammy gets up from the couch and returns to her room, music again softly seeping through her closed door.

Chapter Twenty Four

I found out some good news and some disturbing, no, some very disturbing news this morning: Tup's in my second period English class this year, but so is Joni Iachello. I came by that information from Tupperware when he called and we compared our class schedules. So this year I got Brock in my history class, and Tup in my English class, along with Joni, and oddly Fig and I have the same lunch period again. Thinking about and doing all this schedule comparing has got me to wondering if I'm going to have Linda in any of my classes. And that gets me to thinking about what my cousin Gene said to me way back when, when I told him all about Linda and the science class project and everything, when he suggested about me calling Linda up. So I take the phone book out from the night table drawer and turn to the O section. I find Orken. There's four of them but only three with my exchange number. There's an Alan and Loretta Orken on 32 Newport Road. There's a Frank and Dorothy Orken that has an address of 751 Route 43W. I could be wrong but think that's a house over in bungalow alley. And there's a Stephen and Sandra Orken on 18 Mistview Lane. I not sure where Mistview Lane is so I look it up on the map at the back of the phone book. It's off of Jordan Road just past all the marsh. I'm pretty sure that couldn't be where Linda lives because those houses are pretty large and fancy. So I sit down at the kitchen table and dial the Newport Road number and a lady answers and my heart pounds and I forget how to talk so I quickly hang up the phone. I dial the number from the house on the highway, but there's no answer. I dial the Mistview Lane number and even though I don't act as panic-stricken when another lady answers the phone, I still hang up the phone without uttering a word. So, I go to plan B. So sort of like just running into Linda at the Shop Rite like I did that day, I figure if I ride my bike over to these addresses, then maybe I'll be able to innocently bump into Linda again.

The house on Newport Road and the house along the highway are about the same distance from my house, just in opposite directions. So I choose to ride over to the one on the highway first. And it does turn out to be one of the houses in bungalow alley, and not very far from the corner of Old Branch Road and the highway. But when I get to 751 the house looks deserted. There's no car in the driveway and a few of those free papers are lying around on the front lawn and look as if they've been there a while. And even though it's early afternoon, the blinds are drawn closed in all the windows and the front door is shut. The only sign of life is a full garbage can at the end of the driveway and junk mail in the paper box. So I ride to the next house.

Newport Road is off of Midstream Road and not too far down after crossing over the highway from Roosevelt Street. I ride there next. When I get there, unlike the near abandoned house along Route 43, this house is occupied. But just not with Linda. I'm sure of that because there's a lady out by the mail box as I'm passing by getting the mail, and it is not the same lady I saw at the Shop Rite with Linda. So that leaves the house on Mistview Lane.

I pedal back down Midstreams Road and then along the highway, passing my neighborhood in the process. Jordan Road is about a mile further down. I get there and turn and as I'm pedaling along there's nothing but woods on my right and marsh land on my left. Then there's a spattering of normal sized houses on my right and on my left the larger houses start to come into view. I can see some of the bulkheads in the backyards and I'm questioning myself as to why I'm even coming out here. These people are rich. There's no way Linda lives here. I'm about to just turn around as I'm nearing the end of the marshes when I come to a screeching halt. I look across the marsh and there resting against a little island of small trees is our canoe. At least I think it's our canoe. There's shark's teeth painted on the side of the canoe that I can see. So I turn onto Mistview Lane to find out if I can see the other side of the canoe.

I'm looking between the houses that are sometimes three stories high, keeping my eyes peeled to the lagoon in the backyards and glimpses of the canoe. All the front yards are twice as large as any in my neighborhood and almost all of the driveways look as if they been shellacked. And almost all have fancy and expensive cars parked in them. I pass house 18 and the mailbox says S & S Orken and there's a man about Dad's age on a small tractor cutting the front lawn. So just on a whim I stop and ask the man if Linda's home.

He stops the tractor and idles the engine. "What was that young man?"

"Oh, I was just wondering if Linda Orken lives here."

"No," the man says. "You must have the wrong house."

I nod but don't respond. I knew it was the wrong house.

I ride further down the block. I'm getting near the end of the road. At the next to the last house I hop off my bike. I walk on the grass median that separates two large homes. I think I'll be able to see the other side of the canoe from here. Once in the backyard it's a scene right out of *Better Homes and Gardens*. A picturesque yard with statues and a screen house and patio with nice patio furniture and a grill built right into the patio area. From every yard there's small docks that stretch out into the lagoon with small motor boats and sail boats and kayaks moored to them. I have to walk a little bit out onto the dock to see the other side of the canoe, but when I do, I see that indeed there's a setting sun painted on the other side. "Huh," I say to myself. Then I'm startled.

"Can I help you, young man?" a lady's voice says to me. "I'm sorry to tell you you're on private property."

I turn and see it's a lady between Mom's and Grandma's age with muddy work gloves on and a small trough in one hand. She's wearing one of those floppy beach hats. Not liking the tone of her voice, I say, "Ah, maybe. I'm lookin' for my dog. A lil' brown runty mutt," showing with my hands the size of the made up dog. "Answers to the name Ralph," I add.

"No, I haven't," the lady says. "So…," she says, extending her arm toward my bike and the street.

• • •

Friday afternoon Labor Day Weekend. I got my pitchback set up in the front yard and I'm throwing my basketball at it, catching the rebound and taking turn around jump shots. I'm waiting for the word, when Mom tells me we're going to Two Guys for new school clothes. Going to Two Guys for school clothes is *not* like going to Two Guys for a suit. Or curtains or irons or anything like that. It's sort of like going at Christmas time but being able to choose your own gifts. There's always a scuttle or two, a difference of opinions on what to buy, but it generally works out okay. And even though I'm a few dollars short for my Clydes, I have a pretty good plan on how to get them.

I take a few more shots, hitting NBA championship game winners, when Mom opens the front door and tells me to get ready. I put my pitchback in the garage and walk into the house and put my basketball in my room and grab the money out of my Sucrets tin, stuffing it into my pocket. Mom's in the kitchen sorting out coupons and looking at the Two Guys circular. "You ready, Robby?" she asks out loud.

I walk to the kitchen entrance. "Been ready," I say.

Mom and me get in the car. In years past we used to do this new school clothes shopping all together as a family. Me, Tam, Dad, and Mom. Dad and me would go to the boys department and Tam and Mom would go to the girls and we'd meet up in the little restaurant in the back when we were done for a bite to eat. We don't do it that way anymore. Mom turns the ignition over and I turn the radio to 66, my favorite station. Mom adjusts the inside mirror and puts the car in reverse and starts to back up, Halfway down the driveway she stops the car. I look at Mom and then out the windshield. Tammy's standing in the middle of the driveway. Mom sticks her head out the window. "What's the matter?" she asks.

Tammy walks to the car window. "Mind if I come along?"

"No. Of course not," Mom says.

I take a deep breath as Tammy walks around the car. I'm expecting her to try and push me out of the front seat. Tam's and mine arguments for front seat rights have been epic. But today, there's no such argument. Just a quiet opening and closing of the back door, and a lost puppy face looking out the window. Mom continues to back out of the driveway.

As we start down the street Mom motions for me to change the station to 77, which is Tammy's favorite, by first looking at the radio and motioning toward Tammy. I roll my eyes but oblige. Turns out okay though because for one, I'm going to need all the good will from Mom that I can get and secondly, 77 turns out to be not too bad a choice. Harry Harrison didn't play one bad song during the whole ride.

We pull into the Two Guys parking lot and by the looks of it, it doesn't look very crowded. We get a parking spot pretty close to the front of the store. On our way in Mom asks Tammy where she's going to be. "Just looking around," Tammy says.

"Well, we won't be very long," Mom says. "Maybe forty five minutes," she adds as we walk through the automatic opening doors. "How about we meet you right here by the bench?" Tammy nods okay. "Do you need anything?" Mom asks as we head to the young men's department.

"No, I don't think so," Tammy says, drifting her own way.

Walking down the main aisle of the store I say to Mom, "Boy, Tam's still all down in the dumps about this Baharupa, huh?"

Taking her store circular out from her purse, Mom makes an affirmative face and says, "Yes, your sister was quite taken with Karl."

"So how long do you think she's gonna be like this?" I ask. Mom says she doesn't know. "Do you think her and Brother Davis will get back together? Ya know. Once school starts?" I ask. Mom says she doesn't know. "Do you think we'll ever see the Karl the Baharupa again?" I ask. Mom says she doesn't know. "Well, he certainly was a strange one," I say, grabbing a small push cart as we walk into the young men's department.

We start with pants. Every time I go school clothes shopping with Mom we start with pants. Dad never cared where we started. I like corduroys so I pick out a medium brown pair my size and hand them to Mom. She takes them and looks at the price and then at her circular and they meet with her approval because in then cart they go. Mom shows me a pair of blue denim jeans with the flared out bottoms that's so popular now. I don't like them so I shake my head no. "But this is what everyone's wearing," Mom says.

"I know," I say, (and I do know because even Clyde Fraizer wears them) "but I just don't like them." And I don't. Nor do I like the colorful plaid style pants that are popular now. To me they make it look like you're wearing a picnic table cover.

We walk to the next aisle and I pick out a pair of Lee Rider's with the normal bottoms and hand them over to Mom, who again inspects the price and puts them in the cart. One can never go wrong with a plain old pair of Lee Rider's. We change gears and go over to the dress pants and dress shirts. Mom insists that I get a new dress outfit for school. I ask why I can't just use my new suit pants and shirt. My goal here is to be able to get another pair of corduroys or something else. Doesn't work. She picks out black pants with a maroon button-up shirt. "Because that's your new suit, Robby. This is for school."

From there we're over to the regular shirts. Mom picks out one of those denim shirts with a design on the pockets that makes it look like a cowboy shirt. I don't like those shirts. So Mom then picks out a brown/black/green flannel shirt that isn't too bad so I say okay. I figure if I agree to that she'll agree to the two rugby style shirts I'm holding, one blue and white and the other green and white. Mom says I can have one. I choose the blue and white one. We also agree on a long sleeve, semi-dress shirt that has a zipper front. Mom adds a pull-over sweater for cooler mornings and it's on to socks and underwear. I stay away from the embarrassment of Mom picking out a new package of underwear for me, but I am interested in the socks. I don't want the plain white ones. I want the ones that have four to a bag, two with blue/gold/blue stripes on top and the other two with red/black/red stripes. Mom doesn't care so I get the socks I want and when we're done here, it's onto the sneakers and my ingenious plan.

As Mom inspects the Kedz, the Chuck Taylor hightops, and the usual sneakers I get, I slide over to the expensive sneaker aisle. The Adidas Superstars and the Nike Cortez's and of course the Puma's. Once there I scan the Puma Clyde boxes. I find my size. I open the box. That intoxicating suede smell meets my nostrils. The golden color illuminates the box. I walk them over to where Mom is. She has a few pairs picked out for me to try on. She sees the box I'm carrying. I don't even get there and she's already shaking her head no. "Robby, they're far too much. You know that." She takes the box from my hands and looks at the price tag. "Twenty two dollars! For a pair of sneakers!"

That was expected. So I calmly take my money out of my pocket and count it out. Nineteen dollars and twenty five cents. I hand it out to Mom and say, "So with the money you were going to use for those," I point to the Kedz and Chuck Taylors, "if I add this here money, I can get those," now pointing to the Puma Clydes

Mom looks at me. More stares at me. Holding the box of twenty two dollar Puma Clydes she looks at them and the price again and says, "This is what you saved your money for all summer? An overpriced pair of sneakers?" I nod as if that shouldn't even be a question. "And you sure? I mean, this is a lot of money for a pair of sneakers," she says. I vigorously nod yes again. "Well, it's your money," she says. "Try them on."

I take the golden suede beauties out of the box and put them on. Even Dorothy's red shoes didn't look this good. Mom tells me to walk around in them. I walk to the end of the aisle and back.

"How do they feel?"

"Like a million dollars," I say.

Mom stoops down and presses her thumb against the toes of the sneakers. Then against the sides. "There's enough room?"

"Positively," I say. "Wanna see me run down the aisle in them?" Mom shakes her head no. I carefully take the sneakers off and gently put them back in the box, making sure the thin paper covering goes over them. I put the box in the shopping cart. "Thanks Mom," I say.

Mom shrugs her shoulders with indifference. "It's your money," she says again. "If this is how you want to spend it."

We start to head our way to the checkout lanes and I ask Mom why she thinks Karl calls himself Baharupa. "It's just a name, Robby."

"Yeah but, Baharupa?" I say. "What kind of name is that? Ya know he used to call Tammy…."

"Sona," mom says, cutting me off. "I know, Robby. And I've also heard you called Birdbrain, Birdclaw, Birdbeak, and Bird everything else but your real name. What do you guys call Tommy? Horsehead? Andy? Brockwurst? What kind of a names are those?"

I think about what Mom just said as we walk up to the checkout lane. Still seems different to me. We pay for everything and head for the exit. Near the doors there's Tammy, sitting on the bench near the front of the store, still looking sad.

Chapter Twenty Five

Tommy and Brock got the canoe back. When I got back from my Linda Orken excursion the other day I told them where I saw it. So what they did was they got two old tires from the Citgo, roped them together, took an old piece of paneling from Brock's basement, and put it over the tires and made a small raft. They then floated down the creek to where the canoe was. Luckily, the front of the canoe had gotten lodged into a small sand bar. If not for that, Brock said, it would have been clear sailing for the canoe all the way to the river. So that's how they got the canoe back. And so right after lunch time, Labor Day afternoon, we're riding our bikes down Constitution Street heading for the big woods and a canoe ride.

When we get to the canoe Brock and Tommy have it hid in another spot, not real far from the original place. We drag the canoe through the underbrush to the creek's edge. "Let's go this way, today," Brock says, pointing northward. "Since we already know where that way leads. Whadda ya think there Horsehead?"

"No argument from me," Tommy says.

We drag the canoe into the creek and jump in and start paddling. The creek doesn't change much at first but when we clear the area of the big woods the creek expands and there's tall grass everywhere and small marsh islands. Some of the islands have grass taller than us. To our right and further out we can see the river. Sailboats with different colored sails dot the landscape. Other boats motor along in either direction. We paddle on, staying on the creek side of the marsh. "So where do ya think this leads to?" I ask.

"I'm thinkin' the stream," Brock says. "Or maybe the pond."

"Probably the stream, then back out to the river," Tommy says.

We paddle a little further on and it turns out we'll never know. As the creek drifts away from the river and becomes narrow again, not too far down from here what looks like what was once a small bridge has collapsed into the water with the tree that fell on it. It's impassable. So we turn around and head back.

On the way we start to talk about the girls we'd like to have in our classes this year. Of course the usual names of Diane Lindsay and Robyn Luft roll off our tongues. Stephanie Reznik's name comes up and is agreed upon. Pamela Crawford's name is mentioned. Brock says he's always thought Michelle Hopka was really cute. Tommy and me agree. Then Broccoli says, "And I have to repeat this again, Joni looked really good that day at Fig's pool."

I have to admit that she did, I just keep quiet about that, along with keeping Linda's name to myself.

. . .

Labor Day has got to be one of the strangest days of the whole year, at least for us school kids. That's because we start the day with the early September sun still in summer mode, but by late afternoon and right now, supper time, real shadowy thoughts descend, knowing that by tomorrow morning we'll all be on that bright yellow school bus that'll bring us to the first day of school, with the scents of new clothes and new book bags and new lunch boxes accompanying us along the way.

Everyone's home for supper which has been a rare thing this summer and when we're done, mom tells me not to roam too far away. So I ask dad if he can move his car and I shoot some hoops. I play a game of 21, that granny shooting Rick Barry against Clyde Frazier. Clyde easily wins, but then again, I'm not used to shooting foul shots like Rick Barry. And it took every ounce of restraint for me not to wear my new Puma's. I want them to look brand new for tomorrow.

When I'm finished with the game I walk in the house and put my ball away in my closet. I walk into the kitchen and open the 'fridge. It take a cherry Hi-C and grab a couple of Hydrox cookies. Through the kitchen window I spot Tammy outside in her garden. I haven't seen Tammy in her garden lately. So I walk out the back door and over to where she is. I finish one of the cookies. I watch as Tammy picks and trims things. "Things got a lil' bit overgrown in there, huh?" I say.

Tammy acknowledges, quietly says, "Nothing that a little time and care won't help."

I don't say anything. I finish the second cookie and sip on the Hi-C. "Need any help?" I ask, not knowing why I did, because any previous mention of me being anywhere near Tammy's garden has always been met with death threats and or certain bodily dismemberments.

"No…thank you," Tammy says.

I feel a sense of relief because I really didn't want to help anyway. I finish the Hi-C when mom sticks her head out the back door, telling me to start packing it in, reminding me that it's a school night.